MURDER OF CROWS

ANDREW JAMES GREIG

Storm

PUBLISHING

Ebook ISBN: 978-1-80508-988-9
Paperback ISBN: 978-1-80508-989-6

Cover design: Blacksheep
Cover images: Depositphotos, Shutterstock

Published by Storm Publishing.
For further information, visit:
www.stormpublishing.co

ALSO BY ANDREW JAMES GREIG

Private Investigator Teàrlach Paterson

The Girl in the Loch

Silent Ritual

The Graveyard Bell

Detective Corstorphine

The Bone Clock

The Devil's Cut

Standalones

A Song of Winter

You people with hearts have something to guide you,
and need never do wrong;
but I have no heart, and so I must be very careful.
L. Frank Baum
The Wonderful Wizard of Oz

PROLOGUE

He opened his eyes in the dark, blinked away tears blurring his vision. Where was he? Pinpricks of cold light resolved into stars – more stars than he could ever remember seeing. It had been the cramp in his leg that had woken him, building in agony until he surfaced from a deep sleep with the urgent need to stretch away the pain. His leg refused to obey the command and muscles knotted under the skin, making him cry out. Except his mouth was covered, his limbs were bound – and judging by the unyielding metal rods under his back, he wasn't in his bed.

Fear bubbled in his veins as he fought through the fog of memory to make sense of where he was – what had happened. The strangeness of his predicament was like a nightmare, a peculiarly vivid nightmare where the pain and cold were all too real.

Richard Bryce remembered going to his allotment after tea. The day had been uneventful. A round of the wards with his trolley of medicines. Double-checking doses, dates and delivery before moving onto the next closed cell. Providing first-aid for the minor bumps, scratches and fights that were a regular occurrence during the working day. Then home to his bungalow in Cleghorn – looking out over fields and Mouse Water. He struggled to remember what had happened. He'd felt faint and had collapsed.

Richard found he could raise his head, although it felt as if it had doubled in size. The realisation that he'd been drugged occurred at the same time as two other startling discoveries. The first was that he was still dressed in his casual clothes, proving ineffectual against the cold of the night. The second, more alarming realisation, was that he was lying across a railway line next to a putrid deer carcass.

When the rails underneath his back began to vibrate, Richard's eyes opened wide enough for the whites to show. The cramp in his leg for now forgotten, he frantically tried to caterpillar himself off the rails and to safety. All thoughts of how and why he was here faded when the first sound of an approaching train echoed down the line. His attempts at moving only served to confirm his limbs had been securely bound to the rails.

There was the level-crossing to his right, traffic lights casting a pulsating red glow like a premonition of the blood about to be spilt. A clanging bell heralded two gates dropping down to block the road. He searched desperately for any signs of life, his shouts muffled, but the road remained eerily empty.

The rails hummed underneath his back. A bright light threw the trees and overhead power lines into sharp relief, and he drank in the details like a man thirsty for life.

The train's horn blared a warning. It was the last sound he'd ever hear.

ONE
WEDDING

'I call upon those present to witness, that I, James Corstorphine accept you, Shamila Mallick, as my lawful wife. To be by your side as your best friend, soul mate and lover. I will be faithful and support you in your dreams. I will be there for you always. Everything I am and everything I have is yours, from this moment forth and for eternity.'

Corstorphine felt the weight of the gold ring heavy in his waistcoat pocket. Time had stopped. The celebrant turned her attention to Shamila, offering a smile as if to encourage her to respond. She had bowed her head as he'd spoken, and now raised it to look directly into his eyes. He saw tears forming, the sunlight streaming through the high banqueting hall windows reflected back at him in the curved mirror of her cornea. He had a moment of panic thinking that she had changed her mind, that she had come to her senses.

Shamila's hand gripped his. She smiled reassuringly and for a moment he lost himself in her eyes.

'The ring?'

He jolted back to reality, fumbled in his waistcoat pocket to produce the ring and gently placed it on her finger.

Someone whooped in the audience; it sounded like Frankie.

The rest of the ceremony passed him by. He could never be this happy again, with the woman he loved by his side. Even the knowledge that PC Lamb's bagpipe playing was to come couldn't take the edge off his happiness.

James and Shamila had met last year when he'd asked for her help in profiling a murderer. Love must have been in the air, because Frankie had met her new man around the same time. Now PC Phil Lamb remained the only member of their small police team without a partner – and since he'd started learning the bagpipes that was likely to remain his condition.

Corstorphine kissed Shamila, and the threatened skirl of the pipes faded away until they parted.

A row of truncheons waited for them outside the anteroom where they'd signed the marriage certificate. PCs Phil Lamb and Bill McAdam, DC Frankie McKenzie and Sergeant Hamish McKee held their arms aloft to make a tunnel through which they had to duck. Corstorphine had worried she'd find this part of the ceremony too much, but Shamila was enjoying every second. Her laughter echoed through the castle, bouncing off the grey walls and bringing life and vitality to the great hall.

Life was going to be good.

TWO
CEDAR

Autumn arrived in the small Highland town overnight. An unusually warm September had lulled everyone into forgetting that winter lay in wait, now snow dusted the distant mountaintops like a premonition. For the first time this autumn, DC Frankie McKenzie felt a sharp edge to the wind and a foretaste of what was to come. Corstorphine would return from his honeymoon tomorrow, and until then she was the lead detective. Not that there was much call for her speciality. Tourists were largely away, not wishing to risk being caught in a random snowstorm and trapped for weeks on end. Seasonal shops were beginning to close now the lucrative summer trade was ending, wood stores being filled, gardens tidied and songbirds turning mute with foreboding.

Frankie stared out over the mountains encircling the town, bored from typing out the week's crime summary in readiness for sending in a report. Why were they even interested, those desk-bound career jockeys at Tulliallan Castle in Fife? Home to Scottish Police HQ, the place demanded weekly summaries from outlying area commanders so that crime figures could be massaged into statistics that reflected well on the leadership. *Lies, damn lies and statistics.* Frankie was with Mark Twain on that.

Graphs sprang into being on her screen. Road traffic accidents down, fatalities down, drug/drink driving offences up, speeding up. Frankie ticked the box from notes Corstorphine had left her. Operation CEDAR – tick.

Someone above her pay grade came out with this stuff – CEDAR: Challenge, Educate, Detect and Reduce road traffic accidents and improve driver behaviour. PCs McAdam and Lamb weren't complaining. Spending the colder months in warm patrol cars was preferable to walking the beat. Not that the dour desk sergeant approved. Hamish came from a generation where policing meant walking the streets, catching trouble before it began. Now she often felt they were only reactive, clearing up the mess society was too mean-spirited to attend to themselves.

Anti-Social Behaviour, Disorder and Violence

Here at least Frankie had some positive news. Unlike earlier years, they could justifiably say that murders and violence had decreased. She stared out of the window again, imagined the murders from last year and shook her head in denial. So many people dying in their quiet little corner of Scotland. She felt that not only had the year turned a corner, leaving the warmth of summer as a memory, but the inhabitants of this wee police station had also changed. She with her fireman, Alex. Corstorphine with his new wife, Shamila.

A smile played around the corners of her mouth. He'd changed completely when Shamila had come into his life. For the first time since she'd met him, Corstorphine had stopped looking back to his past and was excited for the future. That faraway look was gone.

Welcome back to life, she thought silently to herself.

The office was empty. PCs McAdam and Lamb were tasked with adding more convictions to the traffic violation results. Hamish occupied his habitual stance at the front desk, more so he could keep an eye on everything and everyone on the streets outside. She wondered how Corstorphine was getting on – two weeks' enforced rest would do him the power of good. Frankie blew her cheeks out in frustration. Still another four headings to fill according to his handwritten guide: *Acquisitive Crime; Protecting Vulnerable People; Serious and Organised Crime; Counter Terrorism.* That last section shouldn't take her long.

Another set of statistics joined her spreadsheet and she hit save just as Hamish poked his head around the office door with an expectant expression. It was a welcome interruption.

'I've a farmer come in.' His slow highland brogue was the prologue to whatever it was he wanted to say.

Frankie waited patiently. Dealing with the sergeant's tortoise-like deliberations was preferable to entering another column of numbers onto her spreadsheet.

'He wants to report missing property, only I don't see how we can help.'

'What's missing?' Frankie asked reasonably enough.

Farmers were being subjected to a crime wave across the entire country. The machinery was expensive, locations remote and easy to access. There had been so many thefts of machinery and live-stock that she suspected organised crime was behind it – not simply some opportunistic light-fingered thieving. Maybe she should move the rural crime figures into Serious and Organised Crime?

'A scarecrow, ma'am.'

The sergeant wasn't renowned for his practical jokes. Frankie watched him carefully, assessing whether boredom had finally cracked his dour demeaner and produced what must surely be his first joke. His face remained serious.

'Someone's taken his scarecrow?' Frankie had trouble concealing her smile.

'He was very attached to it by all accounts. Been in the family a while. He's asking for a detective to be assigned to the case.' Hamish had exhausted his word count for the day and waited for her to respond.

What the hell, it would make a diversion from all the bloody paperwork. How did Corstorphine keep sane with all the reports they were obliged to create on a weekly basis?

'Send him through to the interview room. I'll have a chat, but as you say, I'm not sure how we can help him. What's his name?'

'William Haddow. I'll bring him through now.'

Sergeant McKee shut the door behind him on his way out. Frankie caught the satisfied look on his face now that he'd successfully negotiated one of the more random enquiries to have come across his desk.

Frankie closed the spreadsheet, picked up her notebook and made for the interview room. Corstorphine would have appreciated this one – shame he wouldn't be back until tomorrow.

THREE
SCARECROW

'William Haddow?' Frankie shut the interview room door behind her out of habit. With only herself and the sergeant on the premises it really wouldn't have mattered if she'd left it wide open.

The man sitting opposite her was in his late fifties, possibly well into his sixties. A life lived outside and exposed to the elements had had an aging effect, weathering exposed skin into leather. His hands were overlarge – great slabs of meat resting awkwardly on the table surface. Sausage fingers interlinked whilst his thumbs described circles around one another. Unused to not having anything useful to do.

'Aye. I've come about my scarecrow.' Belligerent brown eyes dared her to treat his complaint lightly, thin lips turned down in disappointment at not seeing the DI.

She saw the results of a lifetime's hardship – coarse red hair that had been cut by himself for so many years that his fringe reminded her of a highland cow. His work clothes had an unidentifiable odour emanating from them – farmyard mainly with something sour underneath. She regretted having closed the door.

'I see.' Frankie opened her notebook, smoothed out a new page and began writing. 'And when did you first notice your scarecrow had gone missing?'

The farmer visibly relaxed now that he could see Frankie taking the case seriously.

'This morning. I was driving the tractor past the winter wheat field and noticed he'd gone missing. At first, I thought he'd fallen over, with the wind and storms we've been having, so I went in to put him back on his feet and he wasn't there!'

Frankie adopted a suitably shocked expression.

'Where do you think he could have gone, Mr Haddow?' She imagined the scarecrow marching off across the fields, belongings tied up in a spotted handkerchief on the end of a stick slung over his shoulder.

The farmer's thick neck jutted towards her, his head angling in for a closer look.

'Well, he wouldn't have gone anywhere, would he? He's a bloody scarecrow. That's the point.'

He sat back in the chair with his arms crossed over his chest and looked at her as if she was daft.

Frankie regarded him calmly from her side of the table. His face had flushed purple with frustration and was slowly returning to more of a ruddy hue now he'd said his piece. She decided his head resembled a neep, particularly so when it had turned purple.

'Yes, I appreciate that your scarecrow wouldn't have made much progress without external forces being applied.' Frankie began to wonder at the wisdom of interviewing someone about a missing scarecrow. 'Could the wind have blown him into an adjacent field, or even further away?' She realised the scarecrow was being discussed as a him, which sparked an absurd train of thought about scarecrow pronouns that she quickly dismissed.

'No. He couldn't have blown anywhere. I put him there myself, see. He was well into the ground. Would have taken a tornado to shift him and we haven't had one of them around here.'

The mention of tornado brought the memory of the film she'd been trying to think of into focus – *The Wizard of Oz*. That particular scarecrow had been missing a brain as far as she remembered. Or was it a heart? No, the tin woodman was missing a heart. She pulled her attention back to the man sitting impatiently in front of her.

'Are you suggesting someone has stolen your scarecrow?'

'That's exactly what I'm suggesting. The Harvest Festival's this weekend and I don't have time to make another.'

One hand curled into a fist, strong fingers turning white with pressure.

'If I find who's taken it, I won't be responsible for my actions!' Veins in his cheeks filled with blood until his metamorphosis to neep was again complete.

Frankie wrote in her notebook, hoping her smile remained hidden from view.

'Do you have a description? I'll ask everyone to look out for it. Probably kids having a laugh, you know what they're like.'

The look he gave her suggested farmer Haddow had long forgotten what it was like to be young and foolish.

'Here's a picture.' His phone displayed the photograph of an archetypal scarecrow, from straw hat and carrot nose all the way down to the bottom of blue overalls tied with string. Straw stuck out for hands and feet. An unpleasant leer had been drawn on the sacking comprising a face.

'He doesn't look very friendly,' Frankie observed.

'Not meant to be friendly. He's a scarecrow. It's got the word scare in it for a reason.'

'Can I have a copy of the photograph?'

'How do I do that?'

Frankie pointed out the share button, then the AirDrop option.

'Right. I'll make sure our constables keep a lookout. I expect it will turn up soon enough and we'll call you to collect.'

'Is that it?' William Haddow viewed her suspiciously from underneath bushy red eyebrows.

'That's all we can do for now, Mr Haddow. We'll keep an eye out for your missing property – and if someone does return it, could you let us know?'

'Aye, alright then. I'll do that.'

He stood, towering above her as he unwound from his chair.

'I'll see you out. Thanks for bringing this to our attention.'

Frankie smiled disarmingly as the farmer was handed back to Hamish, printed out the farmer's photograph and laid it on her desk before returning to her paperwork. The scarecrow's disturbing leer proved too much, and she turned the picture over so she could concentrate on finishing the report.

FOUR
SUZIE

Suzie counted out her money, painstakingly taking the notes and coins one by one from her purse, double-checking each one before handing them over to the cashier. She became aware a queue had formed behind her, becoming more irritable by the second.

'Oh, for God's sake.'

'Hurry up, will you.'

'Shouldn't be let out on her own.'

The cashier stared them back into silence, helped Suzie pack her few groceries into her bag and gave her an encouraging smile.

'There you are, Suzie. Take care now. See you tomorrow.'

Suzie dared to raise her head, shyly meeting her eyes.

'Thank you.'

It was what her mother had taught her to do, when people are kind. A rare enough occurrence these days. Mostly she kept her face down, tried not to show she was frightened or hurt or confused by how she was treated.

The walk home wasn't far. She knew the way back along the main road – wait for the green man to show before crossing the busy road. Look right, look left, look right again. Familiar and reassuring habits that should have protected her. Except the ritual let her down today.

The bike came out of nowhere. Silent except for the shout that came too late.

'Out the fucking way!'

The collision knocked her to the ground. Suzie's hand stretched out ineffectually to break her fall, but her forehead hit the tarmac with a sickeningly hard smack. She lay there dazed, tins of soup rolling further out into the road. The lights changed and a double-decker bus rolled over a tin of tomato soup, exploding the tin and spreading red goo around like blood. People stared down at her through the windows. She touched her forehead; fingers came away sticky and red.

'You stupid cow! Look what you've done.'

Suzie struggled to her feet. The green man had turned as red as her fingers. It was dangerous to be on the road when the man turned red. Her mother had taught her that.

The cyclist blocked her return to the pavement. A car horn made her jump to the side as the driver mouthed angry obscenities through the window.

'What are you going to do about this then?' The cyclist was pointing to his front wheel, buckled by the impact into Suzie's leg. She realised she was hobbling and suddenly felt frightened in case she'd broken a bone. Her mother had never taught her what to do about broken bones.

'You'll have to pay for a new wheel.' The young man squinted at her, as if trying to work out if she had any money.

He stood to one side so she could make the refuge of the pavement. She stooped to collect the tins that had rolled into the kerb. The others were too far out, causing vehicles to attempt slaloming around them. In short succession, three explosive noises announced the termination of chicken, mushroom and mixed vegetable soups. How was she going to feed herself now?

'I'll follow you home. You can give me the money for my bike there.'

Suzie kept her face averted, not daring to see if she was being followed. Her block of flats was ahead. Children were playing in the dog-shitty grass outside.

'Simple Suzie, simple Suzie.'

The chant often accompanied her entry and exit – so much so that she preferred to stay in her flat all day and night, only risking a trip to the shops when her cupboard was bare, or it was time to sign on at the benefits office again.

A stone whizzed past, then another. She hurried as fast as her bruised leg would allow her.

'Fuck off ye wee bastards!'

The missiles ceased and Suzie wondered if she'd found a friend.

'If my bike's not here when I come back, I'll murder the lot of yous.'

He entered the lift with her. Suzie pressed the button and kept her gaze fixed to the floor. They travelled upwards in silence, accompanied only by the whine of cables pulling them higher and the sour smell of piss.

She opened her door and he pushed past her, looking into each room as if he'd already moved in.

'You got any money for me then?'

She shook her head. It felt sore, her leg felt sore.

'Didn't think so.' He didn't seem bothered by her admission. 'You live here on your own then?'

Suzie nodded, untrusting of her voice. *When will he leave me alone?*

'Anyone looking after you like?'

A shake of her head. There was no one to look after her – not since her mum died. Social workers used to visit regularly, but they'd said something about budget cuts and had apologised. Shame-faced like they'd done something wrong, except Suzie didn't know what that was.

'OK. Suzie, is it? Is that right?'

She dared to look at him. He was smiling. Like he was being

friendly. But something wasn't right about his smile. Suzie felt afraid.

'Well!' He spoke harshly, making her jump. 'Or are you dumb as well as daft?'

'My name's Suzie.'

'OK, Suzie. This is how it's going to work. You owe me money for my bike, see?'

He was waiting for her to respond.

She nodded again, wanting him to leave her alone. There was blood on her face, and her hands. She needed to wash and lie down.

'OK. I'm going to move in, see? I'll sleep here.' He indicated her bedroom. 'And you can sleep on the couch. Got it?'

Another nod. *Please leave me alone.*

'Good. All you have to do is keep your mouth shut. Can you do that, Suzie? Can you keep yer mouth shut for me?'

Suzie wanted to cry.

'Yes.'

'Good. You get yourself cleaned up and I'll come back with some food for you. That's more than fair, isn't it?'

Suzie looked hopefully at her benefactor. If he replaced the tins she'd lost, then she would have enough to last the week.

'Where's your spare key?' He spotted the empty key rack by the door.

Suzie opened her bloodied hand to reveal her house key, the one she wasn't allowed to lose or 'all hell would break loose'. He took it, wiping the blood off on a curtain and pocketed it.

'I'll be back later.'

Suzie wished her mum was there to tell her he was a nice man, and that his smile was genuine. But Mum was dead. Suzie wasn't that simple, despite what the children said. She was on her own now, and 'had to make her own decisions'.

Why then, did she feel like someone had made the decision for her?

FIVE
PERP

The white protective suit was designed for working in an abattoir –
an appropriate choice. The body was limp and had started to leak
noxious fluids from the severed neck and ankles. He'd considered
that, which is why he was wearing chemical-resistant black rubber
gloves and wellington boots as he manhandled a bloated corpse
from the back of the car and into the old church interior. In the
dark recesses of the abandoned building, a bound man stared up at
him. Ropes hogtied him into a parody of extreme bondage – a ball
gag stifling any comments whilst the corpse was forced into scarecrow clothes. Only eyes expressed emotion, opened wide in shock
at the scene playing out in front of him.

He worked meticulously, pulling jacket sleeves up over unre-
sisting arms and trousers over truncated legs, the limbs turning
green in decomposition. Discarded straw from the dismembered
scarecrow provided an artistic touch, poking out at the neck, hands
and feet – or where the head and feet should have been. Those
missing body parts were stored in plastic bags and would be assembled at the last minute. A metal rod was hammered into the neck to
take the head, wire wrapped around lower legs ready to attach the
feet.

The finished article was manoeuvred back inside the car with difficulty, the body sliding on thick plastic sheets placed there to contain any evidential DNA. He stood back to admire his creation, much as the fictional Dr Frankenstein may have viewed his monster, then added a wheelbarrow to the back. He'd found it convenient for transporting bodies.

With a final check that all the parts were inside, he shut the car doors with a smile of satisfaction. There was one last task he had to complete before taking the body to its chosen location.

'I need more of your blood.' He reached for a syringe and stood over his immobilised captive, pulling up a sleeve and wrapping a cord around the wrist until a vein pulsed purple under white skin.

'You may feel a slight prick.' His voice betrayed the falsity of his bedside manner, the laughter following his remark directed at his hapless patient. Blood filled the syringe as the plunger lifted.

'And I'll have some hair.' Pliers tugged at the man's face, ripping hairs out of a nascent beard. 'Sorry, didn't mean to take that much,' he said unconvincingly. He placed the hair and syringe inside a plastic bag, then a plaster hurriedly pressed where a drop of blood had formed on the man's white skin.

It was pitch dark outside. He'd planned for that. What he hadn't planned for was the smell of the dismembered corpse. The sound of a wheelbarrow provided a surreal soundtrack as it bounced around in the back of the car beside the only passenger. He didn't mind – he was beyond minding about anything.

SIX

MCKEOWN

Frankie pressed send and the monthly figures went their electronic way to Scottish Police HQ. Relieved to be free of her administrative task, she logged out and made for the door.

'See you tomorrow, Hamish.'

The sergeant held a hand up in response and she realised he was on a call.

'Sorry,' she mouthed. Frankie moved more quickly than usual so she could make her escape in case he called her back. A familiar honking came from the darkening sky. She looked up to watch a skein of geese encouraging each other onwards. Of all the signs of autumn, these migratory arrivals were the surest indication that winter would soon be here. She pulled her winter jacket in tighter and drove out of the station car park towards home, looking forward to an evening by the fire.

That small moment of peaceful reflection was spoilt by Hamish's name displayed on an incoming call.

'What the hell, I've only just left work!' Frankie grumbled, accepting the call. 'Hamish, did I forget something?'

'Not that I'm aware of.' His lugubrious voice paused for an unreasonably long time. 'We've had another missing scarecrow reported, from Glenarty. It's their harvest festival—'

'Why is this worth calling me on the way home?' she interrupted, then felt guilty for snapping at him. 'Can't it wait until tomorrow?' Frankie tried for a more conciliatory tone.

'Aye. I just thought you should know. In case you wanted to investigate.'

She couldn't be certain that the desk sergeant wasn't winding her up on purpose.

'I'm sure it can wait. I'll deal with any other missing property in the morning. Night, Hamish.'

'This one was taken from outside Mart McKeown's house,' he added quickly.

Her finger paused over the end call button. Mart McKeown was the closest thing to rock star royalty hiding away in the Highland hills. A string of hits in the Nineties, some of which she could still sing along to without needing the lyrics.

'Can't Lamb or McAdam deal?'

'They've just come from the village and are in pursuit of a stolen tractor. I can ask them to call in tomorrow morning?'

'No, it's OK.' Frankie made the calculation, balancing how much time the detour would take out of her evening against the grief she'd experience if Mart McKeown made a complaint.

'I'll call in on my way home. Is he still at the same address?'

'Aye. The big house in Glenarty.'

'OK. I'll go there now, although what he expects us to be able to do...'

In a village full of outlandish houses, the McKeown house at first glance appeared unremarkable. A little larger than the others, and the turrets were an unnecessary nod to Scottish baronial – only electric gates and substantial gardens differentiated this house from its neighbours. Frankie introduced herself at an intercom and the gates swept smoothly open, allowing access to a gravelled drive. She parked in front of an imposing front door, which started opening in expectation of her arrival.

'Mart McKeown?'

Frankie stretched a hand towards the figure revealed by the opening door. His face was instantly recognisable, more so from the floppy blond quiff that had been his trademark. Her gaze lowered to take in a plaid shirt, baggy denims and white trainers before returning to meet his eyes. He'd had work done. The skin around his eyes was devoid of the wrinkles that age should have bestowed, pulled taut and shiny over high cheekbones. He might have been smiling a welcome, but he gave the impression of only being capable of manifesting the one, fixed expression beneath immobile eyebrows.

'And you are?' His voice retained the same tonality and cadence she remembered from his songs.

'Frankie. DC Frankie McKenzie.' She stumbled over her words, momentarily starstruck. *Jesus, Frankie, pull yourself together. You've seen better-looking waxworks.*

'Please, do come in.' He gestured for her to enter.

The hall was decorated with gold and silver disks. Frankie read the titles, bringing back early memories of school discos.

'A few mementos.'

His voice came from by her ear. She turned to find him standing close, too close for comfort. Frankie took a step away, ostensibly to peer at the only gold disk displayed on the wall.

'"Done With Crying" – I remember that one.'

'Aye. My only song to reach over 100,000 sales.'

He might have been wistful. Frankie couldn't tell. His inability to display anything other than the one fixed emotion was making her feel uncomfortable.

'You reported a missing scarecrow?' Frankie concentrated on the job at hand. The sooner she took a statement and left, the better.

'Rufus was taken last night. I wouldn't have minded, but he was dressed in some of my old stage clothes.'

He must have noticed Frankie's bewilderment.

'Rufus is the name I gave him. He's meant to be a caricature – I gave him a guitar as well. He was on our side of the gate, that's what I don't understand. If kids had taken him, then he'd have turned up by now. I put out a message on the Glenarty Facebook page asking for him to be brought back – no questions asked.'

'Facebook page?' Frankie asked.

'The residents use it to keep in touch. Which bins this week? Whose dog keeps shitting on the pavement? Anyone know a plumber who knows what he's doing and doesn't charge an arm and a leg? That sort of thing.'

Frankie made a note on her phone.

'Do you have a photo?'

Now it was Mart McKeown's turn to look bewildered.

'Photo?'

'Of Rufus. Your missing scarecrow?'

'No. At least, I haven't. Trudi will have something.' He took a few steps further down the hallway, stood at the bottom of a polished oak staircase that wound its way upwards via sharp right-angled bends to an upper floor.

'Trudi! Can you come down please?' His shout was loud enough to make Frankie's ears ring.

An attractive young woman came into view, treading the stairs like a model. She trailed a long, blue dress behind her that wouldn't have looked out of place on a film set.

'My daughter, Trudi.'

Cool eyes met hers. Frankie felt judged.

'This policewoman is looking into Rufus's disappearance for us. She wants a photo – do you have one?'

Trudi joined them at ground level. She was almost the same height as her dad, both taller than the DC.

'I'll have a look.' Father and daughter looked intently at Trudi's phone screen as she swiped repeatedly. She must have realised her father was peering too closely because she pulled the screen near to her face. He turned his frozen expression back to Frankie.

'Here.' Trudi held the screen for her to see.

The picture was of a guitarist wearing much the same clothes as Mart McKeown had on now, topped with a leather jacket and bright red scarf wrapped around its neck. The head drew her attention – no pumpkin or stuffed sacking for this one, instead the scarecrow had Mart's face.

'Uncanny, isn't it?' he asked with obvious pride.

Frankie wasn't sure how to respond.

'It looks just like you.' That at least was true.

His daughter looked on with boredom. 'Do you want a copy then?'

'Can you share it with my phone?' Frankie asked.

'I'll have to add you as a contact first. Hold your phone close to mine.'

Trudi swiped her screen and the photo appeared on Frankie's phone once she'd accepted.

'Thanks. How does it look so much like you?' Frankie asked with complete seriousness.

'It's a waxwork,' Mart replied. 'Tussauds were going to melt me down, so I bought it. I've grown rather attached over the years and I'd like it back.' He fixed Frankie with his expressionless eyes. 'Can you do that for me?'

'We can certainly try.' Frankie made purposefully for the door. 'Thanks for sharing the photograph. It gives us something to work with.'

Mart opened the door for her. 'The gates will open automatically for you,' he advised.

'Thanks. We'll, eh, let you know.' She walked to her car and caught a glimpse of them standing motionless in the doorway as she swept back down the drive. The song 'Done With Crying' started playing in her head as the gates opened.

Something about the similarities between Mart McKeown and his waxwork scarecrow doppelganger had completely unsettled her – the last face she'd seen so lacking in movement or emotion had belonged to a corpse.

SEVEN

PUB

The pub was filling up when Frankie arrived. She scanned the volunteer firefighters by the jukebox, recognising the usual crowd: the woman with the crewcut, the lanky youngster towering above her, Sandy with his ginger hair and loud laugh – but no sign of Alex. She felt a pang of disappointment at his absence. They'd arranged to meet here – he could have let her know he was going to be late. She ordered a drink, took it over to the firefighters.

'Hey, Jo.' Frankie caught the firefighter's eye before closing the gap between them.

A woman with a crewcut appraised Frankie through cool blue eyes as she approached.

'Frank.' She raised a glass in greeting, but not before she'd made a show of admiring Frankie's body.

Frankie's smile felt forced. She wasn't sure about how she felt having her name shortened to a male moniker. The men were so used to her now they'd forgotten how misogynistic they'd been when she'd first been introduced as their new driver.

Now they'd forgotten Jo was even a woman.

'Have you seen Alex? I was meant to be meeting him here tonight.'

Jo's blue eyes continued to blatantly drink her in.

'Not since the shift ended. He'll be along later I expect – or maybe not.' Her enigmatic expression hinted that she'd prefer if he left the field wide open.

'Frankie!' Sandy's loud voice boomed from somewhere deep in his chest. Ginger stubble had colonised his chin since the morning, short hairs catching the artificial light and throwing red highlights into the air. She could easily imagine his chin completely hidden by a few days' growth – except regulations prevented such an obvious fire risk.

'Hi, Sandy, Coll.' She directed this to the lanky lad whose height was only exaggerated by the leanness of his build.

'Who's keeping us all safe if you're in the pub?' Coll asked. His voice, coming from near the pub ceiling, sounded like he breathed helium instead of normal air.

Frankie risked straining her neck to respond.

'I could say the same about you lot.' Her riposte was met with a collective unconcerned shrug.

'You looking for Alex?' Sandy's bass contrasted with Coll's treble.

'Aye – is he coming? We'd arranged to meet.' She instantly regretted making their arrangements public. If Alex didn't show, for whatever reason, they'd be viewing her with pity.

'He said he'd be along later,' Sandy confirmed. 'How's your week been, without the DI keeping an eye on you?'

Frankie was grateful for a change of subject.

'Not much happening, I'm pleased to say. There's been a spate of scarecrow thefts.'

They stopped drinking to focus on her.

'Did you say scarecrows?' Coll squeaked.

She nodded, sipping at her drink.

Three faces expressed incredulity.

'Thank God Corstorphine's on his way back to put a stop to it!' Sandy spoke with mock conviction, then spoilt it all by laughing.

'It will be kids,' Jo stated simply. 'Or Coll looking for trousers that fit him.'

Frankie's attention shifted to the tall firefighter's legs with trousers hanging short of their destination.

'It's not easy when everyone else is a short arse.'

She didn't need to risk straining her neck to detect the peeved tones came from Coll.

'Aye. We don't need the ladders with you on a call,' Jo added for good measure, exchanging a wink with Sandy.

'Aye, aye. Very funny.'

Coll gave Frankie a nudge. 'Here's your fancy man.'

She followed his line of sight, taking advantage of his elevated view from above a sea of heads, and saw Alex's dark curls approaching from the door.

'Hi, Frankie.' He leaned in for a kiss. 'Sorry I'm late. Got caught up with something.'

Frankie's interest was roused. 'What? Anything I can help with?'

'No, it's all good.' He gave her a look that said *not here*. 'I'll get a round in, what are you all having?'

As the orders were placed, the firefighters forgot to follow up on their interest in Alex's enigmatic comment and talk turned to football.

'Do you want to come back to mine?' Frankie asked quietly as the evening drew to a close.

'I can't. Not tonight.' Alex looked uncharacteristically troubled.

'Is there anything wrong?'

'No, everything's fine. Just, not a good time – that's all.' His smile lasted all of a second. 'I'll be in touch. Have to go.'

He placed his empty glass down on the bar, then turned back with the smile firmly fixed in place.

'See you all tomorrow. Have to dash.'

Four pairs of eyes watched him depart with varying degrees of interest, then pulled faces to express their reactions.

'Right. I'll call it a day as well. Work tomorrow.' Frankie put on a brave front to dispel the inevitable post-mortem that would follow her departure. Only Jo's gaze lingered on her. She could feel the heat of her eyes on her back until the pub door closed behind her.

Alex was nowhere to be seen. She debated going after him, taking the direction to his flat in the hope that she'd catch up and they could talk in private.

Frankie checked her watch. Whatever was troubling Alex would have to wait, but his sudden departure had left her with a sense of unease.

At least Corstorphine was due back tomorrow. Perhaps then things would return to normal.

EIGHT
THREAT

DI James Corstorphine entered the station with a spring in his step.

'Morning, Hamish. Town hasn't burned down in my absence then?'

The desk sergeant viewed him without expression.

'Morning, sir. Did you have a good break?'

'Couldn't have been better, thanks, Hamish.'

Corstorphine made straight for his office, straightened the picture of Shamila that now adorned his desk and logged onto the computer. He saw that Frankie had copied him into the report and opened the document. He'd been concerned that for her first attempt she'd miss sections, or not present it in the way he'd painstakingly set out for her to copy, but it was all good. Relieved to have delegated that tedious task, he headed for the small kitchen area off the main office and filled the kettle.

'Tea, Hamish?' he called out to the front desk.

The sergeant made an appearance, holding a mug so stained with the patina of time and tea it wouldn't have looked out of place in an archaeological dig.

'That would hit the mark, sir. Thanks.'

'So, tell me. What have I missed?'

Corstorphine busied himself with teabags, pulling milk out of the wee fridge, sniffing it out of habit to check it hadn't gone off.

'It's been quiet, now the tourists have gone,' Hamish intoned. 'McAdam and Lamb have been out trying to find a stolen tractor. They lost it on the A85 yesterday evening.'

Corstorphine raised his eyebrows enquiringly as he poured the boiling contents of the kettle into two mugs.

'Was it a Ferrari?'

'No, sir. Massey Ferguson.'

He stood aside to let the sergeant attend to his own tea, disappointed his attempt at humour had fallen flat.

Hamish approached teamaking with the same ponderous intent he gave to everything in his life. By the time he lifted the teabag out of his mug, the water would be stained the colour of peat.

'One thing, sir,' Hamish continued stirring the tea bag until it had given up every last drop of tea. 'There's been a spate of scarecrow abductions.'

Corstorphine waited for the punch line that didn't arrive.

'Abductions?'

'Aye, sir. One stolen from a farmer's field, the other from that pop star's garden in Glenarty. Mart McKeown.'

Corstorphine regarded the sergeant with concern, wondering if senility had finally gained a foothold.

'Frankie's dealing with it,' Hamish added. The teabag was pressed into the side of his mug in case any tea remained trapped, then the bag transferred into a bin.

'Thanks, Hamish. I'm sure she'll provide an update when she's in.'

The sergeant made slow progress towards the front desk as the telephone started to ring. He picked it up once he'd settled into his seat and placed his mug on the desk.

'Police.'

Corstorphine smiled at Hamish's economy with words. He returned to his office, sat down and sipped at his tea. The computer screen was ignored as he cradled the hot mug in his hands and stared happily at Shamila's photograph.

She was smiling as if sharing a private joke, her dark eyes watching him with amusement.

Corstorphine was a good enough judge of character, and his hearing acute enough, to know his colleagues believed Shamila saw him as a 'work in progress'. Whatever the truth in that, he was grateful every day to wake up next to her.

His mobile rang, Shamila's picture on the screen.

'Hi, love.' The words still tasted strange on his tongue.

'Jim. I've had a call from my last place of work.' She sounded hesitant. 'They've issued a warning to all staff – and ex staff.'

Corstorphine's heart missed a beat. Shamila's previous job was working with some of the most dangerous members of society – those deemed so criminally insane they were destined to spend their lives locked away in Carstairs State Hospital.

'Has there been an escape?'

He knew from talking with her that the hospital siren sounded on the third Thursday of every month to announce the all-clear. Local residents might have found the sound comforting; it chilled him to the bone that such a siren should be required at all.

'No, nothing like that.'

Shamila's tone did nothing to assuage his fears.

'What is it then? Why have they contacted you?'

'I'm sure it's nothing to worry about. A member of staff has gone missing over the weekend. There's no sign of him, no panic calls, nobody knows where he's gone. It's enough for the hospital to issue an alert – more an abundance of care than anything else.'

She'd failed to convince him that this was a mere administrative problem.

'You say no one has escaped?'

'That's right. One of the first things they do is make sure all the patients are secure. Whatever this is, it's not one of the patients.'

Corstorphine's heart returned to a more normal rhythm.

'Why the alert then?'

'Automatic. Any member of staff goes missing in unusual circumstances and it triggers an immediate alert for personnel to be on their guard. Just in case.'

'Are you under any kind of threat?' He spoke urgently, feeling the need to be with her.

'No, don't be daft. I'm sure it's all fine. They'll probably find he just forgot to update personnel on his holiday plans.'

Her buoyant tone sounded forced.

'I'll come home.'

'No, you won't,' Shamila countered, just as firmly. 'I'm only telling you because that's the procedure we were trained to follow. It's nothing for you to worry about, honestly.'

'All the same...'

'Honestly, Jim. It's fine. I'm going to work. God, look at the time! I'll see you this evening.' She blew a kiss down the line and ended the call.

'Love you.' His words came too late.

Corstorphine glanced at the photograph of the two of them lost in each other, their hands entwined. He was probably being over-protective but couldn't shake off the dread that had followed her call. If anything was to happen to Shamila...

He closed down the thought before it took hold. They'd only just found one another – he couldn't bear imagining life without her.

NINE
BEAT

Hamish stood at the back of the office as Corstorphine started the morning brief in his customary fashion.

'Morning all. Thanks for all your cards and presents. Shamila sends her thanks too. Though we didn't make use of these.'

He held up a pair of fluffy pink handcuffs and fixed Phil Lamb with a look that left little doubt that he knew where that gift had originated.

'Frankie's done a good job filling out the report in my absence, so thanks for that. I see we're keeping on top of traffic violations, so good work, McAdam and Lamb. General crime figures are low, which is good. Been an increase in rural crime – tipping and theft, so we'll have to encourage landowners to fit more security. Frankie, could you download the relevant advice sheets and print off a load?'

Hamish saw Frankie making a note in response. He let the words wash over him, paying scant attention to the team brief. Everything in his life was concentrating down to the one, inescapable event. His world was becoming as focussed as the vanishing dot that the old TVs displayed when they were finally turned off at the end of the evening.

'Apart from that it looks like I picked a good time to go away. Does anyone have anything they want to add?'

'The scarecrow epidemic, sir,' PC Lamb piped up, only to be met with raised eyes and shaking heads.

'Yes, thanks, Lamb. I've already made a note of that.' He waited for anyone else to comment before continuing, 'I'd like you to keep a close eye on my house and Shamila's place of work – she's had a warning through from Carstairs that a member of staff has gone missing recently.'

'Is she at risk, sir?' Hamish lost his distracted air to focus on Corstorphine.

'I don't think so, Hamish. She had an alert come through this morning but said it's routine. She hasn't worked there for months, and the missing staff member may just be on holiday or something. I was told not to worry.'

'I'll include those locations in the daily patrols, sir,' he volunteered from the back of the room.

'Thanks, Hamish. If there's nothing else?'

The team exchanged questioning glances.

'OK then. Let's get to it.' The DI returned to his office and Hamish joined the two PCs.

'Leave the traffic for today. I think it would be best if you both took a car out and made yourselves seen around the town. Foot patrols as well. Phil, you patrol the High Street and shopping area. Bill, you take the top end of town and both of you pass by the DI's house and his wife's clinic on the industrial estate – just in case.'

The constables picked up their hats and left the office empty except for Frankie busily tapping on her keyboard.

Hamish watched her thoughtfully for a moment, saw that her focus was on the job at hand. The sun was shining, autumn leaves catching the light in shades of gold and red. It was too good a day to spend waiting behind a desk.

'I'll take myself out on foot patrol for an hour, if you don't mind looking after the front desk? I could do with stretching my legs.'

Frankie looked up in surprise.

'Sure. I'll listen out for the door buzzer. See you in a bit.'

Hamish wanted to say more, but this wasn't the time. Not that there ever was a right time for what he needed to say.

He began an unhurried but purposeful pounding of the pavement, giving him time to think. Walking the pavements instantly brought back memories. He saw the town through old eyes. Those timbers left rotting in the loch were all that remained of the small passenger ferry that had plied a steady passage up and down the water. The gleaming glass and steel offices on a hill where heather once stained the ground purple until the air was thick with bees. Every street was haunted with the ghosts of his past.

Those memories came easily to him, which made it all the sadder. For months, Molly had been slipping away from him. They'd been married for over thirty years and Corstorphine's wedding had been the lowest point. He'd accepted the confusion over every shopping expedition, the forgetfulness. He'd put it down to age. They were both affected by the passage of time – his muscles weaker now, held in loose folds of skin. The backs of his hands wrinkled when he straightened them, his eyesight useless without glasses. Ahead of him lay retirement and what was euphemistically termed his 'Golden Years'.

Hamish remained sharp enough to know this was fool's gold. Molly had Alzheimer's. They both knew it without having to see the doctor and subject her to the undignified process of clinical appraisal. And to what end? Being offered a label that was worse than any sentence handed down by a judge? The condition sat at their table like an unwelcome guest they were powerless to send away.

'Who's that?' She'd pointed at Shamila as Corstorphine fumbled for the ring, her voice loud in the quiet of the moment.

'Shush, dear. That's Jim. Jim Corstorphine and Shamila. It's their wedding.'

He'd surreptitiously searched around to see if anyone had overheard, breathed deeply when everyone's attention remained fixed on the couple.

'Jim? But he's already married.'

Frankie's whoop as they kissed drowned out her words.

Hamish's blurry vision couldn't be helped by the glasses this time. He stopped, wiped his eyes with the corner of his handkerchief and mimed having a piece of grit in his eye which required his full attention.

Why was life so fucking cruel?

It was a question he'd asked many times over the years – faced with mindless acts of violence or stupidity, or writ large on the news with bombings or famine.

Hamish was not a religious man, or he'd gladly have been on his knees praying for divine intervention every bloody day. He'd not lost his faith as much as never found it, to begin with. The whole church pantomime had always left him feeling faintly bewildered and wondering what it was he was missing. Now he'd offer his own life in exchange for Molly to return from wherever this journey was taking her.

His steps took him home and he opened his front door to find Molly in her favourite chair staring into space as he knew she would.

'Hello, dear.' She rose unsteadily, planted a kiss on his cheek. 'I don't know where the time's gone – I haven't even started tea.'

Hamish took her hands, held them tightly in his.

'It's not even ten, love. I thought I'd stretch my legs, see what's happening in the town instead of staying put in the station all day.'

'Keeping us all safe, like you always do.' She patted his hand, then sat back down as if the effort of standing had been too much.

He sat down with her in companionable silence. Too long together for words needing to be said, too short a time left. Keeping her safe was all he could do now.

TEN

CARSTAIRS

Corstorphine looked up from his computer to see the office was empty, apart from Frankie bent over her own keyboard. The call from Shamila had unsettled him, despite her repeated assurances that there was nothing to worry about. Carstairs State Hospital housed the most dangerous people – those too violent, unpredictable or insanely cunning for the normal prison service to deal with. He dialled the number for Lanark police.

'My name's DI James Corstorphine. My wife...' He paused, the two words still tasting strange in his mouth. 'My wife, Shamila Mallick, has received a warning from Carstairs Hospital about a member of staff who's missing. I just wanted to check with you how worried I should be?'

'What was your wife's name again, can you spell it?'

Corstorphine frowned at the telephone.

'Can you put me through to a detective involved with the case?'

He was asked for his full details, warrant card number and location before being passed on to the detective running the investigation.

'DI Anderson here, your wife's had a security alert from the hospital – is that correct?'

'Aye. Shamila Mallick. She used to be a clinical psychologist at the unit until six months ago. I know these things are routine but wondered how worried we should be?'

'No, you're right to check. It's a strange one, to be honest. A member of staff hasn't shown up for work this week. We've checked his home address – he lives on his own so we've no way of knowing why he's not around.'

'Do you suspect criminal intent?'

'I think it's more likely he's forgotten to notify the hospital of his holidays, or there's some sort of administrative cock-up. Gives us all a bloody headache!'

'And there's no sign of foul play or forced entry?'

'No. I don't think there's anything for you to be worried about. The hospital is understandably cautious whenever a member of staff is absent, but notifying ex-staff is just standard procedure. If I hear anything to the contrary, I'll get straight back to you, but no patients are missing and there's no sign of anything amiss. Does that help?'

'Aye. Thank you, DI Anderson. Like you say, probably a surfeit of caution.'

Corstorphine hung up and wondered why the detective's words had failed to reassure him.

'Sir!' Frankie called out from the main office.

He pushed himself out of his seat, headed towards her desk with an enquiring look on his face.

'Have you seen this?' She pointed to her screen.

Corstorphine moved around her desk. Frankie's screen showed a night-time video taken from a poor-quality camera. Two drunks were staggering around someone's driveway, one of them so paralytic he had to be carried.

'I'm sorry, Frankie. What are we looking at?'

She pointed to the top of the screen where Glenarty Facebook Group displayed as a header.

'This was recorded last night on a resident's doorbell camera. It shows the scarecrow thief in action.'

Corstorphine re-ran the video. Now he knew what he was looking at, he could see that one of the figures was less than human. The picture quality was too poor to make out the thief's features.

'Have they raised a complaint?' The irritation was clear in his voice.

'No, sir, not yet at any rate. I was looking to see if there was any update on Mart McKeown's missing property and this popped up on the page.'

Why would anyone spend their evenings stealing scarecrows? Corstorphine shook his head in exasperation. 'We've enough to be dealing with, Frankie. Whoever this is will have to wait – we've more important problems than this.'

He regretted the sharpness of his tone, realised he was still concerned about Shamila's warning. He followed up his outburst with a more conciliatory compromise.

'Look – the rural crime figures are too high, and now the nights are drawing in, opportunities for the thieving fraternity are only going to improve. Why don't you take a few hours out of the office, visit some of the farmers who've been targeted and give them some reassurance that we're keeping on top of it?'

'I printed out a pile of advice notes, I'll take them with me.'

Corstorphine offered her a smile of encouragement. Frankie knew as well as he did how stretched they were and how farmers were mostly left to deal with rural crime themselves. The missing scarecrows, though – he'd thought it was just youthful high spirits but not over this wide an area. Try as he might, Corstorphine couldn't shake off the unease that had been building since Shamila's call. What would make anyone steal scarecrows?

ELEVEN
FLY-TIPPING

The previous evening was still playing in Frankie's mind. Alex had made some lame excuse for not coming back with her last night – *not a good time* – before leaving without any other explanation. The pain of rejection still made itself known with flashes of worry that he'd found someone else. She was acutely aware that she was swimming in a diminishing gene pool – one where being a detective constable had negative connotations.

The sun failed to lift her spirits, proving more of an irritant every time the road twisted south and highlighted every smear on the windscreen, so she had to repeatedly squint, then activate the screen wash to see the road ahead. What had seemed a blessing when Corstorphine asked her to visit farms that had reported trouble had turned into a curse. This was the fourth farmer she'd seen. The others had thefts of machinery, attempted break-ins or stolen livestock. The farm she'd just left had been the victim of fly-tipping. Builder's rubble and black bin bags blocking a gate, a discarded settee left on top of a beech hedge like an art installation. Her proffered leaflets were an inadequate response, but what else could a small police team do? She made for William Haddow's farm with its missing scarecrow.

Frankie attempted to analyse the source of her disquiet as she drove. Over the last few days, she'd felt herself fading away. It was not a sensation she'd ever before experienced, and not one she welcomed. The cause wasn't Alex's sudden loss of libido or his unwillingness to spend the night together, although that didn't help. She'd felt it in the station, in the other members of their close-knit team. Hamish had become strangely distant of late; Phil Lamb's excruciating jokes and enthusiasm for the next training course had lessened; Bill McAdam was more stoical than usual. Even Corstorphine had a distracted air about him this morning.

Maybe it was the onset of winter. All she really wanted to do was curl up in front of a fire and dream the next few months away.

The farm turn-off was just ahead, Frankie slowed right down to avoid the worst potholes as the car suspension began to protest. There was a tractor parked up, a man waving frantically at her to stop. She recognised William Haddow as he ran to meet her, his beetroot face twisted in shock.

'What's wrong?' Frankie called out of the car window, feeling slightly worried as he flailed towards her.

She cast a look around for the source of his unusual behaviour, but saw nothing out of the ordinary. The tractor was parked normally, not tilted in a ditch or involved in a collision. Fields green with regimented rows of green shoots complete with a scarecrow overseer. Was he excited because he had his scarecrow back?

His overlarge hand hit the patrol car with a heavy thump.

'The scarecrow,' he managed between panicked gulps of air. 'You have to see for yourself.'

Frankie followed William's shaking arm and extended finger. Far from scaring the local corvid population, the scarecrow had become a magnet, attracting newcomers to the irritation of those already perched on outstretched limbs.

She linked the farmer's horrified expression to the crows tearing chunks off the scarecrow's face.

Frankie felt her blood chill as she climbed out of the car and followed the farmer's unwilling steps towards the figure tied to a wooden cross.

TWELVE
RAG'N'BONE

The big, black birds waited until the last possible moment before abandoning their prize, flapping heavily into the air with angry caws of displeasure. Frankie was close enough to see dark beaks stained red, alien intelligence in the dark beads of their eyes. As the black shroud of birds lifted, Frankie desperately hoped their newly vacated perch would resolve into a stuffed mannequin of sacking and straw.

Once her eyes had explained the truth of what she was seeing, her first impulse was to retch. She turned away, hand covering her mouth to stop the first wave of bile forcing its way out of her stomach.

'Fuck!'

William Haddow stared at the figure with the same shocked expression that was written across her own face. She risked another look, swallowing hard to counter the initial surge from her stomach. There was enough left to confirm this had once been human. The face had been the focus of the birds' attention. Tasty morsels such as the eyes were long gone. Strong, dagger-like beaks had rendered cheeks into tattered strips of flesh. Fingers poked out of an old jacket, stained red with blood. Straw turned crimson where it showed in collars and cuffs in deference to the scarecrow's provenance. The shape of jacket and trousers hinted at the body contained therein, strangely shapeless as if further horrors lay in wait.

'When?' It was all Frankie could manage without risking contaminating the scene.

'Just seen it now,' he said weakly. 'Spotted it from the tractor. I thought someone had returned it but then...' The farmer's words spluttered into silence.

'Didn't see anything?' She felt a sense of déjà vu.

'No, nothing. I can't see this track from the farm.'

'I have to call it in. We'll need scene of crime, forensics.' Frankie realised she was babbling, forced herself to take control. 'I'll use the car radio. Ask for help.'

The crows had settled nearby, patrolling the ground like cloaked assassins awaiting their next move.

'Can you keep the crows off? We have to preserve what's left, for identification.'

The farmer nodded wordlessly, and she hurried back to the patrol car trying to ignore the hysterical voice in her head laughing about having the farmer keeping crows off his own scarecrow.

'Sir?'

Frankie realised DI Corstorphine had picked up the call.

'Hello, Frankie. Hamish has taken himself off on foot patrol for a while. What's up?'

'You'd better come and see for yourself. I'm at William Haddow's farm. Someone's returned his scarecrow, except they've put a real body in it.'

'Is this a joke?'

'No. Crows have made a real mess of him – least I think it's a him. We'll need SOC, forensics.'

'I'm coming now. Keep the scene as clean as you can. I'll call in the other services. Are you safe? There's no sign of anyone else around?'

Frankie heard the concern in his voice.

'Just me and William Haddow here, sir. He's in shock. I had to leave him with the body to keep the birds off.'

'Be with you shortly.'

Frankie risked another glance over at the scarecrow. William Haddow had positioned himself a good few metres away from the figure, his back to the macabre sight. Sombre suited crows stood hunched as if in mourning, the more adventurous hopping purposively forward and testing the farmer's resolve. She could see more black dots approaching in the autumnal sky, no doubt attracted by the presence of the earlier arrivals.

Frankie reluctantly left the safe confines of her car and crossed the field towards the farmer and his cohort of crows. The scene was almost biblical – a crucified figure, William standing with arms slightly outstretched and his black-clad congregation shuffling uneasily under the sightless gaze of their host.

'Do you have any idea who that might be?' Frankie took refuge in procedure, attempting to normalise the bizarre.

William Haddow's eyes were still wide with shock as he turned towards the sound of her voice.

'There's nothing left to recognise.'

He purposely averted his gaze from the torn and bloodied mess.

Frankie tried another tack. 'The clothes he's wearing. Are they the same that your scarecrow wore?'

She flapped her arms to warn off a crow that had made a stealthy approach from behind their backs. It hopped a few steps and stood its ground, fixing her with a malevolent black eye.

William's head was nodding when she returned her attention to him.

'Aye. Those are the rags I dressed him in.'

His arms dropped to his sides, all thoughts of warding off the crows apparently forgotten.

'Who'd do such a thing?'

Frankie had no answer.

THIRTEEN
A MURDER OF CROWS

Corstorphine threw the heavy police Land Rover around every twisting corner, cursing the vehicle's top-heavy handling. The SOC unit were on their way from Inverness – almost two hours away. He'd delayed calling in the mortuary van. From Frankie's description, they'd need several body bags rather than a stretcher.

His feeling of unease only intensified as he approached William Haddow's farm. He passed a scattering of stone cottages almost hidden in trees until a weatherbeaten sign pointed the way to Halfway Farm. The Land Rover felt more at home here, taking potholes in its stride and affording him a view over neatly trimmed beech hedges to fields each side. Frankie's patrol car was parked next to a tractor, looking like a toy in comparison. Corstorphine's gaze was drawn to the comical sight of a scarecrow being defended from a growing number of crows.

Frankie came to meet him – trailing a line of police tape behind her.

'Over here, sir.' She pointed at the raggedy figure slumped on its makeshift perch in the middle of the field. The ground had been recently worked, brown soil turned to expose stones to the sun like bleached bones.

Corstorphine sat on the back of the Land Rover, exchanging

his footwear for wellington boots. He struggled to pull on forensic overshoes whilst Frankie wrapped police tape to the gatepost, waiting for him to enter the field before closing the gap with the last of her tape.

'Did you see any footprints, signs of a vehicle being driven into the field?'

He could see the clear imprint of two pairs of feet left in the soil where Frankie had just been. The footsteps joined those of the farmer's to leave a confused trail towards the scarecrow.

'I only saw the one set of prints. William Haddow had already been over to investigate the return of his scarecrow, then ran back to his tractor to call us in – except I arrived before he had a chance.'

Corstorphine viewed the scarecrow with apprehension.

'We need to keep to your footprints otherwise forensics will have nothing to work with.' He placed his feet as closely to Frankie's steps as he could, taking a shorter pace than felt comfortable.

'Why's he staying on top of the crime scene?' Corstorphine kept his voice low enough for only Frankie to hear above the displeased cawing from the crows.

'To keep the birds off. Every time we move away, they're back, taking chunks off the body.'

He grimaced. 'I've asked Lamb and McAdam to join us. They can look after the scene until SOC give us the all-clear. William Haddow?' Corstorphine fought to keep his emotions under control as he called to the farmer and the birds lifted into the air, mocking calls aimed earthwards. 'I'm DI James Corstorphine. What can you tell me about this?'

He didn't need to elaborate. Even from ten metres away he could see skin hanging off in white threads. Only dark shadows remained where eyes should have been. The farmer made reluctant progress towards them, boots held by the wet soil at the field's edge and released with a squelch at each step. He positioned himself so he didn't have to see the scarecrow, nervously turning his head as if to confirm the thing stayed still.

'Nothing I can say. Wasn't there yesterday, so someone must have put it there overnight.'

'You didn't see anything, hear a vehicle?'

A flicker of annoyance crossed his face. 'I've already told her. I can't see this field from the farm and it's too far to hear any vehicle. Whoever did it came last night.'

He shivered at the thought, forced himself to look at the corpse tied to a pole embedded in the ground.

'Those are the same clothes your scarecrow wore?' Corstorphine asked the question as if this was a normal investigation – not that there was anything remotely normal about the three of them standing in a field next to a mutilated body. His feeling of being in a surreal nightmare only intensified as the crows wheeled back to land, carpeting fresh shoots in black undertaker garb.

'Aye.'

Corstorphine had to be content with that. One glance at his face was enough for him to know William Haddow wasn't going to be adding anything else to the investigation.

'OK. Thanks, William. Can you wait by the tractor until we're done here?'

The farmer's normally ruddy complexion had turned ashen, his head jerked a few times and his hand lifted to cover his mouth as he hurried away.

Corstorphine and Frankie tactfully looked the other way as William threw up in the hedgerow.

'What do you make of it, sir?'

He shook his head. 'I don't know, Frankie. Whatever we're dealing with, it was planned. When was his scarecrow reported missing?'

'Yesterday, sir.' Frankie pulled out her notebook, flicked through the pages. 'William came in to report it at 4:55 p.m.' She continued reading. 'He said it must have been taken sometime overnight on Sunday. Do you think this is premeditated? Taking his scarecrow to replace with a body? Why would you even do something like that?'

Corstorphine exchanged a look with the nearest crow as it strutted closer to the corpse, watching cold avian intelligence make the calculation that maybe that was close enough. It altered course like an innocent hiker out for a ramble.

'I don't know, Frankie. Whoever it is, I hope to hell this isn't the start of something. We'll have to wait for forensics to tell us what we're dealing with.'

Dread threatened to overwhelm him. Corstorphine's intuition that the scarecrow thefts weren't as innocent as they first appeared had been proved correct. He scanned the area for clues, taking refuge in working the scene.

The crows pecked insects out of the soil without any enthusiasm, waiting for their opportunity to return to the main feast. Corstorphine's eyes narrowed as he watched the birds pecking at the field's margin.

'Wait here.' He left Frankie and cautiously made his way towards the unkempt field's edge. There was a single tyre track heavily embedded in the loose soil until scuff marks erased it as it headed towards the scarecrow.

Corstorphine took a snap on his phone before returning to Frankie.

'Stay here until the constables turn up. I'll take William home – he's in shock. Last thing he needs is to be driving a tractor in that state. Ask forensics to check the field edge, it looks like some sort of vehicle may have been used to transport the corpse here. I'll see you back at the station.'

Frankie raised a hand in farewell and a few crows lifted off the ground before settling down again.

A murder of crows – the thought occurred to Corstorphine as he made for the tractor and the solitary figure sat motionless in the cab. Whoever chose that word for a collective noun knew what they were dealing with – if only he could say the same.

FOURTEEN

DI

The dour sergeant was back behind his desk at reception when Corstorphine returned to the station. He'd barely looked up from his screen to acknowledge Corstorphine's greeting, leading the DI to wonder what had captured Hamish's attention. Corstorphine returned to his office, typed up the visit to William Haddow's farm. The constables should be arriving there any moment to take over from Frankie – he needed the DC here to help begin piecing together the investigation into the body.

Forensics were expected on site in the next two hours. He checked his watch – just after 12:30 p.m. That would leave them a good four hours until sunset. Enough time for them to process the scene and hopefully find something that could identify the victim, or a clue as to who had placed the body there.

Corstorphine leaned back in his chair, searching the ceiling for inspiration. He was expecting the first day back at work after his honeymoon to be undemanding, a gradual easing back into the daily routine. Instead, he was faced with a homicide – and the replacement of scarecrow with a human body suggested a killer who was intent on being noticed.

He read Frankie's interview notes from yesterday. According to William Haddow, his scarecrow went missing Sunday night. Then

Mart McKeown reported that his was taken that same evening. He checked his diary – the 26th October.

Corstorphine made his way to the main office, stood in front of the blank crazy wall in silent contemplation before committing the recent events to the board. The homicide took central position, leaving enough space for the investigation to grow. He gave the unknown body the name John Doe, linked to William Haddow – forensics would hopefully furnish him with a name soon enough. To the left of John Doe went Mart McKeown's name, with a line connecting him to his missing scarecrow. Corstorphine elaborated on the stick figure he'd drawn, adding a guitar. On the right, he wrote *Glenarty Facebook Page* with a line connecting another stick figure.

The three minimalistic figures were arranged in a row like a child's game of hangman. Corstorphine hoped his prescience that the two other missing scarecrows would come back in the same manner as William Haddow's was simply his imagination working overtime.

'That's Bill arrived at the Haddow farm now, sir.'

Corstorphine turned from contemplation of his primitive artwork as Hamish spoke.

'Thanks, Hamish.' He observed the sergeant closely, his age showing in the way his body appeared to sink into itself, the movements slow and deliberate as if the man was under water.

'Is Lamb joining him?'

'On his way.' Hamish hesitated in the doorway, his cue to wait for a further announcement. 'Do we know who it is, sir? The body?'

Corstorphine shook his head. 'No idea.' The image of crows reluctantly leaving the scarecrow's disfigured face appeared in his mind so vividly he could hear their harsh calls of displeasure.

'Forensics should be on site soon enough – they're our best bet unless someone calls in a missing person.'

'Aye. Right you are, sir. I'll get back to it.'

Corstorphine frowned as Hamish turned away. There was

something bothering the sergeant. He might be slow, but he'd always been focussed, his steady presence a counterbalance to Lamb and McAdam's more youthful exuberance. Maybe it was because he'd been away on honeymoon and was able to notice changes more readily than if he'd been in the office every day for the last few weeks. Whatever the reason, he'd swear those had looked like tears in Hamish's eyes before he had turned away.

The phone rang, breaking into his thoughts.

'DI James Corstorphine?' The voice sounded familiar. He struggled to remember where he'd heard it before.

'Yes, speaking.'

'DI Anderson, Lanark police. You called this morning, about Carstairs Hospital?'

Something in the caller's tone sent a chill down his spine.

'Yes, have you found the missing member of staff?' Corstorphine's imagination threatened to pre-empt the detective's response.

'I'm afraid not, but we have a match for prints found at his house which has given us cause for concern.'

Corstorphine willed the man to get to the point.

'One of Carstairs' patients, Duncan Lewis. We found his fingerprints on a glass.'

Corstorphine puzzled to make sense of the DI's statement.

'Duncan Lewis – is he interned at the state hospital?' The name was familiar. He struggled to remember where from.

'No, an outpatient. He was discharged a year ago following a psychiatric evaluation.'

'Discharged?' Corstorphine asked. 'I thought the state hospital was for those cases who posed such a threat to society that they were in for life?'

'It's a common misconception. The hospital has around three hundred patients at any one time, and typically ten to twenty are discharged back into the community each year.'

An icy knot had settled in his stomach.

'He's now a suspect in the search for the missing staff member. He'd had dealings with him at the hospital.'

'Who was responsible for the psychiatric evaluation that enabled his release?' Corstorphine felt his mouth go dry.

'Your wife, Shamila Mallick.'

The ice in Corstorphine's stomach reached cold fingers up his spine.

'I advise you both to be cautious until we've caught him. Duncan is a dangerous individual, as your wife will be able to attest. I'm sending his file over to you now in case he appears in your locality.'

A ping from the computer alerted him that the file had arrived.

'We'll watch out for him.' Corstorphine's own voice sounded distant to him. 'Thanks for letting me know.'

FIFTEEN
DUNCAN LEWIS

'Hamish! Is Lamb still anywhere near Shamila's office?'

The sergeant must have detected the note of panic in his voice, his head jerking up with unusual alacrity.

'He's almost at the Haddow farm, sir. Is there a problem?'

Corstorphine swore under his breath, grabbing his coat and car keys from his office as the sergeant looked on with concern.

'I hope not, Hamish. I've had a call warning me that Shamila may be in danger due to one of her former Carstairs patients. I'll go there myself. Can you let Frankie know when she arrives?'

He flew out of the door, leaving Hamish's response to fade into the air behind him.

Shamila's office was in one of the small business parks that surrounded the town – built in the optimism of bringing new jobs to the Highlands and now mostly let to accountants, builders and craft brewers. Shamila's clinic was the odd one out, next door to a private gym so both body and soul could be treated in symbiotic proximity. He slewed to a halt in front of her clinic, feeling slightly foolish to have made such a dramatic entrance in the zen-like calm of the car park.

His panic subsided as soon as he tried the door and found it locked, as it normally was. Shamila didn't accept walk-ins – all her clients were referred through professional channels and given appointments. He peered through a frosted glass pane set in the door to see the receptionist moving behind her desk, the glass breaking her image into fractured shapes which his brain had to reassemble like a puzzle. An intercom clicked beside him as she triggered the audio.

'Mallick Psychotherapy, can I help you?'

'Hi, Kira, it's James Corstorphine.' He searched for the words that could explain his unexpected arrival and wondered whether she'd picked up the sound of his tyres screeching to a halt outside the unit. 'Is Shamila busy? I just wanted a quick word.'

He glanced at the doorbell, aware that his face was being displayed on a small screen on Kira's desk. He attempted a carefree smile which felt unnaturally forced.

'Oh, hi, Mr Corstorphine. I'm sorry, but Shamila's with a client at the moment. Is it urgent?'

The normality of the exchange was reassuring. He checked his watch, 1:18 p.m. She'd be finished at 2 p.m. at the latest. Tuesday was a half day.

'No, nothing urgent. How's your day been?'

He could imagine the receptionist's quizzical expression even if the glass made such an observation impossible.

'Yeah, it's been good, thanks.' An awkward silence followed before she added, 'and you?'

Corstorphine didn't need to reflect on his first day back to know it hadn't been the best.

'Quite busy. I'll wait in the car park for her. Could you let her know I'm out here?'

'Is there a problem? Anything I can help with?'

'No, it's alright. I thought Shamila might have been free so we could have an early finish.'

'I'll pass that on, Mr Corstorphine.'

'Thanks, Kira.'

The intercom gave a final click as he remained marooned on the other side of the door. The situation gave him comfort – if Kira wasn't going to open the door for him, then anyone other than registered appointments would have a hard time accessing the clinic.

He returned to the Land Rover, confident that the presence of a marked police vehicle was enough to deter anyone from attempting to harm Shamila, and opened the file sent from Lanark police.

Duncan Lewis's photograph stared back at him from the small iPhone screen. He was a powerfully built man in his fifties, bald head giving his rounded face the appearance of a boiled egg. Intense blue eyes shone with intelligence. He smiled for the camera, but there was something false about his expression as if he was attempting to appear open and friendly. Maybe it was a police thing, this ability to see beneath the mask people present to the world. Whatever Duncan Lewis was hiding, it left Corstorphine feeling worried.

He prepared to read the accompanying notes, in between quick glances around the car park in search of any lurking figures as the afternoon wound on. Duncan Lewis had been admitted to Carstairs State Hospital in the June of 2000. Aged thirty, he'd been convicted of the murder of his then wife – Sandra Lewis – whose body had been found dismembered and hidden in isolated locations around the Highlands. Originally treated as a missing person, the discovery of her murder had only come to light due to Duncan Lewis's inexplicable decision to write a novel featuring his own crime. The significance of the name suddenly came back into memory – he was better known as the author Daemon Aticus.

He'd created a fictitious world describing his crime and cryptic clues pointing to burial sites. It was enough to attract the attention of a retired detective who thought it would be amusing to try and solve the mystery. When the first body part was discovered, decomposed but identifiable as human remains, Daemon Aticus's debut novel became an overnight sensation.

Corstorphine had heard of the case, it would have been impossible not to have known. The police had been unable to stop the hordes of amateur sleuths, geocache enthusiasts and thrill-seekers from trying to break the code. As a result, crime scenes were so badly damaged that forensics had a tough job pinning the wife's murder on her husband. In the space of two weeks, every part of her anatomy had been found – buried under bridges, left inside caves and deserted buildings. In the end, the strongest evidence the procurator fiscal could bring to bear was the codified evidence in Duncan Lewis's novel.

Corstorphine hadn't realised Shamila had any involvement with Duncan Lewis, but then she didn't share any of her clinical work with him. He looked into the author's eyes and wondered how sick he had to be to commit such a horrendous crime – and how correct was Sharmila's decision to have him released a year ago.

The missing staff member had also been included in the file – a Richard Bryce who was employed as a pharmaceutical nurse. He added the name to his notebook.

Light spilled from the clinic's door as it opened and Corstorphine watched as a middle-aged woman wrapped her coat around her as she left, making for a nearby car. He caught Shamila's eye as she turned towards him in the doorway, giving her a wave. She held up four fingers to advise him how much longer she'd be, then placed them to her lips before throwing a kiss his way and returning into the clinic.

His smile faded. Duncan Lewis had taken his wife apart piece by piece. The scarecrow in Haddow's field had been assembled much the same way.

SIXTEEN

DECAPITATED

'The DI said Shamila's in danger. He's gone to her clinic.'

Frankie paused on her way into the office, the sergeant's unhurried pronouncement reverberating around her skull.

'In danger? Does he need backup?' She willed Hamish to react to the urgency in her voice.

'He didn't ask for any backup. Just wanted to know if Lamb was anywhere near her clinic, then left in a bit of a hurry when I informed him he was on his way to the Haddow farm. The DI said it was to do with one of her Carstairs patients?'

'I'll give him a call on the radio. Jesus! Why does everything have to happen at once?'

She left Hamish pondering her question without any expectation of an answer and reached for her radio.

'Charlie six-four. Charlie six-four from Foxtrot Kilo, over.'

She waited impatiently for the radio to splutter into life.

'Foxtrot Kilo, this is Charlie six-four. I'm with Shamila now and heading home. I'll update you tomorrow morning. Send Duncan Lewis's details to Lamb and McAdam. He's being sought by the Lanark police. I emailed them to you. Over.'

'Do you require any assistance, over?'

'No. We're in control of the situation here. I'll brief you tomorrow, Frankie. Out.'

She sat at her desk and opened up the email Corstorphine had mentioned. The face that appeared on the screen was one she remembered from the news. Frankie read the accompanying notes to refresh her memory of a case that still resonated after twenty-five years, long before she had joined the force. Corstorphine's notes had been added at the end, and she read about Shamila's involvement with growing disbelief.

'Jesus! She was the one who recommended him as fit for parole!'

She pulled out her iPhone, looked at the photographs she'd taken of the scarecrow figure and zoomed in for a closer inspection. The head sat unnaturally on the body, reinforcing the impression that it had been assembled from parts rather than a complete person. Like Corstorphine, she made an immediate connection to the infamous author's dismembering of his wife. Had this been left as a message for Shamila?

Frankie leaned back in her seat and spotted Corstorphine's stick figures on the crazy wall. The Haddow scarecrow took centre position, the two other missing scarecrows arranged each side of it. She stood and walked over for a closer look, confirming the crude outline of a guitar under Mart McKeown's stick figure and gave a wry smile. At least the boss retained some semblance of humour in the face of the day's macabre find. She selected red string and added Duncan Lewis's name to the missing Carstairs nurse.

If the Lanark police had issued an alert for his arrest, then she could understand why the DI had left in such a hurry. Shamila's previous involvement with Duncan Lewis would be enough for him to have concerns. Would the ex-patient go after the woman who'd essentially set him free? It seemed unlikely, but his fingerprints found at the missing nurse's home was cause enough to bring him in.

She re-read the briefing notes issued by the Lanark police. All they had on Duncan Lewis was his home address, with current whereabouts unknown. He'd been released into the community for a year without any trouble or missing any parole meetings. Frankie delved deeper into his case files, finding he'd been convicted for manslaughter by reason of diminished responsibility. That explained him being sent to Carstairs State Hospital. It also went some way to explaining why he had been released so early if the parole board were convinced of his mental well-being – a decision Corstorphine's new wife was instrumental in bringing about.

Frankie parked it there. If Corstorphine said he had it under control, then Shamila was safe. Meanwhile, they had other problems that needed her full concentration. The missing scarecrows had rapidly turned from farce to horror. She only hoped that the other two missing scarecrows were the actions of high-spirited teenagers and not the precursor to further atrocities.

She'd left the farm when forensics arrived, leaving PCs Lamb and McAdam to stop any inquisitive locals or the press from taking a diversion up the farm track. The two forensics officers had suited up in sterile white oversuits, scaring off the crows more successfully than she'd managed to do. It was almost as if they knew the game was up and there'd be no further opportunities for rich pickings.

Even from a distance she'd seen the technicians' expressions turn to shock when they drew closer to the body. Death and mutilation, these were their constant reminders of mortality and the fragility of life. But a corpse dressed up to look like a scarecrow...

'I've had word from McAdam.'

Frankie jerked in surprise, turning to face Hamish who'd managed to enter the office without her noticing. She regained her composure, gave him a brief nod to continue whilst hoping he hadn't noticed how easily she'd been spooked.

'Forensics are working at the scene. They'll be taking the body back to the Inverness lab for further investigation. I'll be standing the constables down when SOC leave.' He consulted his watch, ignoring the wall clock beside him. 'There's not anything more they can usefully do at the scene.'

'Did forensics have anything to say about the body? Anything we can work with until they come back with lab results?'

The sergeant's lips pressed together as if he had no wish to pass on further information.

'Only that he'd been decapitated – and his feet taken off at the ankles.' Hamish lowered his voice. 'Hadn't been done cleanly either, according to what Bill McAdam had to say.'

Frankie's heart lurched at the confirmation of what she'd already suspected. The head hadn't sat right on the body, making the resemblance to a scarecrow even more acute. Whoever had committed such an atrocity would be capable of worse. Now he had the taste, he'd be searching for more victims.

'Who'd do such a thing?' The sergeant's rheumy eyes focussed on her face.

She realised he'd aged.

'I don't know, Hamish.' Frankie spoke softly, her mind still focussed on the sergeant's health. 'That's for us to find out.'

The sergeant couldn't be her major concern, not now there was a killer on the loose. They had to find him before the next victim was discovered. She mentally counted the missing scarecrows. Could there be more bodies to come?

SEVENTEEN
HOME SWEET HOME

Corstorphine followed Shamila's car on the journey back, parking the police Land Rover in the drive to advertise the fact that this was a policeman's home.

'Wait a second. Let me go in first.' He had to hurry before she opened the door ahead of him.

Shamila stood poised on the doorstep, key in her hand and the first hint of exasperation crossing her features.

'James, are you not overreacting slightly?'

Her smile was an attempt to placate his worry, but he'd not settle until Duncan Lewis had been found.

'Humour me. I have a policeman's jaundiced view of threats like this, and I'm not taking any chances where you're concerned.'

He'd already scanned the doors and windows for sign of forced entry, now turned the key in the lock and cautiously pushed the door open. The house was undisturbed, waiting for them to return. Corstorphine scooped up the mail and walked down the hall to drop the small collection of envelopes and marketing flyers on the kitchen table. The burglar alarm control screen showed no alerts. He began to relax.

'Safe for me to come in?' Shamila called from the doorstep.

He heard the laughter in her voice. It didn't matter if she

thought he was being overly careful – a career as a detective made him suspicious of almost everyone. Particularly if a psychotic murderer was on the loose.

'Aye. It's fine.' He tried for a reassuring smile as she walked past him, a cryptic expression etched on her face.

'I'll just check upstairs – and can we keep the front door closed?' Corstorphine heard her sigh as he took the stairs two at a time. He returned to the kitchen once he'd assured himself the house was safe. Shamila had filled the kettle and was spooning ground coffee into a cafetière.

'Want a cup?'

'Aye. Please.' He forced himself to sit at the kitchen island when all he wanted was to prowl the house and garden.

'How was your day?' Shamila asked as she poured boiling water over the ground coffee. 'Good to be back?'

Corstorphine thought of the crows and the body tied to a rough cross in the farmer's field.

'It's been busy.'

She sat beside him, pushing a steaming mug in his direction.

'Do you want to tell me about it?'

Corstorphine still wasn't used to having his own personal therapist to hand. He felt like he was turning into an American. Not that Shamila meant it that way – this was merely an entirely standard exploration of each other's day.

'There's been a body left in a farmer's field.'

'Oh no! That's dreadful! Do you think it's murder?'

The sightless eyes remained in his memory. The strange way the head had sat lopsided on the shapeless body.

'Aye. I don't think there's any doubt. Someone had gone to the trouble of replacing a scarecrow with the body, using the scarecrow's rags. Left in the same place as well so no attempt at hiding it.'

Shamila lost any vestige of humour and shivered involuntarily. 'It's the one thing I can't stand.'

Corstorphine shot her an inquisitive glance. 'What do you mean?'

'Formidophobia.' She must have seen he hadn't the faintest idea what she was talking about. 'An irrational fear of scarecrows,' she explained. 'I've no idea why – I just find them so... creepy.'

He felt the hairs rising on the back of his neck. Corstorphine didn't like coincidences, but didn't want to worry her any more.

'Well, this one was enough to give anyone a phobia.' Corstorphine filed away her newly disclosed fear for future consideration. Maybe *she* needed therapy?

'Do you know who it is? Was,' Shamila corrected herself.

'No. Forensics are looking into it now. Not much left of his face, but dental records or fingerprints should help.'

'Have you any idea who might be responsible?'

Corstorphine did – he only hoped it was wrong.

'This patient of yours, Duncan Lewis – the one you advised the parole board was fit to be released.'

'You think he's involved?' Shamila's eyes narrowed imperceptibly.

'I'm not saying that.' Corstorphine took a deep breath. 'The Lanark police found his fingerprints at the home of a missing member of staff. Duncan's not at his registered address and there's an arrest warrant out for him.'

'Has he missed any parole meetings?' She remained unbothered by his revelation.

'I don't think so. It's just with you having an involvement with him...' Corstorphine struggled to put his thoughts into the right words. 'What can you tell me about him? Am I right to be concerned if the local CID have issued an arrest warrant?'

He searched her face, seeing nothing other than calm acceptance.

'You think he may be coming for me? Is that what this is all about?'

Corstorphine nodded.

'OK.' Shamila sipped at her coffee, watching him with seriousness. 'I can't say much because of client confidentiality, but I can tell you Duncan has no reason to harm me – nor do I think he's likely to be the murderer.'

'What makes you so sure?'

Her hand reached out to cover his.

'Duncan Lewis experienced a psychotic episode. He believed his wife was a demon and the only way of completely destroying her was to cut her body into pieces and spread them far and wide.'

'How do you know that? Couldn't he just be an evil bastard?'

She sighed before giving him a pitying glance.

'That's the line the papers went with. I dealt with him, James. I know Duncan Lewis better than anyone, even himself.'

Shamila withdrew her hand and took hold of her mug, sipping at her coffee with apparent unconcern. She raised her head, looked directly into his eyes.

'Duncan's condition was a mental illness. No different to any physical sickness we're all prone to. People have this strange idea that those unlucky enough to suffer from psychosis or even depression have brought it on themselves. That it can't be fixed and they should be outcasts from society, but with the right treatment and medical intervention many can make a good recovery and have a quality of life unimaginable in earlier times.'

Corstorphine tried to look reassured, but he could tell she wasn't convinced.

'In Duncan's case, there was a chemical imbalance in his brain. We don't fully understand what can cause these episodes, but he managed to keep his psychosis hidden from his family and work colleagues until it was too late. By the time anyone knew how sick he was, he'd already disposed of his wife. The rest you know about.'

'I didn't know you'd been the one treating him,' Corstorphine replied, quite reasonably in his view.

'I don't discuss my clients. You know that.' She stared at him, her brows creased in irritation.

Corstorphine attempted to calm the rising tension.

'I know that. I'm sorry – I'm just worried. For you.'

'Duncan Lewis isn't your murderer, James. He had the one episode due to a condition which has been successfully controlled with anti-psychotic medicine. I wasn't the only professional involved in his treatment, or providing recommendations to the parole board. Believe me, we're used to patients trying to outsmart us – seeing us as a challenge. Many are above average intelligence; it can be difficult.'

She paused, deep in thought.

'Duncan has regular meetings with a clinical psychologist as part of the terms of his parole. His anti-psychotic medicine usage is checked, interactions with people monitored. He couldn't fool everyone. Besides, the fact that his psychosis was so deep that he created a complete alter-ego is the main reason we let him go.'

'I don't understand.'

'He became an author. I mean, he *really* became an author. It was a classic case of dissociative identity disorder. Duncan Lewis had no knowledge of his alter ego – Daemon Aticus.

'What? You're saying he murdered his wife and wrote a book about it but has no memory of doing either?'

'He's not the first case where a completely separate identity can exist concurrently in the same mind. Duncan Lewis was an extreme example, but in terms of the law you could argue the wrong man was convicted for the crime.'

Corstorphine wrestled with the concept. 'The only reason he was brought in for murder was thanks to a reader taking his book seriously enough to decipher the locations he'd given for the body parts.'

'*Outgrave,*' Shamila clarified.

'Aye.' He carefully selected his words before continuing. 'You believe Duncan Lewis had no memory of killing his wife – that this other personality Daemon Aticus was responsible even though they're the same person?'

'Exactly! And no sane murderer would have documented exactly where he'd buried every part of his wife's body. Once

Daemon Aticus had been erased from his mind, Duncan was as sane as you or I.'

Corstorphine remained unconvinced. He reached for his notebook and searched for the name of the missing staff member he'd jotted down earlier.

'Do you remember Richard Bryce from your time at Carstairs?'

Shamila drank the last of her coffee and placed her cup down on the counter.

'Yes, I worked with him. Is he the one who's missing and started this alert?'

He nodded. 'Can you tell me anything about him?'

'Richard's one of the nurses. His job is to ensure the patients are correctly medicated. He's a good man, takes pride in his work. He's not the sort to just take time off without clearing it with HR first.'

'Why would Duncan Lewis be visiting Richard's house?'

She showed the first hint of unease since he'd first asked her about the automatic hospital alert.

'It's not usual but then Duncan Lewis has been an outpatient for a year now. They may well have developed a friendship outside of their clinical relationship over that time. It's a small place, people naturally see a lot of each other outside of the hospital.'

Shamila sighed with frustration as she saw his cynical expression remained in place and tried again to reassure him.

'You remember Gyles Lambert, from our wedding reception?'

Corstorphine's memory supplied the details. A face that looked as if it had been hewn out of rock, square jaw, powerful frame, a handshake that threatened to break his fingers if he hadn't grasped back equally as firmly. He'd arrived alone, hadn't made much of an effort at mingling and then had been one of the first to leave the reception.

'Dr Lambert was employed under me. He became the lead clinical psychologist when I handed in my notice. He never really agreed with my clinical assessment of Duncan Lewis.'

'How's that meant to reassure me?'

Shamila's eyes crinkled in amusement. 'Because he's been managing Duncan's case and seeing him regularly. If Duncan showed the slightest hint of mental instability, he'd have him back behind bars and under a chemical cosh instantly. Nothing would please him more than to prove me wrong and have him re-committed. Believe me, so long as Gyles allows Duncan Lewis to be free in the community, then he's no threat to anyone.'

Corstorphine picked up on the first mention of professional conflict.

'Did you two get on?'

Her mouth twisted before responding. 'He propositioned me once – I liked him but not in that way!' Her expression turned serious. 'Gyles Lambert is a competent clinician. If he had the slightest concern about Duncan Lewis, then he'd be back inside.'

'Well, can you just take extra care until Duncan Lewis is found. I couldn't bear if anything happened to you.'

'I'll be careful. Here, give me a kiss.'

EIGHTEEN
NEWSHOUND

PC Phil Lamb spotted the local newspaper reporter before she'd managed to park her car, pulling up onto a grass verge at the edge of the farm track.

'Who's this?' Bill McAdam was alerted by the sound of the car door slamming.

Both constables had been fixated on the forensics activity happening in front of them. The white-suited technicians had first carefully removed the head, sliding it off a metal pole until it came free with a glutinous slurp before sealing it inside a large, clear plastic bag. As soon as the body had been released, both feet had detached and fallen to the ground. The constables had been so fascinated by the gruesome activity happening in front of them that the job of safeguarding the site had slipped both their minds.

'I'll deal with it,' Phil grabbed his chance to impress the woman he'd already made several unsuccessful attempts to court. 'It's that French reporter who works for *The Courier*.'

'Don't say anything!' The older constable shouted advice to his back.

PC Lamb held a hand up in acknowledgement, then raised it higher to sweep hair back from his forehead and patting it into place.

'I'm sorry, you'll have to stop there.' The hand returned to traffic duty, palm held flat facing her.

'Oh, PC Lamb. I'm so glad to see a friendly face in uniform. I was just driving back into town when I saw police activity.' She kept on coming, angling her neck around him for a closer look. 'Is that a body?'

Phil almost tripped over his own feet when he saw the phone in her hand already rising for a photograph.

'You can't do that! I have to ask you to leave. This is an active investigation.'

He caught her judging how serious he was, making the snap decision whether to risk a photograph or not. The phone lowered and was replaced in her bag.

'OK. OK.' She held her hands up to show they were now empty. 'What's the story here, Phil? You can tell me.'

He couldn't. Not with Bill within earshot at any rate.

'I'll have to ask you to take your car back onto the public road. We need to keep the track free.' He took a few steps towards her, both hands now raised as if he was herding a stray sheep.

'That's a body they're taking down, isn't it?'

'Seriously. You can't stay here. I'm going to have to ask you to leave.'

She looked at him in disappointment. 'Phil. You're usually so good with the press.'

He checked behind him, relieved to see his colleague paying full attention to the forensics team collecting severed feet from between deep furrows and placing them in plastic bags. They looked as if they were being prepared for the freezer.

She'd taken out a notebook in the time he'd taken to risk a quick backwards glance, and he caught her writing notes. Had he said anything he shouldn't have? Phil nervously ran through the conversation they'd just had. No, he'd not given anything away.

'What's that?' She pointed towards the scene with a biro aimed over his right shoulder.

Phil turned instinctively to catch sight of one of the forensics officers carrying what was unmistakably a human head towards his vehicle, a ruined face visible through clear plastic.

'It's a head, isn't it?' she asked brightly.

The PC saw the biro hovering over the notebook page in readiness for a response. Shit! He should have left her to Bill. He'd know how to deal with her. If it wasn't for the hope that she'd find him interesting enough to go out with...

'I'm not at liberty to provide any information. Now, if you'd return to your car and clear the track...'

'A head.' Her biro made a definitive mark on the page. 'We have a murder investigation then. Can you tell me who it is? Looks very much like a man's head.'

Phil watched in increasing desperation as her biro added more squiggles to the page.

'You're going to have to leave.'

'OK, officer. I have enough information for now. Tell your DI Corstorphine that I'll be in touch. Will you be in the pub later, it would be nice to see you out of uniform?' Her eyes swept seductively from the peak of his cap all the way down to his muddied boots.

'I could. Eh, I mean aye.' Phil hoped his blush wasn't as evident as it felt. 'I was going there anyway – after my shift. About eight?'

'I'll see you then, officer. Bye.'

Phil waited until her car returned back down the track and his blush receded before he rejoined the other PC.

'She saw the body, didn't she?' Bill stated simply.

'Aye.' PC Lamb spoke tiredly. 'Now it's going to be in the paper and I'll be the one who gets the blame.'

The thought of meeting her later made all other concerns fade into insignificance.

NINETEEN
PANDORA'S BOX

Frankie read through the notes sent from Lanark Police Station and studied Duncan Lewis's photograph. His expressionless face stared back at her like a man devoid of a soul. She tried to picture him killing and dismembering his wife. In his case it wasn't difficult to imagine.

Hamish said that Corstorphine had hurried off. That explained his leaving the crazy board unfinished. She'd have done the same if someone she loved was in immediate danger of being murdered. The thought unsettled her in a way she wasn't keen to dwell on. Her own relationship with Alex wasn't exactly setting the world on fire. Maybe she shouldn't have expected the flames of passion to survive with him being a fireman.

The Lanark DI hadn't sounded unduly concerned to have a member of staff missing. Corstorphine had mentioned in passing that he'd probably not filed his leave correctly. But there was an unidentified body on its way to the Inverness morgue, and she'd give even odds on it matching the name on the crazy board.

The DI had left work early to keep Shamila close – that was sufficient cause for her to take the threat seriously. Would Duncan Lewis have reason to come after Shamila if she was the one who marked him as no longer a danger to society? What if she'd made a terrible mistake?

Corstorphine's stick figures representing the three missing scarecrows mocked her concerns.

She heard the phone ringing in reception, then Hamish's measured tones as he took the call. Her own phone buzzed moments later, and Frankie crossed over to her desk to answer.

'What is it, Hamish?' It was too soon for forensics to have made an identification on the body – unless they'd struck lucky with some form of ID on the corpse.

'I've Josephine Sables on the line, from *The Courier*. She wanted to talk with the DI about the decapitated body found at Halfway Farm.'

'Shit!' The French reporter was well-known to them, and too bloody good at her job!

'Has Lamb been talking to her?' The young PC's infatuation with the reporter was an open secret in the station. 'Pass her through to me, Hamish. I'll have to deal in the DI's absence.'

She waited for the click which signified the call had been transferred and ordered her thoughts in readiness.

'DC Frankie McKenzie, how can I help you?'

'Ah, Frankie – I was hoping to talk to DI Corstorphine. Is he busy?'

Frankie frowned at the familiarity, but then it was a small town and they all knew one another – besides, she quite liked the way her name always sounded exotic in that French accent.

'The DI's not here at the moment. Can I help?' she asked in the certain knowledge that the recently discovered body was the only item on the reporter's agenda.

'I was hoping you'd be able to tell me about the body that was found today?'

There was no point in trying to obfuscate, the reporter had already seen enough.

'We can't comment this early into an investigation as you well know. The DI will release a statement once next of kin have been notified – until then, it would be helpful if you refrained from publishing anything that may have a detrimental impact upon our enquiry.' She gave a tight smile at her delivery and choice of words. That should slow the reporter down at the very least.

'Yes, of course. We wouldn't want to interfere with your enquiries, but...'

Here we go, Frankie thought. She waited for the next salvo.

'But why was he dressed as a scarecrow and his head decapitated? Also, it very much looked to me as if his feet had become detached. Should people be worried? We have a duty to tell our readers the news.'

Frankie sought for a way of replacing the lid on Pandora's box.

'If any of these details are made public, then you run the very real risk of being prosecuted for defeating the ends of justice.'

'I was hoping that we might be able to work together, Frankie.' The reporter was trying for a conciliatory approach, her voice hopeful.

'Just keep a lid on it. At least until DI Corstorphine has had a chance to ID the body. You'll be the first to know, OK?'

The line went silent for a few, long seconds before the reporter's voice came back. Frankie could imagine her having a hasty conversation with her editor in the interim.

'We'll run the story but leave some detail out until tomorrow. Nice talking to you, Frankie. Bye.'

Frankie stared at the phone in disgust. They'd be running what they had past their legal team and coming to the conclusion that they could print the whole damn story. She slammed the phone down. This wasn't the first time the local newspaper had run rings around them.

'Where's Corstorphine when you need him?' Frankie asked of the empty office.

The crazy wall had no answer.

TWENTY
SHOTGUN

Josephine Sables raised her perfectly shaped eyebrows to silently interrogate the short, rotund man who'd been listening in to the call with the DC. Jack Hammond had been the editor at *The Courier* for so many years that his face was synonymous with the publication. Josephine had often thought when he finally retired, that would be the end of the newspaper and of an era. Who else would have the passion to keep the paper going when sales figures dropped every year?

'What do you want to do?' Josephine questioned when her raised eyebrows had failed to elicit a response.

'We'll be pushing it for tomorrow's print run, but I want us to lead on this for Thursday's edition. The nationals aren't going to get wind of this if DI Corstorphine keeps it under wraps and that provides us with an opportunity.' His eyes shone with undisguised enthusiasm. 'This is why we do what we do, Josephine. Local news brought by local reporters. The big boys can't compete, so let's make the headlines, eh?'

'I could talk to the farmer, Haddow?'

Jack's round head bobbed in agreement.

'Yes – go back there and interview him now. Check the police have left before approaching the farmer and see what you can get out of him. I'll do a bit of research from here. There's the Halloween Harvest Festival coming up on Friday the 31ˢᵗ at Glenarty village, we may be able to do a tie-in with the scarecrows there.'

'A Halloween special?' Josephine suggested.

'That's the idea! Pumpkins and scarecrows, dead bodies and harvest festivals. What's not to like?'

She left him newly energised, rushing off to his office on short, fat legs with a pronounced wheeze coming from his lungs.

If he dies now, he'll die happy. The thought crossed her mind as he shut his office door and was lost to view. Josephine picked up her notebook and biro, swept the camera over her shoulder and headed downstairs for her car.

There was no sign of a police presence as she negotiated the rough track towards Halfway Farm. The farmer's tractor lay abandoned beside the field where she'd spotted the scarecrow. Now the field lay empty apart from furrows containing the first, green shoots of winter wheat. No police tape adorned the farm gate or hedgerows which told her forensics must have swept the area clean of whatever clues remained for them to find. She continued along the track until the farm came into view.

Halfway Farm consisted of a solidly built farmhouse, not pretty to look at but constructed from such huge slabs of rock that it resembled a glacial erratic left behind by the retreating ice. Stone outbuildings held various items of green or red agricultural machinery. Smoke trailed out of a chimney; electric lights painted the downstairs windows in a welcome shade of yellow. Josephine parked in the sheltered courtyard and rapped on the door.

She saw movement out of the corner of her eye, spotted the farmer she'd seen earlier holding back a curtain to view her with suspicion. Her heart rate picked up when she saw him lowering a shotgun; it had been all but invisible when he'd been aiming it directly at her. Her hand fluttered a wave, the other held tight onto her notepad as if it offered some protection from a trigger-happy farmer.

The door opened, and Farmer Haddow's suspicious eyes glowered at her from underneath bushy, ginger eyebrows.

'What do you want?' He looked over her head and around the courtyard to check if she was alone, then visibly relaxed when he'd confirmed that was the case.

'Mr Haddow? My name is Josephine Sables. I'm the reporter for *The Courier*.'

The ginger brows drew down again in irritation.

'Is this about the scarecrow?'

She nodded. 'It must have been such a shock for you, finding a human body. Have the police said who it was?'

The farmer's mouth worked as if he was chewing on something unpleasant.

'They've not said nothing.'

His eyes remained locked on hers and she knew he was debating whether to talk to her or not. She'd seen the same calculation being made many times before.

'Our readers would very much like to hear the story from your point of view, Mr Haddow. It's not every day a farmer discovers a body masquerading as a scarecrow. I think it would be good to have your perspective rather than just a police statement. Do you mind if I come in?' She shivered for effect.

'Aye, alright. You'd better come in. I could do with the company, to be honest. It fair unsettled me.'

Josephine followed him into the farmhouse, trying not to react to the rustic smell of the place. It was clear Mr Haddow lived on his own. She followed him into the kitchen, scanning the surfaces covered with dirty plates and pots.

'Tea?' Bushy ginger eyebrows quizzed her.

'Please,' she replied with false enthusiasm. She looked for a seat, and after quickly inspecting the few chairs available decided instead to remain standing.

'When did you first notice the scarecrow had been put into your field?'

He filled the kettle before setting it down on an old gas hob, struck a match to ignite the flame and a ghostly blue fireball engulfed the stove before settling down.

'It's more a case of when I first noticed it missing,' he responded. Two mugs were scooped off the wooden kitchen table, given a cursory inspection and rinsed in a stained sink.

'I told the police on Monday he'd been taken. Gave them a photograph and everything. Don't think they took it seriously and then look what happened!'

Josephine's biro raced across the page.

'Do you have a picture of the scarecrow, Mr Haddow? What's your first name? I can't keep calling you Mr Haddow.'

'William,' he answered in surprise. 'I've a photo here, on my phone. Hang on, I have to share it somehow...'

Josephine helped him to transfer the photograph across to her own phone.

'Looks scary,' she ventured once the picture was viewable on her screen.

'That's the point of it, isn't it?' William spoke tiredly as if he was repeating a statement made before.

'I suppose so,' Josephine admitted.

He spooned tealeaves into a large, brown teapot as the kettle began a low whistle from the hob. William attended to the ritual, turning off the gas which gave a final small explosive pop, then poured boiling water into the teapot.

'I've got some milk and sugar here somewhere.'

'Just milk would be fine, thanks,' she added quickly. 'What did the police say? About your scarecrow going missing?'

'Well, they said it was probably kids. I told 'em it weren't. Don't get kids here. Then they said maybe it had been blown away. I said how? I put 'im in the ground myself. It would take a force ten to shift 'im. Then they said they'd keep an eye out. Like he'd be marching around somewhere.'

'When did you notice he'd been replaced?'

'This morning. I was taking the tractor back up from the south field up to the farm and saw the scarecrow back where he used to be. I thought someone was playing silly buggers.'

Tea poured blackly out of the teapot spout and into two mugs. William opened a fridge door to retrieve a bottle of milk and poured a generous helping into each.

'There you go.'

Josephine tried not to look suspiciously at her mug contents and placed it on the nearest surface.

'Oh, too hot!' She smiled disarmingly and carried on writing.

'Well, then I went up to 'im to see if he'd been damaged at all. He looked a bit strange from the cab of my tractor.' A slurp of tea provided the lubrication required to force the next words out.

'I couldn't work out what had happened to 'im at first. He was dressed in the same rags, but someone had added shoes and the face was wrong.'

She looked up from her notepad at the sound of another slurp, saw the mug shaking in the farmer's large hand.

'When I got closer, I saw they were real hands.' His voice expressed wonder. 'Then when the crows left his face, I could see it was... It was human. Someone had dressed a body in my scarecrow's rags and left 'im in my field. I almost shat meself.'

He stared wide-eyed at the reporter, the mug shaking sufficiently for small waves of tea to overlap the rim and drip down to the floor.

'Don't put that last bit in,' he added urgently as she committed his words to shorthand.

Josephine obediently deleted the last few squiggles.

'Then what happened?'

'Well, I ran back to the tractor so I could call the police, and that policewoman I'd seen earlier came up the track. I thought that was fast, but it turned out she was handing out leaflets or something. Anyway, she called in all the others and then the detective took me back here.'

'DI Corstorphine?' Josephine quizzed.

'Aye, that's the one. He said they'd sort it all out and not to worry and I could get back in my field once the forensics had left.'

'And no one's been in touch since?'

'No. Easy for him to say don't worry. He's not living on his own with some madman out on the loose leaving bodies in your fields!'

Josephine thought of the shotgun. He'd be safe enough.

'OK. Well, thank you, William. You've been a great help. We'll be printing your side of the story. I wouldn't be surprised if there's a lot of interest. Maybe even a TV crew.'

He looked at her in shock. 'TV? Coming here?'

'Thanks for your time, William. I'll see myself out.'

Josephine's mug remained untouched. She had a photograph of the farmer's scarecrow, and the one she'd taken of the body before the PCs had spotted her. That was more than enough.

TWENTY-ONE
PRETENDER

'Bye, sarge. See you tomorrow.' PC Phil Lamb waved cheerily to the sergeant as he left the station, glad to see the back of another shift. Bill McAdam was putting in another few hours and had taken himself off in the patrol car after they'd been given the all-clear to leave Haddow's farm. His wife was expecting, hence grabbing all the overtime going and her working long shifts at the supermarket. That went some way to explain Bill's recent dour mood – the responsibility was weighing heavy on him.

Responsibilities that he didn't have, and that fact alone put a spring in his step. Phil gave a moment's consideration to the old sergeant. Was it his imagination or was he even more miserable than usual? The thought was fleeting, brushed away by the possibility of meeting the French reporter later in the pub. She'd practically invited him out! He knew everyone else in the station saw him as reaching for the unattainable. Josephine might be older than him, might have a level of worldliness and sophistication that he didn't, but she was definitely interested.

The walk to his flat took twenty minutes. He couldn't shake the image of the body and the way the head had rolled off once forensics had released it from the stake. It had taken all his willpower not to throw up at the sight. Then when the feet had followed suit, both he and Bill McAdam had exchanged a shared look which clearly said WTF!

'That's not good,' Bill had stated. 'Looks like there's a fucking madman on the loose.'

Phil had nodded wordlessly, still concerned about the contents of his stomach making an unwelcome return.

It wasn't good. The occasional dead body came with the job: RTAs, accidental deaths, suicides or the odd domestic getting out of hand. The only real murders he'd experienced had been the carefully engineered killings of a few years ago and then the fallout from the distillery owner's death last year. None of them had involved the deliberate dismemberment that they'd seen laid out in full technicolour on top of Farmer Haddow's winter wheat. Like Bill had said – it looked like the work of a madman.

The connection to the other missing scarecrows was also preying on his mind. At least they had DI Corstorphine. He'd managed to solve all the other cases they'd dealt with. Him and Frankie, he added mentally. Maybe there was a chance Phil could get into the CID? All he had to do was pass the National Investigators Exam and he could be a DC like her? If he could find out where the murderer was before Corstorphine or Frankie...

The Old Pretender was just off the High Street. The pub was one of the oldest buildings in the town and somehow managed to be so unobtrusive that tourists often passed it by. The grimy windows likely helped, lending an air of abandonment to the favoured watering hole for a mostly older clientele. Phil would normally head for one of the newer establishments, where the loud music and brash lighting affirmed that life was for the young, but he knew the reporter favoured this place. It also offered quiet nooks where they might be able to speak in private without everyone seeing them.

He'd gone easy on the aftershave following Frankie's frequent admonishments about his smelling like the perfume counter in the local chemist's, brushed his hair and gargled with mouthwash. Phil entered the bar with the confidence that tonight would be the night.

Josephine was already standing at the bar, deep in discussion with the woman who owned the hairdresser's on the High Street. He stood pointedly beside her, ordered a drink and expressed surprise when she turned around at the sound of his voice.

'Oh, hello, Josephine.'

'Phil. What a lovely surprise.' Her smile lit up the dark interior. 'Let's go somewhere quieter – like over here.'

She led the way towards one of the quiet booths, telling the hairdresser that she'd see her later. Phil grabbed his pint and followed in her footsteps.

'Here'. She indicated a seat across from hers, a small table between them. 'This is cozy.' Josephine raised her cocktail, and they clinked glasses.

'The body!' Josephine shuddered theatrically. 'I don't know how you can deal with things like that.'

'Oh, it's part of the job. You get used to it after a bit.' Phil took a sip from his pint and wondered when it had ever become normal to have a scarecrow's head fall off and turn out to be human.

'Still. You're so brave.'

He thought she might be laying it on with a trowel, but her expression remained sincere.

'Just doing my job.' Phil wondered how he could get off the subject and turn the conversation away from the murder and towards something more pleasant.

'I talked to the farmer, William Haddow, after everyone had gone.' Her eyes shone from over the top of her cocktail and fixed on his.

'Oh.'

She waited as if he was about to add something, but his mind had gone completely blank.

'Yes, he told me all about his missing scarecrow and how it had returned. The poor man is in shock.'

Phil sympathised with the farmer.

'What did he tell you?' He attempted to take control of a conversation that had left him more of an onlooker.

'Just about how he'd been to the police to report the theft of his property and how Frankie had said it was probably children.' She tilted her head to one side in a manner that he considered to be decidedly French. 'But children don't do that.'

Phil didn't need her to elaborate.

'I think it's caught us all by surprise. Nobody expects to find something like that in the middle of a field.'

'Do you have any idea who might have done it?' She'd lowered her voice to a conspiratorial whisper and leaned in so close that he could have kissed her lips with the smallest effort.

'We haven't got a clue,' he answered, then saw her interest fading as rapidly as it had arrived. 'Although we do have a lead,' he blurted.

The interest returned and Phil felt she could hypnotise him with her eyes.

'Who?' she asked simply.

'There's a patient, from Carstairs State Hospital. There's an arrest warrant out for him. He's a person of interest,' Phil added with self-importance.

'Goodness,' Josephine breathed out.

He could feel her breath on his skin and was grateful for the fact he was sitting down as his knees had turned to jelly.

'Who is he, this patient?'

Phil knew he shouldn't be telling her anything else, but he felt a prize was within reach. All of her attention was focussed on him. She had eyes he could drown in.

'Duncan Lewis. He murdered his wife – left her body parts scattered all around Scotland and then wrote a book about it.'

Phil had played his trump card. If that didn't do it, nothing would.

'Duncan Lewis,' she repeated thoughtfully. 'I remember the name. Escaped from Carstairs, you say?'

'No, not escaped. He used to be a patient until Shamila Mallick decided he was cured.'

'DI Corstorphine's wife?'

Phil had the feeling that he might have said too much.

'Aye but keep it to yourself. It's not really meant to be public knowledge.' He grinned at her hopefully.

'But I'm a reporter, Phil. Public knowledge is what we provide.'

Her smile left a sinking feeling in the pit of his stomach.

'I keep my sources anonymous.'

Her words were meant to reassure him, but as she stood to leave him alone with his pint, he felt anything but reassured.

TWENTY-TWO
OUTGRAVE

Corstorphine's choice of bedtime reading glowed from an electronic screen. Shamila had already drifted off to sleep by his side, but he couldn't relax. The book he'd downloaded was still selling well, sufficiently for Duncan Lewis to make a comfortable living from the proceeds. There was talk of a screenplay, except his murdered wife's remaining family were objecting to anyone wanting to dramatise such a traumatic event in their lives.

The author's face stared back at him from the rear cover. Did he have the face of a madman? There was something mocking in the calmness of his expression as the photographer pressed the shutter. Shamila was convinced that his split persona was no more, that a combination of therapy and drugs had eradicated the personality he'd named Daemon Aticus.

Corstorphine puzzled over the name Duncan Lewis had chosen for his evil self. Like Dr Jekyll and Mr Hyde, his alter ego could only exist once the other had been completely subsumed. The name Daemon was self-evident, a description of the character he'd accused of possessing his wife. He entered it into the search tool, adjusted for loose spelling.

A demon from hell has taken her soul. I can taste sulphur on her lips, see fire curling in her eyes. There is crawling evil in her movements, darkness follows each step. I can no longer live in peace. She has to be destroyed.

Corstorphine could feel his eyebrows raise. The only way this prose made it to the top of the bestseller lists was due to the story hidden within its pages. A gory treasure-hunt for thrill-seekers. He tried Aticus in the search tool, pressed the enter symbol.

What does she keep hidden in the attic? I've looked, searched through boxes of books and chests full of old clothes, curling photographs of people we once knew or once were. Something draws her there. It's on the edge of my hearing, that call. Is it a child? How can a child be hiding here?

The next suggestion offered nothing any more illuminating.

No, not the attic. It's the first place they'd look. The attic or the garden. Or the basement, or in the walls or up the chimney. Except a body is too big. Even a head. How do you lose a head? In the bin? Cut a body into small enough pieces and flush away.

'You need a pig farmer. Pigs eat anything.'

I've a better idea.

He gave up searching for Aticus. Perhaps Duncan had misspelt Atticus Finch? What connection would Duncan Lewis have made between the eponymous lawyer defending a black man against a charge of rape in the American deep south? Could he have foreseen his conviction for murder as injustice if he truly believed that he was ridding the world of evil?

These were metaphysical constructs beyond his reach as a small-town detective. Undeterred, Corstorphine ploughed on through the dense prose, skipping page after page until he came to the first clue. This was what had inspired the retired detective to start searching for himself, poring over maps and identifying arcane references until he'd identified the first location – and the missing wife's head. He read the paragraph closely, if only to pitch his detective capabilities against the man who'd began the search in earnest. This was something he *could* do.

False! Every word you spoke I'll stop your mouth with rock and earth. Under the first king's foot, under a royal roof beset with jewels and sapphires. Where the gold of morning first touches the sacred hill as day balances night after the long death. Your coronation will be with a crown of thistles. Neither the living nor the dead shall claim you. Here you'll lie until your flesh returns to soil and your skull is taken by the ancient people who wait to carry you away on the wild boar that watches over you.

It wasn't difficult, but then he already had the answer. Her head had been buried at Dunadd in Argyllshire and that discovery had sparked pure mayhem. It was a macabre treasure hunt from hell.

TWENTY-THREE
JOHN DOE

Corstorphine drew up at the clinic, watching Shamila as she walked the few steps to the door. He waited until he heard the lock click shut behind her. They'd hardly spoken during the short journey, apart from her irritably telling him that he was overreacting.

'I don't know how you think I coped when I worked at Carstairs,' had been her parting shot.

He didn't have an answer to give her.

He arrived at the station to find he was the first there. Hamish usually arrived long before anyone else, but just lately Corstorphine had felt the sergeant wasn't quite himself. Perhaps there was a problem at home – the sergeant wasn't the type to be open about anything personal. Corstorphine would try and figure out how to broach it with Hamish and filed the thought away for later.

Corstorphine logged onto his computer and opened the latest email from forensics. He skimmed the photographs of severe trauma wounds separating head from torso, feet from ankles. No matter how long he'd been in the force, pictures displaying butchered human bodies still hadn't lost the ability to shock. He had to physically force himself to carry on viewing.

A metal rod had been used to secure the head back onto the body, wire held severed feet onto legs.

He paused there. For the murderer to be comfortable enough to handle a dead body with such callous disregard either pointed to a serial killer or someone suffering from a serious mental illness. Duncan Lewis's featureless expression reappeared in his imagination – much as it had in his nightmares.

Cause of death was evident enough. The procurator fiscal had added a note stating the measurement between neck wound and ankle separation was 1435mm, together with evidence that rope had been used at both locations. A close-up of the rope fibres embedded in raw meat accompanied the note, together with the procurator fiscal's observation that 1435mm was the standard railway gauge. The report added that the injuries were comparable to those experienced after a body has been run over by a train. Time of death was approximately four days from discovery of the body.

They didn't have a positive ID yet. The facial features had been so badly damaged by corvids feeding on the flesh that they would require dental records, or DNA matches which could take a while.

Corstorphine sat at his desk, taking in the ramifications of the report. The officer dealing with the investigation knew what he was looking at. He'd been the same forensics technician who'd dealt with the body of the young woman who'd thrown herself under a train last year.

There were two problems staring him in the face. How could a train driver not realise they'd run over a body, especially if that body had been tied to the tracks as the forensics report hinted at? And who in their right mind takes the dismembered corpse and turns it into one of Farmer Haddow's scarecrows?

Halloween was literally two days away and Corstorphine had the uneasy feeling that this was just the prelude to something. There were two other scarecrows missing – the thought that they'd be replaced in a similar fashion provided the fuel for his nightmares.

He forwarded the report to DI Anderson at Lanark Police with the fervent hope that the detective's missing person wasn't presently laid out in pieces on an Inverness forensics slab. Until he had the positive ID, it was best to assume the worst.

The team arrived one by one, Hamish giving a curt nod through the glass partition wall, then Frankie, McAdam and Lamb, last as always. He gave them time to settle, the kettle working harder than the small police team, then called them to gather around for the day's briefing.

'Morning, everyone. Our focus is on the body discovered yesterday. Forensics haven't come up with a positive ID, so for now we'll concentrate on finding how John Doe arrived at William Haddow's field. Time of death has been estimated at around three days ago. Whoever was responsible, they placed the body there some time between the farmer's last trip up the farm track leading to that field the previous evening and his discovery yesterday morning. William Haddow last saw his scarecrow on the afternoon of Sunday 26th October. Later that same night, Mart McKeown's scarecrow was also taken, and the Glenarty community Facebook page reports another one missing.'

'Are we expecting more bodies, sir?' Lamb had his hand raised like a schoolboy, putting voice to the entire team's concerns.

'Short answer is I don't know, Phil. This may be unconnected to the other missing scarecrows – chances are they're just the result of teenagers' high spirits. One thing forensics have suggested is that the body we found may have been run over by a train.'

'Is that cause of death, sir?' Frankie asked.

'As far as the preliminary results show, yes. It appears the train caught him as he lay on the rails. Both head and feet were separated from the rest of his body and the distance between them corresponds to the standard UK railway gauge.'

'Wouldn't a train just splatter the body all over the place?' Frankie argued.

'Forensics kindly provided research on the depth of trough a body would require positioned between the rails to avoid impact.

They can be up to twenty-four inches deep which is a survivable option if you find yourself in that predicament.'

'Not if you're tied to the rails.' Lamb's comment was loud enough for everyone to hear.

Corstorphine took a deep breath before continuing.

'Very perceptive, Phil. The preliminary report also mentions rope fibres present in the flesh where it had been severed by the train wheels, inferring that John Doe had been tied to the railway tracks on purpose.'

He looked out on a sea of sombre faces. Even PC Lamb failed to make a humorous quip for the occasion.

'Whoever murdered him must have collected the parts and dressed them in William Haddow's scarecrow clothes.' Frankie spelt it out for the rest of them.

'Aye,' Corstorphine agreed. 'Then risked being discovered by planting the human remains where they'd be found, in his field.'

He waited for them to settle.

'One other thing. I've had a call from a DI Anderson at Lanark police. They have the responsibility for informing the local population if there are any escapes from Carstairs State Hospital.'

'They set off a siren in the town, don't they, sir? One of my friends moved down there and didn't know about the monthly test. Almost shat himself when they all went off!'

'Thank you, Lamb. Yes, same as Broadmoor they use sirens to alert the local population if any prisoners are unaccounted for. Only in this case, it's a member of staff that has gone amiss. All patients are securely locked away.'

He pressed his lips together at the thought of what he had to say next.

'As you all know, I've been contacted due to Shamila's involvement with a patient who has since been released on parole. DI Anderson from Lanark CID wants to interview Duncan Lewis as his fingerprints have been found at the home of the missing staff member. You've all been sent his details.'

'Do you think he's somehow involved with the body here, sir?' PC Bill McAdam broke his silence.

'I don't know, Bill. But we can't ignore the possibility. Frankie – can you contact Scottish Rail – see if any of their drivers or line workers reported seeing anything. Bill, Phil – keep your eyes open for Duncan Lewis, just in case he's in the area. I'll check Glenarty, see if I can find who else has lost a scarecrow or whether there's any more video footage.'

He paused to clear this throat. 'Can I also ask you all to keep eyes on Shamila's clinic?'

A chorus of affirmatives followed his request, and with a grim nod to the team, he returned to his office. Shamila might not be concerned about Duncan Lewis or his whereabouts, but Corstorphine knew he wouldn't rest until he'd been found.

TWENTY-FOUR
BLOOD ON THE TRACKS

Frankie parked in front of the railway station, viewing the 1960s brutalist architecture with the same resignation that she occasionally felt for her choice of profession. Today was very much one of those days.

She'd driven to see Alex last night after binning her supper. When he informed her his son was missing, her first thought was of the body they'd discovered. There hadn't been an ID made yet, but she had seen enough to reassure her it wasn't a body belonging to a sixteen-year-old gangly youth.

'Why didn't you tell me, at the pub? I could have helped.' She'd released him from a hug with the distinct impression he'd been going through the motions when he'd returned her embrace.

'I didn't want everyone to know. It's bad enough being a single dad without advertising the fact I'm fucking useless at it.'

'He's not phoned?'

Alex had shaken his head.

'Do you have him on your mobile – able to track him I mean?'

'That's what I've been trying to do. He's switched his phone off since Monday night.'

He'd looked straight at her without trying to conceal the worry etched on his face.

'I've not seen him since Monday, Frankie. Without telling me where he was going or calling to let me know where he was. He knows I'd be bloody worried. I just want to know he's alright.'

'How's he been doing at school?'

Her attempt at making casual conversation was met with a stony stare.

'He's not. Half the time he doesn't bother going in, the other half he plays up, so they want to ban him. He sees it as a win-win. I've tried to tell him he has to knuckle down, but he just laughs in my face. He asked me what's the worst that could happen if he leaves school without any exams – "be a fireman like you?"'

Alex had stared blankly into space as if Frankie was no longer there.

'We can raise a missing person report, Alex. He's only sixteen.'

'I don't want to do that. Not yet. What if he comes back tonight? I'd have only made things worse with that on record. Can you do it unofficial-like? Just ask your coppers to keep a watch for him? I love him to bits, you know that? It's just sometimes all I get is he detests me and then I hate him so much I could murder the wee bastard!'

He'd looked shocked at his own outburst. 'I'm not saying I would do that.'

She'd nodded in understanding. 'I know, of course you wouldn't.'

'He just knows how to push my buttons, you ken? Can you help?' Alex had looked like a man out of his depth.

She'd agreed. Taken a photograph of a happier, younger Mikey from its frame and reassured Alex that in the vast majority of cases kids came back.

The photograph was still in her pocket. The morning's briefing hadn't been the right time to bring up her boyfriend's missing teenager. Not if it wasn't his body they were dealing with.

Frankie approached the stationmaster's door and knocked in the no-nonsense way favoured by police everywhere.

'Come in.'

They'd had enough history between them to recognise each other.

'Good morning, detective. Is this a social call or business?'

Frankie corrected his all too obvious attempt at flattery. 'Detective Constable. I wouldn't want the paperwork involved with being a detective – although I wouldn't mind the salary.'

'Do you want a tea?' He made to stand.

'No, you're alright. I'm here on business.'

He sank back down in his chair. A bank of CCTV monitors shone unblinking eyes down on the platforms, entrance foyer and the local environs. Frankie realised he'd have seen her arriving and sat motionless in her car whilst she'd gone over last night in her head.

'What can we do for you?'

The news would be out soon enough, she didn't need to keep anything other than the detail under wraps.

'We found a body, yesterday. Forensics have suggested that the injuries sustained are typical of being run over by a train.'

The stationmaster sat up. 'Hit by a train?'

'Not as such. From the injuries they think he was lying down on the tracks and a train went over him. Preliminary reports suggest this happened around three days ago.'

The stationmaster's expression had turned from querying to shock.

'And this happened here? Somewhere local?' His voice expressed disbelief. 'We've not had any incidents reported by the drivers. It's not the sort of thing they'd not notice.'

'We don't know where it may have occurred. That's one of the things we need to find out. I was hoping you may have heard something?'

'No. Good God no. Transport police would be all over something like that. Do you have their number?'

'Aye, of course. I just wanted to start here. Who do I need to talk to in case there's blood on the tracks?' She pushed aside the Bob Dylan track playing in her head.

'Transport police. They'd liaise with the maintenance crews and ask them to report anything unusual like that. Are we talking a lot of blood?'

Frankie imagined head and legs separated by the steel wheels of a train.

'Aye. A lot. You'll let me know if you hear of anything?'

'Of course. I'll get onto it now. Is this related to the body you found at Halfway Farm?'

Frankie stopped in her tracks, turned back to see the stationmaster holding up *The Courier*.

Headless Corpse Dressed as Scarecrow. Local Halloween Horror.

Her heart sank. The DI had specifically asked for the case to be kept quiet for as long as possible. They'd managed a few hours at most – this report must have been filed last night to reach the newsstands for this morning. Her conversation with the French reporter played in her memory. Corstorphine wasn't going to be happy.

'Can I see?' Frankie took the newspaper out of his hands without waiting for a response and skimmed the article. Josephine Sables referenced William Haddow in the piece and she started to relax. There wasn't anything they could have done to prevent her talking to the farmer. But then she read the details about Duncan Lewis which could only have come from someone on the small police team. She handed the newspaper back without comment.

Frankie left the stationmaster with the certain knowledge he was about to spread the news of the body. If anyone in the rail industry had seen or heard anything, this was one way of flushing them out. The second way was via official channels. What she hadn't expected was for details of the case to be plastered across the front page of the local newspaper.

Frankie kept watch for Mikey as she drove back to the police station. She couldn't stop thinking that the man tied to the tracks might have still been alive when the train hit him.

TWENTY-FIVE
PUSSYKINS

Corstorphine entered Glenarty village stores, making straight for the counter.

'Could you tell me which house is Tabitha Richardson's? I'd like to have a word with her.'

The shopkeeper had twisted his mouth in pique.

'Treasury Cottage. Three houses up. It was built in the style of the Treasury in Petra. Of course, not to the same scale. In fact, all it really has is the two stone columns by the front door topped by a triangular carved stone lintel...' He stopped as the jangling bell announced the detective's imminent departure.

'Rude.' He stared at the door with real anger, then stroked the cat in its basket on the counter. 'We don't like rude people, do we, Pussykins?'

The cat purred in agreement.

Corstorphine walked up the main street, taking a closer look at the scarecrows leering at him from the tops of hedges or from upper floor windows where they dangled like would-be suicides. There was one in a wheelbarrow, and he compared the single tyre to the track he'd photographed in Farmer Haddow's field.

The third house was a modest cottage with preposterous stone pillars flanking a red door. A stonemason had made valiant if primitive attempts at depicting two Grecian urns and a Romanesque figure above a triangular architrave. He'd heard the shopkeeper's description as he'd left the shop, but the house bore a greater resemblance to a tomb than a treasury.

The doorbell held a lens which observed him with a dull electronic eye as he pressed the bell. Beethoven's 'Für Elise' played tinnily in response from the bowels of the house like a tribute to hold music everywhere. It mercifully stopped after eight bars and the door opened to reveal a tall, slender woman. Her head tilted to one side in interrogation. Long, brown tresses cascaded over a bare shoulder where a purple mohair jumper exposed well-tanned skin.

'Tabitha Richardson?' Corstorphine held his warrant card up in readiness.

'Yes. What is it?' She gave the impression of having better things to be doing with her time than standing, chatting on her doorstep.

'I understand you've had a scarecrow taken from outside your house.'

Her chin pulled back into her neck in response. A peculiarly bird-like gesture. He imagined her perched like a heron over the River Arty, preparing to strike at a tasty morsel.

'I wouldn't have expected the police to have much interest in a missing scarecrow.' Two bright eyes interrogated him with humour.

'We believe there may be a link to a wider investigation.' Corstorphine trod carefully, choosing his words with precision. 'I was hoping you'd be able to help us with our enquiries.' He winced internally at the use of such a pat phrase. 'Specifically, if you have doorbell camera footage that may identify who took your property?'

He had her interest.

'What enquiries are those?' Tabitha pressed.

'I can't say due to operational reasons. Not at this stage. But if I could have a look at your doorbell recording?'

She considered his request, looking him up and down as if she was making a judgement on character before acquiescing.

'You'd better come in. I'll show you what I have. It's not anyone from the village; I'll tell you that for free.'

Corstorphine entered the cottage in her wake and realised the house was bigger than it had first appeared from the outside.

'This way.' Tabitha beckoned him onwards, leaving a trail of floral perfume in her wake. The room he was led into was warmed by a log-burning stove. Flames danced in yellow and red. A desk held papers and a computer; a crowded bookcase displayed spines in alphabetical order.

His attention was captured by the painting taking up most of one wall – a floor-to-ceiling depiction of a young girl standing beside a wolf almost twice her size. She held a saltire hanging limply from the staff in her hands, the blue of the flag mirrored in the painted eyes following his. He'd seen it before, or something very similar.

'Here. This is what I have, from Sunday evening. Bold as brass. You can see he wasn't a child.'

Corstorphine reluctantly dragged his gaze away from the portrait and joined Tabitha at her desk. The computer monitor displayed two men drunkenly staggering out of view. It was dark, but he recognised the same footage from the Glenarty social media page.

'This was Sunday evening?' Corstorphine leaned closer to view the date stamp in the top right-hand corner. The time displayed as 23:29.

'Yes. Why would someone want to steal my scarecrow? It makes no sense!' She sounded freshly enraged at the theft.

'I'd put a lot of time into making him,' she continued. 'We all do. They're all judged, did you know?'

Corstorphine must have expressed bewilderment as she immediately continued, 'There's a £500 prize for the best one. The money all goes to charity, naturally.'

'Can you just show me when this person first appears on your recording?'

She rewound the footage to where a figure appeared.

'Hold it there.'

Tabitha stabbed a finger at her keyboard.

The subject of Corstorphine's interest remained in shadow, the hood of a sweatshirt or jacket obscuring the features. A hand reached out towards the edge of the screen.

'Can you press play?'

She gave him a hard look, then poked at the keyboard with irritation.

The figure was busy with something just out of view.

'He's untying my scarecrow,' Tabitha explained. 'He was attached to one of the pillars in case the wind caught him.'

The view now showed the culprit dragging it away out of shot, looking more like two drunks supporting each other than the theft of a stuffed mannequin.

'Can I have a copy of that?' Corstorphine asked as he handed her a card. 'If you can send it to my email address, then we can see if the picture can be enhanced.'

'Are you going to all this trouble just for my scarecrow? Or is this more to do with Mart McKeown?'

The way she said his name gave Corstorphine the definite impression that the retired pop star wasn't the most popular resident in their exclusive village.

'It's part of a wider investigation. Do you happen to know if anyone else in the village had had anything stolen recently – or may have video footage from Sunday night?'

Tabitha looked at him with the same disconcerting directness he'd seen in the large painting.

'What "wider investigation"?'

'I'm not able to comment on a live investigation, but if you know of anyone with video recordings from Sunday, it would be a great help.' He gave her his most disarming smile.

Tabitha's twisting lips showed what she thought of his evasiveness.

'This is all there is. I've already asked around. Thanks to the lack of any regular police presence here, we have to do your job ourselves.' She indicated the door, following him back out until he was stood once again on her doorstep.

'I'll send you the video now. Goodbye, officer.'

The door closed and Corstorphine was face to face with a Neighbourhood Watch sticker. He turned and walked back to his car. Three scarecrows were missing, one had been found. The other two could just be a harmless prank.

The video of a man, deliberately obscuring his features and determined to take Tabitha's scarecrow, didn't fit harmless or prank in Corstorphine's mind.

TWENTY-SIX
LÜSCHER TEST

'Good morning, Phoebe. How are you today?'

Shamila stepped back to let a young woman into her office, shutting the dividing door to reception behind her. Phoebe had already taken a seat, hands arranged demurely on her lap as she waited patiently for the doctor.

'I'm fine, thanks.' Her smile lit up her face.

Shamila studied her carefully as she ran through the standard screening questions – asking Phoebe whether she'd had any strange experiences, was hearing voices, seeing visions or feeling threatened.

Phoebe's responses were calm and normal. She'd been through this so many times before that Shamila suspected she knew which questions would be asked in advance.

The doctor moved onto diagnostic tests, making small conversation as she ascertained Phoebe's personality and emotions. Phoebe treated it all with good-natured humour – suspected this young woman knew exactly what each question was designed to reveal about her.

'Right, Phoebe. I'm going to give you a quick test. There's no right or wrong answer.'

Phoebe leaned forward in eagerness. 'Like the Rorschach inkblot test?'

Shamila had to laugh. 'You know too much about this – perhaps we should change places? No, every time I give you the inkblot test, you see cats. This is the Lüscher colour test.'

'Oh, I like this one as well.'

Shamila placed an iPad on the table. Eight coloured cards waited for Phoebe to arrange in order of preference. Her finger pressed at each colour, then repeated the process on a second trial.

'How did I do?'

Shamila retrieved the iPad. 'It's just a simple test, Phoebe. Like all of these things, the results are open to interpretation. Let's talk about something more important. How's the job going?'

'I'm really enjoying it.' Phoebe spoke with enthusiasm. 'We had a pet snake brought in last week attacked by a cat. Heather found a puncture wound and sewed it together, but the owner brought it back in yesterday because it had swollen up to twice its size.'

'Oh dear, that's terrible. Did it have an infection?' Shamila began writing notes as she listened.

Phoebe giggled and Shamila looked up sharply, alert for behaviour that signalled any hint of psychosis.

'She'd sewn up its arse!'

Shamila's shocked expression sent the young woman into uncontrollable laughter.

'That's not good.' She found herself laughing in turn, sharing the unfortunate reptile's clinical condition.

'We've never had a pet snake before,' Phoebe explained once she'd quietened. 'It's an easy mistake for a vet to have made.'

'I suppose so,' Shamila agreed. She thought of all the different species the surgery had to diagnose in any given day and her sympathy went out to the vet.

'You can't tell anyone.' Phoebe's expression had turned serious.

'Don't worry. Nothing you tell me will ever leave this room. You have my word on that.'

Phoebe looked relieved that her indiscretion wouldn't be broadcast, and the smile returned.

She'd started working at the local veterinary practice as a volunteer. Shamila had made friends with the local vet soon after moving in with Corstorphine. Heather Grant was Corstorphine's neighbour, and they soon became firm friends – close enough for her to make the difficult request that she let Phoebe help out for a few hours a week. Those few hours had turned into days and now Phoebe was an invaluable part of the team. It was the perfect job for her in many ways. A structured environment, limited interactions with the public and all under the watchful eyes of those who understood her troubled past.

Working with small animals brought out Phoebe's natural caring instincts and allowed her to focus on the outside world after a lifetime of living inside her head. She had made extraordinary progress – so much so that her brother, Robb, scarcely recognised his sister. She still needed care, and Robb made sure she was well looked after. In many ways, her progress was healing him as well following the traumatic events they'd both lived through.

Shamila glanced at the notes on her screen – a weekly report from Heather; academic progress from the local college where Phoebe was already catching up with her peers.

'Is there anything you want to discuss?' Shamila gave Phoebe the freedom to steer the conversation in whichever direction she wanted.

Phoebe gave her question serious consideration, searching the ceiling for guidance.

'I've been thinking about Sarah Keir. The girl I blinded.' Phoebe's gaze lowered to engage with Shamila's.

She had wondered how long it would take Phoebe to confront the single crucial episode in her past that had resulted in so many deaths.

'What are your thoughts?' Shamila asked gently. This was a critical moment in Phoebe's treatment, facing the trauma of an event that had happened so many years ago when she was just a young child.

'I never meant it to happen. We were making art – I was making something for Patricia. A cat, she likes cats.' The shy smile fleetingly appeared before the seriousness returned.

Shamila nodded in encouragement.

'Sarah kept knocking into me as I was cutting paper. I needed the cuts to be accurate otherwise the picture wouldn't have worked. I asked her to stop, but she just laughed and did it again, waiting until my back was turned and I was busy concentrating. I spun around the last time she bumped me, pushed her away with all my strength.'

Her voice quietened. 'I forgot the scissors in my hand. They hit her face, and she screamed.'

Phoebe stared down at her hands.

'There was so much blood and screaming. I can't remember what happened next.'

She looked into Shamila's eyes again, tears welling up.

'It was an accident. I'd not hurt anyone on purpose.'

Shamila leaned forward to hold her close.

'It's OK, Phoebe. I know it was an accident.' Under her arms the young woman's body shook silently. She held her until the shaking stopped.

'It's not OK, though, is it? Sarah's dead and all those other people and it's my fault.' She pulled a tissue out of the box on Shamila's desk, dabbed at both eyes.

'You can't blame yourself for everything that happened, Phoebe. You never meant to harm Sarah and you're entirely innocent of everything that happened afterwards. It's not your fault and you don't need to carry the guilt you feel. Do you understand?'

Phoebe's smile returned and she gave one nod of acceptance.

'I know, but I can't help feeling responsible.'

'We'll talk more about it next session. Until then try not to dwell on it. Accidents happen; it's just a fact of life. You have no reason to feel guilty for what happened afterwards.

Shamila stood, signalling their therapy session had come to an end.

'I'm glad you wanted to talk about this, Phoebe. It's important that we deal with that day so you can understand and forgive yourself. You were just a small child. We'll talk some more tomorrow, OK?'

'Yes. Thank you.' Phoebe stood, turned towards the door as Shamila held it open for her. 'Thank you for everything,' she added.

Shamila watched her as she left the unit, climbing into the waiting taxi that her brother always arranged to drive his sister around.

'Your next client is at eleven,' the receptionist advised.

'Thanks, Kira. I'll write up my notes on Phoebe. Let me know when he arrives.'

The colour test results stared her in the face.

Needs release from stress, longs for peace, tranquillity. The situation is difficult, and she is trying to persist in her objectives against resistance. Finds it necessary to conceal her intentions as an added precaution in order to disarm opposition.

It was just a test, Shamila reminded herself. Open to interpretation. She had time before the next appointment to refer to previous Lüscher test results. Her brows creased as she confirmed an identical reading taken several years previously. The subject's name leapt out of the screen at her – Duncan Lewis!

TWENTY-SEVEN
MOLLY

PC Phil Lamb wasn't enjoying his morning breakfast roll. He'd parked at the small industrial park where Shamila had her clinic. They'd been asked to keep an eye on the place until the missing Carstairs outpatient had been found and conveniently enough there was a fast-food van parked nearby. He chewed reflectively on his bacon and egg, catching drips of grease and yolk in a napkin before they stained his uniform. It was the ketchup that was ruining his appetite, he decided. Too similar to the contents that had spilled out of the scarecrow when forensics prised it off the makeshift crucifix. His stomach had felt queasy before he'd taken the first bite.

Phil glanced at the passenger seat, refreshing his memory with the file on Duncan Lewis. The intense face staring out of the page had unsettling blue eyes – open wide as if he'd seen a ghost or something so surprising that he was in a state of shock. His bald head made him easy to recognise.

'OK, Dunk. Let's find you.'

First stop was the town centre. At the very least there were always cars parked on double-yellows he could ticket even if he didn't spot the fugitive. Phil was so busy scanning the pavements for his target that he almost ran over the woman crossing the street in front of him.

'Bloody hell!' His involuntary outburst coincided with his hitting the brakes, the patrol car tyres shuddering with anti-lock on the tarmac accompanied by a familiar screech of burning rubber. Phil's teeth clenched as he waited for the inevitable sickening impact with the clear thought running through his mind that this was the end of his police career.

The car stopped close enough for the woman to stretch out a hand and touch the bonnet. Phil watched in surprise as she did just that, before turning unhurriedly to smile vacantly at him. He recognised her immediately; it was the sergeant's wife. Thoughts of his career ending returned; it would only take a word from her, and Hamish would be down on him like a ton of bricks.

He checked the mirror, confirming no other vehicle was about to plough into the back of him, and turned on the blues.

What the hell is her name? PC Lamb struggled for another mnemonic as he left the vehicle. She was still standing there with a hand on the car and that grin on her face.

Molly – Mollycoddled.

'Molly! I almost ran into you. Here, let me help you across the road.'

He took an arm, held up a hand to stop the traffic and walked her to the safety of the pavement.

She looked up at him with a trusting expression, but he had the strong sense that something was off.

'Are you feeling alright?' He kept looking back to his patrol car stopped in the middle of the road. The traffic was quiet enough for it not to cause an obstruction and drivers negotiated around with their focus very much on the policeman and old lady at the side of the road.

'I'm looking for my mother,' Molly stated. 'Can you help me?'

Phil looked at her askance. 'Your mother?'

He had no idea how old Hamish or his wife were. Anyone on the wrong side of forty belonged to a different epoch. They might as well have been dinosaurs. He made a swift calculation based on the normal retirement age of sixty. Hamish always struck him as being older than that, but he must still be in his late fifties, so Molly must be around the same age.

'Is she out shopping with you?' Phil was anxious to move the car, but the sergeant's wife was behaving oddly. Was her mother even still alive? She'd have to be pushing eighty.

'I've forgotten the way home. I wanted...' She rubbed her forehead in confusion. 'I was shopping and now I'm lost. Isn't that silly?'

The PC recognised what he was dealing with only too well.

'Just wait here for me, Molly, and I'll fetch the car. Don't you worry. I'll take good care of you.'

PC Lamb returned to the car, parked up alongside the sergeant's wife who waited as trusting as a child.

'Here. Let's make you comfortable in the back. Make sure you're strapped in.' He leaned across to fasten her seatbelt. 'Now, we'll get you home.'

He checked the rear-view mirror, saw Molly looking contentedly out of the window and triggered the door locks just to be safe. Phil prepared to take her to Hamish with a sinking feeling in his heart. This wasn't going to be easy.

TWENTY-EIGHT
IRN BRU

PC Bill McAdam stood in the supermarket queue, a bottle of Irn Bru tucked under one arm and a BLT sandwich in his hand. The cashier had caught his eye as soon as he'd entered the store, now she kept sending him a cheeky grin as he waited in turn.

'Just these, thanks.' Bill reached for his credit card and held it in readiness.

'You should have a fruit smoothie. They're much better for you,' the cashier admonished.

The PC rolled his eyes. 'Give over, Caitlin. I need hydrating not a vitamin cocktail.'

'Your stomach's starting to show. Hang on, I have to enter family discount.' Her fingers tapped at the keyboard.'

'Not as much as yours,' he retorted. Bill viewed his partner's swollen womb with a mixture of pride and concern. Their first child and one giant leap for them both!

He held his card to the reader, waited for an electronic beep.

'What time are you home?'

'Usual. Back of five – unless anything else turns up like yesterday.'

'Do they know who it is?' Her voice lowered to a conspiratorial tone as she looked around her.

'Not yet. It will come out soon enough. Poor bastard.'

She touched his arm. 'Bill, can you look into something for me?'

'What is it?'

'There's this young woman that comes in every day. Suzie. She's a bit slow, you know? She always comes to me because she's used to seeing me here, and I think the self-checkout is beyond her.'

'Her and everyone else. Bloody things play up all the time. It's quicker to queue here.'

'And there I was thinking you were being romantic!'

'I was,' Bill countered defensively.

A shopper started placing items on the conveyor belt and it lurched into life, sending a procession of groceries towards them.

'Who do you want me to look at for you? I've got to get back to work.'

'Suzie. She lives in the big flats somewhere. I've not seen her for days now, and I don't think she has anyone to care for her. I'm starting to worry that something might have happened. Could you just have a look?'

PC McAdam tucked the Irn Bru back under his arm, took the sandwich.

'Do you know her full name, address, anything I can actually use?'

Caitlin bit at her lip. 'I don't know anything else about her.'

'Alright. I'll have a patrol around the flats. Wouldn't do any harm. Don't worry, it's probably nothing. See you later, love.'

'Love you.' Caitlin blew him a kiss and began scanning the next shopper's items.

PC McAdam sauntered back to his patrol car, placed his shopping under the dash for later.

The radio had been quiet all morning. Unusually quiet. Hamish was normally on every half hour checking on the two constables, asking where they were. He'd have them fitted with tracking devices if he knew the technology existed, just so he could continually monitor their whereabouts. Bill's mouth turned down at the prospect. It was something that would surely come one day, then he'd be asked to justify trips to the supermarket, or why he was parked in a quiet layby eating his sandwiches. *That's the trouble with progress, Bill thought. It doesn't always make life better.*

He left the supermarket, turned up the hill towards the flats towering over the town. Back in the Sixties, they represented a brand-new start. Now they housed single mums, pensioners, those struggling to earn enough to live on. All conveniently bundled together in a vertical high-density habitat.

He parked next to the main entrance. A playpark of sorts had been created on a stretch of tarmac: swings, see-saw and a wooden fort. A young mum wheeled a pushchair in his direction, a crying child buried under blankets becoming louder as they drew closer. She gave the PC a sullen look as if he was responsible for her child's behaviour.

'I don't know if you can help me?' Bill gave her a friendly smile.

'What do you want?' She stopped reluctantly, rocked the pushchair backwards and forwards in a futile attempt at sending her child to sleep.

'I'm looking for a young woman who lives here. Her name's Suzie?'

'I don't know her,' she said dismissively and began to move off.

'She's maybe a bit slow? Struggles to understand things?'

She stopped, turned to look over her shoulder. 'Simple Suzie, you mean?'

The PC shrugged. 'That could be her. Do you know which flat's hers?'

'5D. Middle block. She's on the same floor as me. What's she done?'

'Nothing. I'm just following up on something to see if she's alright.'

'Be nice if someone checked up on me sometimes.' She walked off, the baby's cries growing fainter.

Bill followed her directions, taking the lift to the fifth floor.

Four identical blue doors stretched along the corridor, two on each side. He searched in vain for a doorknocker and rattled the letterbox at 5D instead.

'Who is it?' a querulous voice responded.

He bent down to peer through the letterbox, seeing a frightened face backing away.

'Hello. Are you Suzie? I'm the police – PC Bill McAdam.' He spoke to her reassuringly through the letterbox. 'Can I come in? I just want to see if you're OK. People are worried about you.'

'I can't.'

Her hands had gone to her mouth, clenched into fists.

'Why can't you?'

'Mum said not to open the door to strangers.'

'I'm not a stranger, though, Suzie. I'm the police. Didn't your mum tell you to trust the police? We're here to help.'

'I don't have my key.' She began crying. 'I can't leave without my key.'

'You've lost your key, is that it?' Bill tried to make sense of what was making her so upset. 'I can get another key cut for you if you've lost it, but you'll have to let me in.' His thigh muscles were beginning to cramp from crouching down at her letterbox.

There was the sound of the lock turning and the door inched open. Suzie's worried face peered around at him.

'He'll be angry that I let a policeman in.'

'Who are you talking about, Suzie? Do you live with someone?' Bill caught sight of a rough bed made up on a couch.

'I don't know his name. He knocked me over with his bike and said I have to pay him, but I've only got enough money for my food.' Suzie started to fret, wringing her hands and stepping from side to side.

'It's OK. It's OK. He'll not bother you anymore. Where is he now?'

Suzie's finger pointed to the door. Bill turned around at the sound of someone running back down the corridor. A young man flew around the corner, heading for the stairs.

'Stay here. I'll be right back,' Bill called out to her as he followed in hot pursuit.

'Police. Stop!'

The DI was in his office when Frankie returned to the station. Hamish had barely responded when she'd entered reception, just a curt nod and then back to his computer monitor. The sergeant was never particularly voluble, using the minimum number of words to get him through each day as if each utterance cost him personally – but this was different.

'Is anything the matter, Hamish?' she'd asked out of a willingness to help. He wasn't the type to ever ask for anything, preferring to stand on his own feet and not have to rely on anyone else.

'No, lass. There's nothing you can help with.' She'd noticed that his eyes were bloodshot, that he was looking older and somehow frailer.

He must be close to retirement. Maybe that was what had been playing on his mind. Frankie tried to imagine what it must be like to be approaching retirement and all she could come up with was the luxury of staying in bed on a winter morning.

She tapped on the DI's door, entered when he waved her in with a distracted air.

'I've talked to the stationmaster. They've not had any reports of a body seen on the line, but he's going to ask around for me.'

'OK. Thanks, Frankie.' His brows drew down in concentration.

'Seems unlikely that a train driver doesn't see a body tied to the tracks – if that's what killed him.'

'I was thinking the same, sir. Unless the train was deliberately driven over the body?'

'A homicidal train driver?' Corstorphine's expression made it clear what he thought of that theory.

Frankie had to agree with him. She hesitated, unwilling to be the first to break the *Courier*'s headlines to him.

'Have you seen *The Courier* this morning, sir?'

Corstorphine's face hardened. 'Have they printed anything about the body?'

She drew a deep breath, thought through her words before speaking.

'The reporter's been to talking to William Haddow. She's printed a picture of his scarecrow and has the details of the body we found. There's another picture of forensics taking the head away in a bag – pixelated, which makes it even worse.'

'Shit! I wanted to keep this under wraps as long as we could. That's...'

She watched uncomfortably as Corstorphine checked the clock and performed mental arithmetic in front of her.

'A little over twenty-four hours since we found the body. What else did they have to say?'

She'd had the small hope that he'd have left it there. Now she was going to drop them all in it.

'They've mentioned Duncan Lewis, sir. As a person of interest – and made the connection to Carstairs State Hospital.'

He wasn't taking the news well. She had no choice but to finish and coughed nervously before risking her voice. 'They also linked Shamila to his release.'

'How in God's name did they make that connection?' His distracted air had been replaced with anger.

Frankie wished she was anywhere instead of standing in front of him.

'Someone here's been talking. Was it you?'

She instantly went on the defensive. 'The reporter, Josephine Sables, called here yesterday afternoon when you were out of the office. She'd already been to the farm and knew about the decapitated body. She took a photo from the track.'

Corstorphine lowered his voice. 'Then how do you explain how she managed to get Lewis's name and the link to Carstairs and Shamila?'

'Sorry, sir. I don't know how she found out.' Frankie had a strong suspicion who had been speaking to her.

'I'll see Lamb as soon as he shows his head. And McAdam,' he added as an afterthought.

It was clear to Frankie which of the two constables he held responsible.

'I'll ask him to see you, sir.'

Corstorphine made for the main office. 'We need to find Duncan Lewis, and fast.'

She followed him to the crazy board.

'If that body turns out to be the missing staff member, Shamila will have to be seen as a potential target.'

The reason for Corstorphine's unusual quickness to anger was laid bare on the noticeboard. Ever since he'd had word from the Lanark police he'd been on edge, worrying about Shamila's safety.

'Still no word from forensics on the ID of that body.'

Frankie wasn't sure if he was asking a question or making a statement of fact.

'I've not heard anything back from them yet, sir.'

He stood in silent study of the few names on the board. There was precious little information there – and most of what they had was conjecture until they had a positive ID linking to the missing Carstairs staff member.

'Whoever took the body to Halfway Farm must have transport – maybe even a van. Check with the local hire companies. See if anyone's taken out a hire in the last week.'

Corstorphine's gaze switched to the ceiling – a sure sign he was searching his memory.

'Make that from Friday 24th October – that's around when forensics estimated his time of death. You'd better check holiday lets as well, the hotel – anywhere he could use to hide out. There's this as well.' He selected a photo on his phone and sent it to Frankie. 'This tyre track was at Haddow's farm by the site of the body – it might be a wheelbarrow. I meant to check forensics had seen it.'

Frankie's pen scratched away at her notebook.

'I'll chase them up. Do you think the murderer *is* him, sir? Duncan Lewis?'

Corstorphine levelled his gaze to meet hers.

'I hope not, Frankie. I really hope it isn't him.'

He made for his office, grabbing his coat and phone.

'I'm going to see Shamila. She may be able to provide some insight as to where Duncan might choose to go if he knows we're looking for him. Thanks to *The Courier* he can hardly not be aware.' He stopped dead in the middle of the office, pointed a finger at Frankie. '*The Courier* might have done us an unexpected favour. See if anyone's cut short their holiday let today. If he's seen the paper, he'd be unlikely to stay put – it might give us the lead we need.'

'I'll get onto it straight away, sir. How's Shamila coping with it all?'

'She refuses to believe it's anything to do with Duncan Lewis, but she said something yesterday that I should have followed up at the time.'

Frankie waited as Corstorphine reached for his jacket, checking the pockets for his car keys. His brows creased in worry before he spoke. 'She told me she's afraid of scarecrows and I need to know if she shared that with any members of Carstairs staff.'

THIRTY

DIAGNOSIS

Bill's muscular bulk proved a disadvantage as he pursued the youth down the stairs, his body slamming into the wall at each sharp turn of the stairwell. The young lad was like a gazelle in comparison, springing off each right-angled turn like a parkour athlete. Bill's shouted commands for the lad to stop only served to make him move faster. By the time he'd run down three floors, Bill was gasping for air and had come to a halt – winded by another collision with the wall.

He took the time to slow his breathing, leaned over the stairwell railings to see his quarry almost at ground level. There was no chance of catching him now. Bill slowly started ascending the stairs again, making for Suzie's flat.

She remained where he'd left her, standing in the open doorway to her apartment with a lost expression etched on her face.

'OK, Suzie. I don't think he'll be bothering you again.' Bill panted. 'I'm going to take you to the police station with me. We can sort this out and make sure you have a new lock fitted. OK?'

Suzie fearfully took a step back.

'I've not done anything wrong!' she wailed like a child.

'I know, Suzie. It's alright, I know you've not done anything 'wrong.' Bill attempted to pacify her. 'Is there anyone here who can help, any neighbours you know or family nearby?'

She shook her head, tears starting from her eyes.

'My mum died. I don't know anyone.'

Bill thought rapidly. He couldn't leave Suzie here in case the youth came back. She was on the verge of hysterics, had no key to her flat and nobody to look after her.

'I'll tell you what we'll do, Suzie. You come with me to the police station where you'll be safe. Are you hungry?'

She nodded, wiping her eyes clear of tears.

'I'll treat you to a takeaway, how about that?'

She smiled shyly, turning a trusting face towards him and offered him her hand. Bill took it in his, pulled the door closed behind her as they exited into the corridor.

'No! I haven't got a key! How am I going to get back in again?' Suzie instantly began to panic, pulling away from him in desperation.

'I'll make sure you have a new key, Suzie. We can do that at the station. Then I'm going to find that young man who's been bullying you and make sure he doesn't bother you again.'

He led Suzie to the lift, his comforting smile at odds to the anger growing in his heart.

Bill returned to the station to face a scene of absolute confusion. Frankie was comforting Hamish's wife, Molly, who was in floods of tears. PC Lamb was standing, twisting his cap in his hands and watching the sergeant with a look of concern. Hamish was sat in his usual position in reception, but holding his head in his hands. By the sounds coming from in between his fingers, Bill had the impression that the sergeant was sobbing.

Suzie peered from behind him, taking in the scene for a second before returning to the protection offered by the PC's wide back.

'What's going on?' Bill's attention switched from one to the other.

'We'd all better go through to the office,' Frankie commanded. 'You as well, Hamish.' She inclined her head at Lamb. 'Give him a hand, Phil.'

Frankie opened the dividing door, ushering Molly in front of her and watching as Lamb helped Hamish out of his seat.

Bill smiled encouragingly at his charge, seeing her wondering at the commotion. Suzie looked as if she was considering making a run for it.

'Let's go through the door, Suzie. I'll put the kettle on.'

His mention of such a domestic routine settled her nerves as he guessed it would. Frankie had commandeered the DI's office, leading Molly and Hamish inside before shutting the door. Lamb looked about as lost as he felt.

'Take a seat here, Suzie.'

She nodded, staring around her in confusion. Bill beckoned PC Lamb to follow him to the small kitchen area where he could keep an eye on Suzie whilst searching for clean mugs.

'What the fuck is going on?' he whispered urgently to the young constable. The sound of the kettle filling masked the sounds of grief coming from Corstorphine's office.

Phil Lamb expelled air from his cheeks as if he'd been storing it.

'That's Molly, Hamish's wife.'

'I know who it is,' Bill snapped. 'What's got them all worked up? I've never seen the sergeant like that!'

'I almost ran her over in town,' the young PC started. 'She was walking along the main road like she was in a trance or something. I had to stop the car in the middle of the road and escort her to the pavement.'

'Is she ill?' Bill questioned. He lined up enough mugs for the lot of them, adding teabags one by one.

'Aye. I think she's got dementia. I had an aunt with it – I recognise the symptoms. She told me she was looking for her mum.'

'So you brought her here?' Bill watched the kettle as the water started to heat up.

'I didn't know what else to do,' Phil explained. 'I couldn't just take her home in case she set off again, and if I took her to the hospital, then Hamish would be down on me like a ton of bricks. What else could I have done?'

He asked the question with an air of desperation, looking back at the DI's office where Frankie switched her attention between Molly and Hamish. 'Do you think I should go in and help?'

Bill shook his head. 'Help me with these teas. Frankie will have to make the call. She knows we're here if she needs us, but fuck knows what we can do.' He gave a mug to the young PC. 'Give this to Suzie and sit with her. She's locked out of her flat – just reassure her that everything's going to be alright. I'll take these three mugs through to the DI's office.'

He looped two handles around one finger, held the third mug in his spare hand and made for the DI's office. Not everything would be alright – not if Lamb's diagnosis was correct.

Corstorphine parked in the industrial estate, choosing his spot so he had a clear view of Shamila's unit. It was coming up lunchtime and she'd be free for the next hour. He hoped it was coincidence that she had expressed a fear of scarecrows at the same time a dismembered body had been left for them to find in farmer Haddow's field. The trouble was that coincidences never remained mere statistical oddities in Corstorphine's experience and often merited a closer inspection.

He held Duncan's mugshot in his mind's eye, sweeping the car park for anyone who might fit the description. Frankie was going through tourist accommodation sites back at the station, and the two constables had been tasked with keeping watch for him. There was nothing more that he could do, for the moment.

What if the body turned out to be one of the Carstairs staff? He'd have to call in the Major Investigation Team, if only so he could make certain Shamila was safe. Their small team couldn't protect her and look for Duncan Lewis. They were spread too thinly as it was.

The clinic door opened, and Shamila stood in the entrance searching for his car. She waved when she caught sight of the police Land Rover and walked over to see him.

'James! Are we going for lunch?'

'We can do. I just wanted to talk with you about Carstairs.'

Shamila climbed in, pulled the door shut behind her and turned towards him with an air of resignation. She sighed theatrically, making her disappointment clear as she strapped the seatbelt into place.

'Is this about Duncan again?' There was an edge to her voice he hadn't heard before.

Corstorphine started the engine and made for the road back into town.

'You said something last night. About your fear of scarecrows.'

She laughed. 'Yes, stupid, isn't it? I don't know why. It's not as if I suffered a trauma when I was younger, but the things just creep me out.'

'I'm worried that our finding that body dressed to look like a scarecrow might be sending you a message.'

Shamila's smile faded. 'I know you're worried about the alert from Carstairs, but it's just procedure. The hospital operates on a surfeit of caution – the staff would all be paranoid if we took every alert personally. Has the body been identified yet?'

'No.'

She sighed with relief. 'Well then, it's probably nothing to do with us – with me at any rate.'

'Did this Duncan Lewis ever know about your phobia?'

'I can see where you're going. No, I never told him about my formidophobia – it's not the sort of subject a clinician would bring up with a patient. My job is to cure them of their psychiatric problems, not discuss my own.'

'So, nobody at the hospital would have known you had a thing about scarecrows – it's not on your medical records or anything?'

Shamila gave his question some thought before responding.

'No, there won't be anything on my file. As for any of the staff being aware of my phobia – I can't remember ever having discussed it.'

'Not even with this Gyles Lambert? Did you work a lot with him?'

'For a few years.'

'Any personal animosity between you and any members of staff?' Corstorphine asked innocently. He thought back to the day of the wedding and Gyles standing apart from all the other guests. He was certain Shamila had invited him more from a sense of duty than any real friendship. Gyles hadn't stayed for the reception either. Taking himself off at the first opportunity.

'Oh, come on, James.' She looked at him in disappointment. 'We're all professionals and well-versed in psychoanalysis and conflict management. Do you really think we'd have the time or inclination for petty feuds between staff?'

Corstorphine felt his level of concern dropping. 'It's just a hell of a coincidence. Someone goes missing from the State Hospital, an arrest warrant out for one of your patients and then this body we found yesterday.'

She reached out and lay her hand on his shoulder. 'Try not to worry, James. I know Duncan Lewis is on your mind, but he is one of the last people I'd suspect of being behind this murder. It's difficult for me to explain in layman terms, but the sickness that drove him to killing his wife has been controlled. If there had been any sign of his psychosis returning, his clinician would have spotted it, but as long as he continues with his medication, then he's as sane as you or I. Saner, probably!'

Corstorphine smiled weakly. 'And what if he stopped taking his medication?'

'Fair comment. Then all bets are off – but Duncan is an intelligent man. He wouldn't want to risk a return of the psychosis that drove him to kill his wife, believe me. It's the last thing he'd want to do.'

'Pub lunch?'

Shamila nodded. 'We should do this more often.'

Corstorphine turned into the driveway of an out-of-town hotel, coming to a halt in front of what was once a country house.

'You've never taken me here before. Is this where you used to meet all your girlfriends before I came along?' Shamila asked mischievously.

'No, not all of them,' he replied, trying to keep a straight face.

As the waitress took them to their table, he tried to take comfort from Shamila's lack of concern and enjoy their time together. In the corner of the room, the sonorous tick from a grandfather clock was an all too present reminder that Duncan Lewis remained at large – and he couldn't shake the fear that the woman he loved was his next target.

THIRTY-TWO
TAKEN

Corstorphine returned to the station only to be given the terrible news about Hamish and Molly as he entered reception.

'Frankie took them both to the medical centre, sir.'

'You'd better stay here, Phil, at least until we hear back from Hamish.'

The young PC buzzed the door lock and slumped back down in Hamish's worn seat, uncharacteristically subdued.

Corstorphine entered the main office with his head bowed. No wonder the sergeant had been so distracted recently. His mind was so preoccupied with worrying about Shamila and trying to juggle his small team that he didn't notice PC McAdam or the young woman sat with him until the last minute.

'Hi, Bill. Do you need me for anything?' He raised an enquiring eyebrow towards the PC and his charge.

'No, thank you, sir. Everything's under control. Suzie here is locked out of her flat, I'm just sorting out a locksmith.'

Corstorphine paid them scant attention and made for his office. A box of tissues had been left on his desk and the chairs rearranged. He guessed that Frankie had probably taken the sergeant and his wife in there for privacy.

There was an email waiting for his attention on the computer.

It had come from the procurator fiscal's office. Forensics had finally made a positive ID, and it was the result he'd feared. The body they'd found belonged to Richard Bryce – the missing nurse from Carstairs. His phone rang almost immediately, sending a jolt of adrenaline through his veins. He almost knocked it onto the floor in his desperation to pick up.

'Corstorphine.' A hollow space opened up in his stomach as he waited to hear Shamila's cry for help.

'DI Anderson, Lanark police. Have you seen the forensics notification about that body you found?' The detective wasted no time in getting straight to the point.

'I'm just back in the office. It's not the news I was wanting to hear.' Corstorphine was relieved not to have heard Shamila's panicked voice. Now he was desperate to end the call so he could warn her.

'No.' There was a pause. 'Will you be notifying Dr Mallick, telling her to increase her security?'

'She's my wife. Of course I'll be increasing security. As soon as I'm off this call.'

'Of course, sorry. Stupid thing to say. What are you planning to do?'

Corstorphine had dreaded this moment ever since Shamila had been given a security warning. He didn't have much choice in deciding the next steps.

'I'll be calling in the Major Investigation Team. We don't have the personnel to conduct an effective manhunt across our geographical region. Besides, I need to keep Shamila safe in case this lunatic comes for her.'

'I understand. We'll offer whatever support we can.'

Corstorphine's imagination took in the missing scarecrows still unaccounted for. He forced himself to concentrate on the job at hand. 'Forensics suggested the body may have been tied to a railway line.'

'Yes, I saw that. Have you had any success with the local rail network?'

'We've drawn a blank so far, neither the train drivers nor rail workers have reported anything. The Scottish transport police are casting a wider net in the hope that we can at least identify where the murder took place. Can you do the same local to you?'

'Good point! Richard Bryce comes from Cleghorn. There's a railway line that goes straight past the village – we'll start with that. I'll be in touch if we make any progress.'

'Thanks.' Corstorphine's finger was ready to end the call.

'Look. I'm sorry. Hell of a thing for you and your wife to go through.'

Corstorphine nodded, then realised the gesture wouldn't translate down the phone.

'Aye. Well – we just have to catch the bastard before he does anything else.'

He immediately hit the speed dial for Shamila, only to go straight through to voicemail.

'Shit! She must have a client. Where's the surgery reception number?' Corstorphine realised he was talking to himself as he hurried past Bill on his way to the staff car park. He hit the contact number and climbed into the Land Rover.

'Come on! Come on!' The engine coughed into life and his mobile routed through to the hands free, a ring tone repeating over and over again. It felt like a block of ice had settled in his stomach when the clinic answerphone clicked in.

'I'm sorry we're not able to take your call at the moment. Please leave your name, number and a brief message and we'll get back to you as soon as possible. The normal clinic opening hours are Monday to Friday, 9:30 a.m. to 4:30 p.m., morning only on Tuesdays.'

Corstorphine tried to stop the images flooding his mind. Crime scenes he'd attended but with Shamila's lifeless body taking the place of any number of murder victims. He switched on the siren and blues, sending kaleidoscopic strobes across the settled surface of the loch and reflected in windows as he accelerated into the traffic. Shamila's clinic was only ten minutes away, but those minutes crept past painfully slowly.

He stopped outside the clinic in a screech of tyres and sprinted for the small industrial unit Shamila had repurposed for her own. It all appeared normal from the outside and Corstorphine began to relax as he reached the door – berating himself for getting into such a panic.

The door opened under his touch. His mouth went dry. Shamila never left it unlocked. His eyes flew to Shamila's receptionist Kira, gagged and tied to her chair, her eyes wide with terror.

Corstorphine rushed towards her and ripped the tape from the receptionist's mouth.

'Kira, where is she? Who's taken her?'

'Mr Samson.' Kira burst into tears. 'He's taken Shamila.'

THIRTY-THREE
SAMSON

Corstorphine felt the world slipping away from him. Kira looked at him for reassurance, her body shaking with fear.

'When was this, Kira? How long ago?'

'He... he... he came in for his appointment at two o'clock.' Kira fought past the shuddering sobs that consumed her. 'Shamila took him into her office. I heard what sounded like a fight. I opened the door and he grabbed me, put his hand over my mouth. He said he'd kill me if I made a sound!' Her wide eyes implored forgiveness.

'It's OK, Kira. He can't hurt you now. What did he do to Shamila?'

She shook her head. 'Shamila just went quietly with him. He wasn't holding her or anything. She told me not to worry, and it would all be over soon.'

'She just walked out with him?' Corstorphine struggled to make sense of her walking out with a violent patient. 'You said there had been a fight?'

'I heard a noise which is why I opened her door. Shamila was standing beside her desk, her chair had been knocked over. And then he grabbed me.'

Kira broke down at the memory. He wanted to put an arm around her for comfort, but forensics would be wanting to check

Kira and her clothes. Corstorphine willed himself to not panic as his heart hammered away in his chest. The time was 3:26 p.m. Shamila had been gone for over an hour.

'Did this Samson character have a car? I need his details – what he looks like, age, height, anything you can remember. Is there a file on him?'

'I can't believe he took Shamila. I tried to help.' Kira was inconsolable.

'Take a deep breath. I can't help Shamila until you calm down and tell me who it is that has taken her. Try and breath normally.'

Kira took a few deep breaths. 'I'm sorry. I'm trying to calm down.'

Corstorphine took the chance to radio through to the station.

'Phil. I need everyone to look out for Shamila. Someone's abducted her from the clinic – one of her patients. A man called Samson. I'll provide more details as soon as I can. Get hold of Frankie and send her here to the clinic, Bill as well. You'd better stay put and handle comms. And ask Inverness to send a forensics team as a matter of urgency.'

'Someone's taken Shamila?' The PC's wondering tones issued tinnily from the radio speaker.

Corstorphine cut him off without bothering with radio protocol.

'What can you tell me about Mr Samson, Kira? Every second counts.'

She bit her lips, wiped the tears away from her eyes and stood up on shaky legs.

'His file's here.' Kira reached for a manilla folder on the edge of her desk.

Corstorphine snatched it out of her hands, searched for his address details.

'What does he look like? Did you see how he arrived here? Did he take Shamila in a car?' He fired the questions at her, willing Kira to answer.

'He's average height, Scottish from his accent. He's got long dark hair. I couldn't make out his features through his bushy beard.'

'What was he wearing?'

'Jeans. Brown shoes. He had a black puffa jacket.'

'What about a car?'

'I didn't see anything. We keep the blinds drawn for privacy.'

Corstorphine glanced at the windows, remembered seeing the blinds always closed. The only view outside was from the door camera.

'The doorcam,' he blurted. 'Is it recorded? Is the video feed recorded or stored on the Cloud?'

'He took the tape.' Her finger pointed towards a VCR on the shelf beside her desk. 'Please, you have to find her!'

Corstorphine pressed eject on the VCR and the machine whirred, revealing an empty slot. He silently cursed before giving his full attention to Kira.

'Believe me, nothing is more important. Just sit quietly and try to think of anything that might help us find them. I have to make some calls.'

He was desperate to leave and begin searching for Shamila, but the crime scene couldn't be left unattended. Neither could Kira. Corstorphine keyed the radio on.

'Foxtrot Kilo. Foxtrot Kilo from Sierra four-five, over.'

Where the hell was Frankie?

'Foxtrot Kilo. Approaching your location. ETA five minutes. Do you have any description, sir?'

'Scottish. Long dark hair, big bushy beard, black puffa jacket, brown shoes. Check this address for me: 37 Balmoral Street. It's where Mr Samson has down as his residence. I'll stay here with Kira – tell McAdam to meet you there. He could be dangerous. Over.'

THIRTY-FOUR
EVA

Frankie had been driving back from the medical centre when she received Phil's garbled message. Her thoughts were still very much with Hamish and his wife, left sitting in the doctor's waiting room for a diagnosis neither wanted to hear. The sergeant was just about keeping it all together, holding onto Molly's hand as if he never wanted to let it go.

'Sorry, can you repeat that more slowly, Phil? I thought you said Corstorphine's wife has been kidnapped.'

'That's exactly what I said. He's at her clinic now and wants you and Bill there as soon as you can.'

'Tell him I'll be there in ten minutes.' She turned on the siren and made straight for the industrial estate out of town where Shamila kept her clinic. Her focus shifted from reading the road ahead to scanning approaching vehicles and pedestrians for any sight of Shamila.

Her radio crackled into life. Corstorphine giving her instructions to search a property in the town. She acknowledged and spun the wheel, making a U-turn to return along the route she'd just taken. Frankie tried to reach Bill on the radio, but he beat her to it.

'On my way to that address now, Frankie. I'll see you there.'

'Kill the sirens and park out of sight. We don't want to give him any warning.'

Balmoral Street consisted of a row of identical houses with coloured bins neatly arranged on the pavement ready for collection. Number 37 lay near enough in the middle. She parked a few doors away, checked she had handcuffs and baton ready for action and made cautious progress towards the house. Bill arrived from the opposite direction, and she beckoned for him to join her. He ducked down beneath a stone wall in front of the property to avoid being seen.

'What's the plan?' Bill spoke urgently, looking back over his shoulder to view the house.

'We don't have a search warrant, so we'll have to play it by the book.' She'd already decided on the course of action. 'I'll try the front door. You stay out of sight and be ready to catch him if he makes a run for it out the back.'

'What if he goes for you?' Bill flicked his gaze towards her baton and cuffs.

'Just stay close. He'll not get past me, and if it turns physical, you can use whatever force is necessary.'

He nodded grimly and they took their positions, Frankie with her hand grasping the door knocker, Bill poised to make a dash in either direction. She gave a quick rap at the door, and they listened intently for any movement from inside. They both heard the sound at the same time – a regular tapping noise growing louder as it approached the front door. Bill McAdam shifted his stance in readiness to rush the door as it opened, only to rock back on his heels in surprise.

'Is this about the zombies?' An old woman leaned on her walking stick, craning her neck to peer around Frankie at the large constable looking as if he was in danger of falling into the well-tended flower beds. 'Are you feeling alright, young man? You seem a bit unsteady on your feet.' She helpfully waved her walking stick in his general direction. 'I have to use this stick now my legs aren't what they used to be.'

Frankie checked the empty hallway behind her.

'Does a Mr Samson live here?'

'Who, dear?'

'Mr Samson. Long, dark hair, beard?'

The woman's shocked expression gave Frankie little hope that they had the correct address.

'Certainly not! I'm a respectable woman.'

Bill McAdam visibly relaxed in the periphery of her vision.

'Are you living here on your own?' Frankie attempted, rephrasing her question.

'Yes!' The reply was loaded with indignation. 'Are you trying to suggest I should be in one of those homes? I can cope perfectly well, thank you!'

Her eyes narrowed with suspicion. 'What are you doing here anyway? Did Hamish send you?'

Frankie struggled to make the connection between this woman and the sergeant, apart from age.

'No, we're investigating a serious crime and looking for Mr Samson. He gave this property as his address.'

'Did he now!' The indignation came back with more force. 'Well, this is *my* house, and I've never heard of this Samson man, whoever he is. He certainly doesn't live here.'

'Do you mind if we have a look?'

'Do you think I've hidden him under my bed?' Her combative eyes challenged Frankie to respond.

'No, Ms... I'm sorry, what's your name?'

'Eva Baldwin. Mrs Eva Baldwin.'

'Well, Eva. Would you mind if the constable and I have a quick check around your house, just to reassure ourselves that you're safe?'

Mrs Baldwin considered her request by apparently chewing on a non-existent lemon.

'I suppose so,' she eventually answered with reluctance. 'Only I've not cleaned the house, so don't look too closely.'

'We'll be as quick as we can, ma'am,' Bill McAdam advised.

'Come on then, you're letting all the heat out!'

It took all of a few minutes for them to confirm Mrs Baldwin did live on her own, even to the extent of checking her dilapidated garden shed and its few tools.

'I'm sorry to disturb you,' Frankie offered. 'You've not seen a gentleman with long dark hair and a bushy beard on the street then?'

'No, and if I had, I'd be keeping a close eye on him, I can tell you.'

Frankie exchanged a look with the PC. The address Corstorphine had was obviously false.

'Thank you for your time, Eva. If you do see anyone matching that description, could you call the station? It's important that we speak to him as soon as possible.'

'What's he done?' Eva leaned on her stick surveying the two police officers like a judge from high on the bench.

'I'm sorry, we're not at liberty to give you that information, but don't approach him yourself if you do see him. Leave it to us, OK?'

'I'll watch out for him – and contact the Neighbourhood Watch team. I'm the chair,' she added self-importantly.

'Thanks. We'll be in touch.'

Frankie and Bill headed back to the street.

'I'll see you at Shamila's clinic,' Frankie said urgently. 'Christ knows what state the DI's in – he'll be out of his mind with worry.'

THIRTY-FIVE
REFERRAL

Corstorphine took the call from Frankie on the radio.

'Have you found Shamila?'

'Sorry, sir. He's given a false address. There's just an old lady living by herself and she's never heard of a Mr Samson nor seen anyone matching the description. Bill and I are heading to you now, ETA 3:50 p.m. Over.'

'Understood.' He ended the call abruptly, unable to concentrate on anything other than finding Shamila.

'Is there anything else you can tell me? Anything he said or did that might help us find her?' He directed the question at Kira, sat wiping at her eyes with a handkerchief.

'I don't know. It all happened so fast...'

'Try and think. Anything you can remember may be the difference between us finding her...' He tailed off at that point, unwilling to give voice to the fear that Shamila might be in mortal danger. 'Tell me everything you remember. How long has Samson been a client?'

Corstorphine was as certain as he could be that Mr Samson's name was as real as the address he'd given, but it was all he had to work with.

'He was referred this week. This was his first session with her.

Everything seemed normal, he was polite and calm. I didn't think there'd be any problem.'

'Who referred him? What was his medical condition?'

Kira indicated the file on her desk which had provided the address details. Corstorphine swept it up, read the attached notes more carefully.

'It says here he was referred by the local council. Is that normal?' Corstorphine continued speed reading as Kira answered.

'He's employed by the council, as a teacher at the local high school. He's been off with stress – his doctor recommended psychological counselling as he's been off a few weeks.'

'Who's his doctor? I can't see a name.'

Kira stretched out her arm and he couldn't help but notice how much she was shaking. She took the file, flicked towards the end and handed it back with a finger indicating a name.

'Here, Dr Selina Edwards.'

Corstorphine searched in vain for any contact details. 'Do you have a number for the doctor?'

'Yes, she should be on the system.' Kira's fingers flew across her keyboard, newly energised at the thought that she could be doing something to help. 'Here we are!'

Corstorphine bent down to read her screen; entered the telephone number directly into his mobile.

'Great work, Kira.' He pressed the phone against his ear, waiting impatiently for someone to pick up.

'Lochside Health Centre, how can I help you?'

'This is Detective Inspector James Corstorphine. I need to speak urgently with Dr Selina Edwards.'

'I'm sorry, Inspector, but Selina is rather busy right now. Can I ask what this is in connection with?'

Corstorphine breathed out as steadily as he could.

'This is an emergency. Tell the doctor this is a matter of life or death and put her through to me now!'

There was a shocked silence as the health centre receptionist digested his words.

'Please hold the line.'

Corstorphine glanced at his watch. Shamila had been taken over an hour ago and he was still wasting time at her clinic.

'This is Dr Edwards. How can I help?'

'Doctor, I'm DI James Corstorphine. You referred one of your patients to my wife, Shamila Mallick for psychological counselling – a Mr Samson. I need his home address details. He's abducted Shamila, and I'm worried that she's in grave danger.'

'Let me stop you there, Inspector. I don't recollect the name – Samson you say?'

'Aye. Samson. He's a teacher, long dark hair and beard?'

'No, I'm sorry. There must be some sort of mistake. I've not referred anyone of that description for psychological assessment or treatment. Where did you get my name?'

'Your name's down on his file here at the Mallick Clinic as his referrer.'

'I'm sorry, but that can't be right. As I said, I've not referred anyone of that name to the Mallick Clinic. I can ask around the practice for you?'

'Please, and could you do that immediately? Every second counts.'

'Leave it with me, Inspector. Can I call you back on this number?'

'Please. Thank you for your help.'

'I'll call you back in a few minutes.'

Corstorphine stared at his phone as if he was willing it to ring.

'Have you had any other referrals from Dr Edwards or the Lochside Health Centre?'

'A few,' Kira replied. 'They tend to deal with a lot of the council staff and we've had a few suffering from work-related stress. That's why it all seemed perfectly normal.'

'You don't check back with the referrer as a matter of course?'

Kira shook her head. 'Not for regular clients. The Lochside Health Centre have sent us a number of patients since we opened. I didn't see any need to check.'

The realisation that she had inadvertently put Shamila in danger suddenly hit home.

'Oh God! It's my fault, isn't it? It's my fault for not looking for confirmation from the health centre.'

Her tear-filled eyes stared up at him, but it was all Corstorphine could do to not give into blind panic himself.

The sound of a siren grew louder. At least now he could begin searching for his wife.

THIRTY-SIX
LAMB TO THE...

PC Phil Lamb sat in Hamish's worn seat behind reception with the radio held tightly in his hands. He listened in on the few rushed exchanges between the DI and the other two members of their team with a sense of disbelief. How could Corstorphine's wife have been taken from her own clinic? He'd never felt so useless, cut off from the action. So much for his plan to be the one to find Duncan Lewis. Instead, he'd been sidelined in the search for Shamila, and what made it worse was the folded copy of *The Courier* Hamish had left unopened on the counter.

He could see the headlines without needing to open the front page. Corstorphine would know someone had talked to the newspaper and he'd be the first to be suspected. The thought lay heavy on his conscience. If he'd compromised the investigation, his career would be over. If it turned out in any way that he had inadvertently placed Shamila's life in danger, he wouldn't be able to live with himself.

The police station was empty, giving the impression of being at the eye of a tornado whilst untold damage was being wrought outside. When the phone rang, he literally jumped in his seat.

'Police, how can I help?'

'Is DI Corstorphine there? I need to speak to him urgently.'

Phil recognised the voice but struggled to put a face or name to the caller.

'I'm sorry, he's responding to an incident. Can I help?'

There was the sound of an exasperated exhale of air rasping tinnily in his ear.

'This is Robb McCoach. I've had a call from the vets saying Phoebe hasn't returned from her lunch break. I can't reach her and I'm starting to get worried.'

Phil's shocked silence lasted long enough for Robb to intervene.

'Hello, are you still there?'

'Yes, I'm sorry. Just taking notes.' Phil followed his own advice and began writing in the sergeant's daybook left on the reception desk.

'What time was she last seen?'

'I don't know. Whenever she left the vets. Around 1 p.m. I suppose. She's never been late back to work. I'm going frantic here. Are you going to look for her or do I have to call Corstorphine's personal number to get a response!' His voice echoed angrily down the line.

Phil thought rapidly. Corstorphine wouldn't want any more distractions and although he'd been told to stay put, he could at least take some of the heat off the DI by dealing with this himself.

'Don't worry, Mr McCoach. I'd recognise Phoebe if I saw her in town. I'll go out now and search for her and put the word out. I'm sure there's no reason to be alarmed.' The image of the scarecrow body came into focus as if to give lie to his words.

'I'll drive around town as well — let me know if you find her.'

'I'll contact you on this mobile number. Is that the best way to reach you?'

'Yes. Thanks. Look... sorry for being abrupt. It's just that she's my young sister and with everything that's happened...'

Robb McCoach didn't need to spell it out for him. The whole town knew the details of what had happened with the McCoach family last year.

'I'll let the DI know, sir. I'll start searching now – call us if she returns and let us know she's safe.'

'Yes, of course. Thanks again.' Robb sounded relieved as he ended the call.

Phil Lamb sat immobile as the implications of Robb's call filtered through. He had to tell the DI and the rest of the team. Chances were that Phoebe was sat in a café and had lost all sense of time – she always had that otherworldly feel to her as if she wasn't really there. But what if there was a connection to the murder and Shamila's kidnap? He keyed the radio.

'Sierra four-five. Sierra four-five from Papa Lima, over.'

A harsh burst of static signalled Corstorphine's picking up the call.

'What is it, Lamb?' His response was curt.

'Sorry to bother you, sir, but I've just had Robb McCoach call. His sister, Phoebe has gone missing and never returned to work this afternoon.'

'Phoebe? What? I can't deal with that now – take yourself into town and look for her. Keep your eyes open for anything that can lead us to Shamila and stay in touch.'

'Sir, Papa Lima out. Over.'

The silence issuing from his radio loudspeaker let him know the DI had left the conversation. At least he now had permission to leave the station.

Phil placed his cap at the regulation angle, locked the police station door behind him and marched briskly into the centre of town. If he couldn't find Duncan Lewis, at least he could try and find Phoebe McCoach. All the patrol cars were out, leaving him no choice but to pound the beat accompanied by his thoughts. He'd wanted to try for CID – if he didn't pull something out of his hat, he'd be lucky to remain a PC.

THIRTY-SEVEN
IMPOSSIBLE

Corstorphine pulled opened the clinic door as Frankie rushed towards the entrance.

'Sir! Any word?' She stopped in front of him, her hopeful expression fading as she caught the shake of his head.

'Nothing. Forensics are on their way.'

'Kira, this must be awful for you.'

Corstorphine saw Frankie's attention switch to Kira.

'She's had a shock. I've not entered Shamila's office to keep it clear for forensics. Careful with reception as well, especially the door handle in case whoever took her has left prints.'

'Understood, sir. Jesus, I'm sorry. I can't imagine how you must be feeling.' Frankie's worried eyes searched his.

How was he feeling? Numb and furious at the same time. 'I'm OK,' he lied. 'The Major Investigation Team are coming from Glasgow. They'll be a couple of hours at least.'

They both turned to face the door as a siren sounded, coming closer until McAdam's patrol car entered the car park. They waited in silence as Bill ran towards them.

'Bill, keep the place secure until SOC arrive in an hour or so. Kira here has had a shock, just look after her. They'll probably want to swab her clothes and the tape he used to tie her up.

Frankie and I will head back to the station. I need to think what to do next.'

He climbed into the Land Rover, feeling his legs shaking in response to shock. Frankie rushed towards her patrol car, waiting to follow him.

'Get a grip!' Corstorphine advised himself angrily. He had to remain calm and focussed if he wanted to find Shamila. He sped back to the station.

It had to be connected to Carstairs. The nurse's body they'd found; the unlikely coincidence of being dressed as a scarecrow and Shamila's phobia; the ex-patient of hers –Duncan Lewis. The man's image was so strong in his imagination that he could have reached out and touched him. Lamb's call about Phoebe – how was she connected to all of this or was her disappearance just another coincidence?

The station door was locked and he fumbled for his key, fingers struggling to fit it into the lock. Frankie pulled in behind him and followed him into the main office.

'Do you think this is connected to Phoebe going missing, sir?' Frankie had joined him in contemplation of the crazy wall.

Corstorphine didn't answer, instead he erased John Doe and wrote Richard Bryce's name in its place.

'I don't know what we're dealing with here, Frankie, if I'm honest. The only common factor is Shamila having worked at Carstairs and being responsible for the release of Duncan Lewis.'

Corstorphine berated himself for not seizing on Shamila's fear and the manner in which the body had been presented. The link couldn't have been any more obvious.

'But Phoebe doesn't fit the narrative, sir. The only connection she has is to Shamila.'

Corstorphine's mind raced. He added Phoebe's name to the board, drew a line linking her to Shamila. He entered a new name at the top – Mr Samson – and picked up a red marker to draw two thick lines connecting him to Richard Bryce and Shamila.

'We can forget the name Samson. It's pretty likely that name is as false as the address he gave. What have we got to work with?'

Corstorphine drew a list of bullet points on the crazy wall.

'One. We're looking for Duncan Lewis as our main suspect.' The pen squeaked as he wrote. 'Two. Mr Samson. We have a description and when SOC have given the clinic a thorough going over, we may have a positive ID.'

He turned to Frankie. 'Ask Carstairs State Hospital if they know of anyone who matches Samson's description – and check with Lanark police. There's a DI Anderson dealing with the case. He needs to be updated on what's happened here.'

Frankie hurried off to her desk, leaving him in silent contemplation of the little they had in way of leads. Whoever this Samson character was, the chances were that he was working with Duncan Lewis. But what motive could they have for murdering a nurse, or of more importance, why take Shamila?

It wouldn't be long before the MIT took over the investigation. He knew the first thing they'd do after he'd been debriefed was to send him home. There was no way they'd allow him to stay on an investigation when his own wife was missing. That gave him one hour, two at the most to try and find her. The task appeared hopeless with so little to go on. He stared out of the window at the mountains looming over the small town. They were surrounded by wild mountains and glens. Without any idea of where she'd been taken, it was an impossible task.

He forced himself to think clearly and logically, to not give in to the panic he felt rising in his chest. Shamila's life depended on him.

THIRTY-EIGHT
WIG

PC Lamb worked his way steadily along the high street, peering into every vehicle and pausing to inspect unattended parked vans in the hope of finding Shamila or Phoebe. When he reached the shops, he asked if anyone had seen Phoebe or could recall seeing someone matching Kira's vague description of Shamila's abductor, drawing a blank in each case.

It was with an increasing air of desperation that he turned towards the veterinary surgery and Phoebe's workplace. He was already in deep trouble for talking to the reporter – this was his only chance to salvage his reputation and get back in Corstorphine's good books.

What would I do if I was a detective?

The thought occupied his mind as he walked steadily towards the end of the high street and the surgery.

Ask if anyone had been hanging around or acting suspiciously. Seen any unknown vehicles parked outside for lengthy periods. Has a man with long black hair and beard brought in a pet for treatment.

The young constable shook his head as he considered the possibility of never being promoted and he realised he must have presented a desultory figure to the group of high school kids coming towards him.

'Afternoon, officer,' a cheeky young man called out, much to the delight of his mates.

Phil had the benefit of height and used it to his advantage, stopping in their path and looming over them so they had to stop or take a detour around him. He fixed the boy who'd called out to him with a hard stare, then looked again at the long black hair which sat strangely on top of the boy's head.

'Hang on, son.' He took a sidestep to block the youth from catching up with his mates who'd all stopped to see how this free sideshow would develop. 'Come here! Closer.'

The boy reached up to the PC's shoulders and after a brazen stare at the PC had decided casting a look towards the pavement may be the better option.

Phil looked more closely at the top of the boy's head and the unlikely hairstyle he presented. The sudden hope that he may be onto something made him grab hold of the boy's hair and pull it up, away from his scalp until it dangled like roadkill from his upstretched hand.

It was a cue for ribaldry and laughter from his mates.

'Oi! That's mine, that is.' The lad jumped up in an attempt to grab the hairpiece out of Phil's hand.

'Not so fast, son. Where did you get this?'

'It's mine,' came the sullen response.

'You in the habit of going to school with a wig on? What's wrong with your own hair?' Phil could see there was no reason to hide the zoomer perm now revealed. It was duplicated on at least half the young men gathered around, so he had the impression of standing in a field full of broccoli.

'You giving it back or what?'

'Let's see about that. Where did you say you bought it?'

A chorus of comments came from the excitable youths gathered around.

'He didn't.'

'Found it in the bin.'

'Manky bastard.'

Phil quietened them with one look.

'What's your name, son?'

He was met with a defiant glare. 'I don't have to tell you my name.'

His bravado was met with cheers from the onlookers along with shouted suggestions.

'Don't give 'im yer name, Murray!'

Phil couldn't help but smile.

'Murray, is it?' Phil enquired, only for the defiant glare to be directed at his mate.

'What you give 'im ma name for?'

'Which bin did you find it in, Murray?' The PC directed at the hapless youngster.

'By the school.'

'Come on. You can show me exactly where you found it.'

'But I'm on my way home.'

'You show me which bin you found this in and then we'll say no more about stolen property, shall we?'

The frightened expression that crossed the schoolboy's face was enough to reassure Phil that the boy would show him where the wig came from.

'I've not done nothing wrong,' Murray said under his breath as the PC led him back the way he'd came.

'When did you find it?' Phil questioned as the boy walked beside him, looking as guilty as his double negative had asserted.

'Just now. I was throwing some stuff in the bin and saw it. Thought it was a dead cat or something.'

'I don't suppose you saw anyone throwing it in the bin?' Phil asked hopefully.

'Nah. It was in here.' The boy pointed to a pavement bin almost overflowing with takeaway wrappers and fizzy drink tins. The council placed them at strategic locations around the school in the hope of containing the worst of the inevitable littering. If only the kids had better aim it might have served its purpose – instead the bin environs resembled one of the illicit tips they'd been dealing with.

Phil pulled on his latex gloves and had an exploratory rummage through the top layers without finding anything of interest.

'OK, lad. What's your full name and address?' He pulled out his notebook.

'But I've not done nothing.'

Phil resisted the urge to provide a quick grammar lesson. 'I know. This is just in case we need to ask you any more questions.' He lowered his voice, looked around furtively. 'This may be important evidence in a case we're working on, so I want you to keep quiet about this, OK?'

The boy nodded, wide-eyed, then gave Phil his details.

'Right. Off you go then.'

The boy hesitated. 'Can I get ma wig back?'

'Just go.' Phil pointed down the road and Murray walked away, turning into a run after a few steps.

'Cheeky wee bastard,' Phil spoke under his breath, seeing himself in the running figure heading back to join his mates.

The wig hung limply from his hand. It could be nothing, or it could be the way back into the DI's good books again. At this stage he didn't really have much to lose.

THIRTY-NINE
POWERLESS

Corstorphine was going out of his mind with worry. He wanted to be searching for Shamila – instead he was trapped in his office waiting for the Major Investigation Team to arrive and take him off the case. The crazy board had provided no additional insights, save a tenuous link between Shamila and Phoebe both reported as missing within hours of each other. Kira had said that Shamila had walked willingly out of the clinic with her abductor, but there had been a short fight in her office. The evidence for that lay in the overturned chair he'd seen. What would make her just walk out without trying to escape or raise the alarm?

Frankie was still working the phones, talking to Carstairs State Hospital and DI Anderson at Lanark. He could hear enough of the one-sided conversation to know she wasn't getting far.

He clenched his fists in frustration, desperately trying to second-guess the abductor's next moves. The link to the State Hospital was no longer in doubt and Duncan Lewis was fixed firmly in his crosshairs as the likely abductor, with the added complication of being aided by this Mr Samson who had somehow managed to arrange an appointment with Shamila. That suggested he knew enough about clinical referrals to have forged an email from the Lochside Health Centre without raising any suspicions.

At the back of his mind lay the dismembered body of the nurse, Richard Bryce, tied to Farmer Haddow's makeshift crucifix. He couldn't let himself begin to imagine that the same fate awaited Shamila.

'Can I speak to Dr Gyles Lambert? This is DI James Corstorphine. It's in connection with Duncan Lewis.'

The receptionist at Carstairs Hospital sounded apologetic as she responded. 'I'm sorry. Dr Lambert isn't available. Can I put you through to someone else?'

'I really need to speak with Dr Lambert. Can you ask him to call me as soon as he can?'

'That won't be possible. He's on holiday this week...'

Corstorphine interrupted. 'Do you have his mobile?'

'I'm sorry, sir. We're not at liberty to pass over those details.'

'OK. Thanks.'

He abruptly ended the call and searched for the Lanark DI's number.

'Is that DI Anderson?'

'Speaking.' A cautious Glaswegian voice sounded in his ear.

'DI James Corstorphine here. Do you have the contact details for Gyles Lambert?'

'DI Corstorphine? Look, I'm sorry to hear about your wife. Have you found out where—'

'We're no further forward. I need to talk to Dr Lambert about Duncan Lewis urgently.' He felt his heart hammering inside his chest.

'Sorry, we've been trying to talk to him ever since Richard Bryce never turned up for work on Monday. He's not answering his phone but then he's on holiday – could be he's just not taken it with him.'

'Fuck!' Corstorphine's fist hit his desk. 'He's responsible for Duncan Lewis's continual assessments, isn't he? Is there anyone else who can help?'

'Look, Corstorphine...' DI Anderson paused. 'I know you've had a shock and believe me I'd be doing exactly the same in your shoes, but Duncan Lewis is our responsibility and is best left for us to deal with. We'll give you every assistance we can, of course...'

Corstorphine slammed the phone down in disgust, only for it to immediately ring with an incoming call – Phil Lamb's name on the screen.

'What is it, Phil?' Corstorphine snapped.

'Sorry to bother you, sir, it's just I've found something that may relate to Shamila's kidnapping.'

The small ember of hope in his chest ignited, only to be extinguished as soon as it had flared. This was Lamb he was dealing with.

'Spit it out.'

'I was patrolling near the high school, sir. On my way to the veterinary surgery to ask about Phoebe and I saw a boy wearing a wig, sir.'

Corstorphine somehow managed to keep his emotions under control. The bar for entry to the police force was set low, but somehow Phil Lamb had managed to limbo his way into a job.

'Get to the point, man!'

'Yes, sir. Sorry, sir. The wig, it's long, black hair. Like the description we were given, sir. I just thought that maybe the kidnapper may have been wearing it; as a disguise.'

He drew a breath deep enough to give Lamb a long overdue assessment of his capabilities as a serving officer, then held it as he reconsidered. If Mr Samson had a false address, almost certainly a false name – then wearing such a distinctive wig wasn't as daft as it at first sounded.

'Good job, Phil. Bring it back to the station and try not to handle it much. Can you find a bag to put it in?'

'I'm near the vets now, sir. I'll ask them for something.'

'Did anyone see anything, any description for who threw it away or when?' He waited hopefully for some tangible evidence they could use.

'No, sir, sorry, sir. It was found in a bin by the high school. None of the kids saw who put it in there.'

'OK.' He thought rapidly. The wig was a long shot, but it could provide crucial forensic evidence if Mr Samson had used it as a disguise. Then again, the bin needed to be collected and analysed in case anything else of value was in there.

Corstorphine cursed under his breath. Hamish was in the medical centre with Molly. They'd be waiting there for hours and given the circumstances the sergeant wasn't going to be of any use in the immediate future. Bill McAdam had to remain at the clinic until SOC took it over, then he'd be needed to take Kira to the hospital for a check-up immediately afterwards. That left him and Frankie. It was coming up to half past four and the light was already fading outside.

Somewhere out there was Shamila, possibly with Phoebe. Both were in danger. Duncan Lewis had killed before, and probably had already killed again.

He'd never felt so powerless in his life.

FORTY
VET

'Here you are.' The veterinary nurse handed over a clear plastic bag, fresh out of a packet. 'We use these for medical waste.' Her voice held the trace of a Welsh accent. She must have caught the look on Phil's face because she quickly added, 'This one's unused.'

'Thanks.' Phil dropped the wig into the equivalent on an over-sized freezer bag and sealed it.

'I thought you were bringing in something that had been run over.' Her open face broke into a wide smile. 'Has Phoebe turned up? She never came back from her lunch break. Her brother said he was going to call you lot – it's nothing serious, is it?'

PC Lamb hesitated in the doorway, turning back to the friendly nurse in her green scrubs. He had the awful suspicion that it was something serious, deadly serious – but telling her wouldn't help.

'I'm sure she'll turn up. You know what kids are like, probably lost track of time. We're all keeping an eye out for her.'

The nurse seemed content with that. 'She's such a sweet girl. We all love her to bits here.'

Phil nodded an acknowledgement, gave her a tight smile and left. The station was a twenty-minute walk away if he upped his pace. The streets were all but emptied of the flood of schoolkids, leaving nothing behind but a few discarded sweet wrappers. It had turned noticeably darker since he'd entered the vets. Streetlights shone their sterile white LED light down, road traffic picked up as workers packed up for the day. He watched every vehicle as they passed him by – tradesmen in their ubiquitous white vans; office and shop workers in small cars; cyclists weaving between potholes. The air chilled as the sun set, leaving fiery red clouds streaked across the western horizon. Phil shivered involuntarily at the colour. Too close to the shade of blood exposed when the scarecrow's head separated, too much a premonition for the two missing people they were no closer to finding.

At least he had the wig. The plastic bag in his hand might be enough for Corstorphine to forget his indiscretion with the newspaper reporter – and with Hamish otherwise occupied...

He instantly felt guilty at using Molly's condition as a salve to his own predicament. Hamish would be going through all sorts of hell and with no hope of a good outcome. He'd seen how that story went when his aunt had been diagnosed and wouldn't wish that painfully slow farewell on anyone.

His phone vibrated inside his uniform pocket, and he fumbled to reach it quickly, hitting accept before reading the screen. The number showed as Josephine Sables, the *Courier* reporter.

'I can't talk, I've said too much already, and you've printed details that shouldn't be in the press. Do you know how much trouble I'm in?'

'Phil. I'm sorry, but we need to tell the people what's going on. I didn't mention your name in the article.'

'Doesn't matter,' Phil cut in. 'The DI will know it's me. I'll be lucky to have a job once this is all over.'

'Hmmm. I may be able to help you with that. Are you anywhere near our offices?'

He glanced up at the building opposite. The windows of *The Courier* displayed the newspaper name. Did she have a tracker on him or something?

'How did you know I'm by your building?'

'Are you? It was meant to be, then. See you in the entrance in a minute. I've something that should make things good again with your inspector.'

'What have you got? I haven't time to play around...' Phil was speaking to himself. 'Fuck's sake!' He looked furtively behind him in case he'd been overheard, relieved his indiscretion hadn't been picked up on. When he looked back at *The Courier*, he could see Josephine standing in the doorway. Should he just ignore her? That would be the sane option. She raised a hand in greeting, holding a parcel.

Something to make things good again.

He held onto that thought, picking his moment to cross the road. The parcel had piqued his interest and if it related to Shamila's whereabouts, then that could be his Golden Ticket.

'Good to see you again, Phil.' She held the parcel out for him. 'This was left at our offices this afternoon. I think your inspector should see the contents urgently.'

He held the brown paper parcel as if it contained a bomb.

'What is it?'

'I could ask the same about that.' Her manicured finger pointed at the discarded wig in its see-through plastic bag.

'What's all this about?' he replied, shifting the bag behind his back.

He could see her deciding whether to push for information, then for whatever reason giving up.

'Somebody posted this in the letterbox and rang the bell. When I went down to see who was there, they'd already gone. I opened the package, of course. There are items there which may belong to Shamila Mallick and Phoebe McCoach together with a note. Are they in trouble?'

Her eyes pierced his. This must be how a mouse feels when a cat has you in its sights. The thought did nothing to settle his already tight nerves.

'I can't say anything, but I'll take this to the DI. Thanks,' he added hurriedly and began marching swiftly away.

'So, they *are* in trouble!' she shouted after him.

Phil picked up the pace. He had to get away from that reporter before she said anything else.

Corstorphine put down his radio after hearing PC Lamb's breathless version of his meeting with Josephine Sables. What could the newspaper have been given? He stood beside Frankie, motioning for her to finish her call.

'What is it, sir? Has she been found?'

'It's Lamb. He's on his way here with what may be the first lead we've had.'

Frankie waited impatiently for him to continue.

'He spotted a schoolkid wearing a long, black wig. He'd found it in one of the bins up by the high school and Phil had the presence of mind to make the connection to Shamila's kidnapper.'

'Good work!' Frankie couldn't help looking surprised.

'Maybe. Another item for forensics to look at. What's more important is that our favourite reporter has handed him a parcel left at their offices, purportedly containing items belonging to Shamila and Phoebe together with a note.'

'What's the note say?'

'He's not opened the parcel, and Josephine didn't say. He'll be with us in a few minutes.'

She hesitated before responding. 'Do you think it's a ransom demand or something?'

'If it is, I'd pay anything to have her back.' Corstorphine spoke under his breath.

He picked up his radio again, put out a call for PC McAdam.

'Bravo Mike. Bravo Mike from Charlie six-four, over.'

'Bravo Mike responding, over.'

'Are forensics finishing up there, Bill? Over.'

'Another thirty minutes or so, sir. Do you want a word? Over?'

'Ask them to pass by the station. We'll have a few items needing looked at. Over.'

'Affirmative, sir. Bravo Mike out.'

Corstorphine's heart leapt at the sight of Phil Lamb entering the office. This was the first break they'd had since Shamila had been taken.

'Put it here, Phil.' Corstorphine indicated the nearest desk. 'Has *The Courier* opened it already?'

He pulled on latex gloves as Phil answered.

'Yes. It was Josephine Sables I talked to, sir.'

Corstorphine exchanged a knowing look with Frankie. There would be a time for that conversation, but not now.

'I handled it as little as I could, sir, to avoid contaminating the evidence.' He placed the plastic bag containing the wig next to it.'

'Good work, Phil.' Corstorphine let out a stored breath, hoping the others didn't hear the shake in his chest. 'Let's see what we've got.'

Frankie and Phil bent over him as he carefully unwrapped the brown paper package, taking one corner at a time as delicately as a surgeon. The first item revealed was a green lanyard with Phoebe's photograph and name emblazoned on the tag.

'That's Phoebe's vet ID,' Phil explained. 'It's the same as the receptionist was wearing when I went there earlier.'

Corstorphine let the PC's words drift over him – his attention was fixed on the glint of gold he'd spotted underneath Phoebe's photograph. His hand visibly shook as he lifted the lanyard out of the package. Shamila's wedding ring.

'Is that...' Frankie began.

'Aye. I'd know it anywhere. It's Shamila's.' Corstorphine's hand went to his own wedding ring, his latex-clad fingers involuntarily confirming the smooth metal remained in place. His voice had died in his throat, an unexpected paralysis taking hold of his body. He could have remained in that catatonic state for longer except for Frankie's voice cutting through the fog enveloping his mind.

'What's the note say?'

With an effort of will, Corstorphine lifted the ring and placed it beside Phoebe's ID, then took out a sheet of crumpled A4 from the brown bag, his hand shaking as he tried to smooth the paper out on the desk for them all to read.

This should be sufficient evidence for a detective to know I have his wife, and the sister of the richest man in town. If you want to see either of them alive again, I suggest you do exactly what I say.

'Is that it?' Frankie asked. 'Nothing on the back?'

He turned the sheet over to reveal a blank page.

His mind raced. Now he had definitive proof that both Shamila and Phoebe had been taken by the same person, or persons, he felt the paralysis of fear fading. Whoever had them was intent on playing a game. A game in which the reward was money, and the forfeit could result in death.

'Phil, you stay here with the evidence. Explain where you found it and then take forensics to the waste bin in case there's something else of use there. Bill will need to accompany Kira to the hospital for a check-up.' The flow of words stopped as he considered the call he had to make.

'I'll have to let Robb McCoach know that Phoebe's been taken.' He started towards his office with his head bowed in pressure.

'I can call him for you, sir,' Frankie offered.

'Thanks, Frankie, but I have to do it.'

He shut the office door and took a deep breath before updating Robb.

'Hi, Robb, it's James Corstorphine.'

'Thank God! Have you found her?' Robb's breathless voice betrayed his relief to finally hear some news of his sister's whereabouts.

'We've had a ransom demand. Someone may have taken her.' He couldn't bring himself to mention Shamila – not without risking losing what little control he still had over his own emotions.

'What do you mean? Where is she?'

'We're doing everything we can to find her, Robb. I've asked for the Major Investigation Team to assist. Try not to worry. We'll get her safely back to you, I promise.' He listened to himself making promises he didn't know if he'd be able to keep.

'Taken her? Why would anyone take Phoebe?' Robb was still playing catchup.

'Stay by your phone in case we need to reach you. We'll keep you updated.'

'Wait! You can't just tell me Phoebe's been taken and leave it at that!' Anger followed hot on the heels of denial.

'I have to go, Robb. I promise you we're doing everything we can. Stay at home if you can, so we know where to reach you.'

He ended the call. Frankie remained standing outside his office.

'You and I are going to visit *The Courier*. I need to know exactly when this parcel was left, whether there are any cameras on the high street that may have captured someone carrying a brown paper package – and confirm we have everything that was delivered.'

He grabbed the Land Rover keys and his jacket, motioning for Frankie to follow, then paused in the office doorway.

'Well done, Phil. This is the first lead we've had.' Corstorphine hurried out of the office, calling behind him. 'Come on, Frankie. We need to move fast!'

FORTY-TWO
HANDS

PC Bill McAdam had never felt so useless. His only job was to sit with the clinic's receptionist and reassure her that everything was going to be alright, whilst ensuring only forensics had access to the unit. A small crowd had gathered outside, alerted by the white van and white-suited technicians going to and forth with various packages and small flightcases containing everything from UV lights to fingerprint kits.

He needed to be doing something – anything to dispel the adrenaline coursing through his veins. Acting as Kira's nursemaid wasn't the best use of his skills.

He'd had to send Suzie back to her flat to wait for the locksmith when Frankie was dealing with the sergeant's wife. The office was already in disarray before the news came through about Shamila's abduction. And now Phoebe McCoach had been taken as well. How they were meant to cope with everything going on and without the sergeant he couldn't imagine. The DI had said he was calling in the Major Investigation Team. That almost certainly meant that he and Phil would be consigned to the most basic of tasks whilst the MIT chased all the leads and took the glory. Or otherwise, he bleakly considered.

'Acrylic fibre,' a technician announced, holding up what

appeared to be a section of Sellotape. He carefully placed a numbered yellow marker on the floor of Shamila's office, joining others left at seemingly random locations. His colleague dutifully photographed both the taped sample and the floor location before moving on to the next item they'd found.

'How much longer do you need?' Bill asked.

'We'll be done in ten minutes. Just have to do a panorama shot of the office and reception. You'll have to move out of the way.'

'Have you finished with Kira here?' Bill gave the receptionist a reassuring smile. She'd been fingerprinted, swabbed and her clothes run over with a device to collect any forensics that may have adhered to her body. 'Only I need to run her to the hospital.'

'Don't be silly. I'm fine,' Kira protested. 'You need to be finding the man who took Shamila – don't worry about me.'

'I'll take you for triage to do a quick check, and then I'm taking you home,' Bill told her in a tone that brooked no argument.

'Yes, she's free to leave,' the technician responded in a businesslike manner. 'Now, if you can go and sit in the patrol car, then we can finish off the panorama here.'

'DI Corstorphine wants you to swing by the station to pick up some items for analysis.' Bill offered an arm for Kira to hold on to. He'd seen the tell-tale shake in her legs – a reaction to the shock she'd had.

'What's he got? Is this related to the abduction?'

'I don't know, he just asked me to pass on the message.'

Bill escorted Kira out to the car, shutting the doors on a sea of questions. At least the newspaper hadn't caught wind of it all. Almost as if his thoughts had been read, Phil saw the portly owner of *The Courier* struggling to lever his body out of his car and begin walking towards Shamila's unit. He was about to leave Kira on her own to stop him when the reporter came to a halt some distance away, aiming a camera at the scene. His arrival coincided with the forensics officers' departure, stowing the tools of their trade into the back of a white van. A swift thumbs-up in Bill's direction from a technician was his signal to lock up the unit.

'Stay here, Kira. I'll just be a moment – and if anyone asks you anything, I'd prefer if you didn't say anything at this stage.'

She nodded in acknowledgement, and he took the keys she'd given him earlier, turning them in the clinic lock with a sense of relief. Finally, he could start doing something useful.

'Good evening, officer. Would you like to comment on the abduction of Shamila Mallick and Phoebe McCoach?' The wheezing *Courier* editor, Jack Hammond, blocked his path with his rotund body.

'How did...' Bill prevented himself from adding anything else. 'I can't say anything at this stage. DI Corstorphine will be releasing a statement in due course, now please step aside.'

Jack Hammond gave Bill sufficient room to press through the growing crowd, hearing them repeat the words *abduction, Shamila* and *Phoebe McCoach* like a giant version of Chinese whispers. There was nothing he could do about it; the news was sure to come out soon enough. But he'd like to know how *The Courier* had the information almost as soon as he did.

'We'll go to the hospital, just so you can be checked over.' Bill ignored her protestations and headed back into the centre of town. 'I know you've told me everything you remember,' he began. 'But was there anything else you can tell me about this Mr Samson? What was his accent? Did he give the impression he was drugged or angry? Anything you can add to what you've already told me?'

Kira concentrated, searching the police car interior for inspiration.

'He was Scottish,' she volunteered. 'He could have been Glaswegian, maybe around Glasgow. His hair didn't look real.'

'How do you mean, didn't look real?' Bill pressed for more detail.

'I don't know. It had that silky texture as if it wasn't really hair at all. Like it was a wig.'

Bill recalled the sample held in clear tape – *acrylic fibre.*

'That's good. Anything else about him?'

'Oh, this is so difficult. It's all turning into a blur.'

'Take your time, Kira. You've been through a frightening event. Try and relax and see if anything else comes to mind.' The hospital was a few minutes away. He made for the emergency vehicle entrance.

'There's something. When he taped me to the chair, I could see the side of his head quite clearly. It sounds daft...'

'No, go on. It doesn't matter what it sounds like, just give me your impressions.' He parked out of the way of the ambulances but close enough to take Kira straight to triage.

'Well, I could swear his beard wasn't real.'

Bill paused before opening the car door. 'What do you mean, wasn't real?'

'I felt it when he brushed into me. It felt artificial, not like real hair. Does that make sense?'

'It may well do, Kira. Now, let's get you seen to.'

As soon as Kira had been taken to a cubicle by a nurse, Bill called Corstorphine on the radio and passed on the latest information Kira had provided.

'Good work, Bill. Frankie and I are almost at *The Courier*'s offices. Pass that onto Phil at the station so forensics know to look for any artificial fibres. When they're through with Kira, bring her back to the station and we can take a formal statement. There's also a wig I'd like her to look at.'

'They've already found some acrylic fibres, sir.'

'OK. Then we better assume Mr Samson's appearance is as false as his address. We'll see if Kira can provide any more information when she's given the all-clear.'

The PC waited impatiently for triage to finish. Whoever had taken Corstorphine's wife had made this crime personal, an attack against them all. Bill couldn't imagine how he'd cope if it had been Caitlin who'd been taken. The thought turned his blood to ice. Whoever it was – they'd pay!

FORTY-THREE
PASS THE PARCEL

They arrived at *The Courier* offices at 5 p.m. Corstorphine worried that Josephine Sables may have left for the day, but the first-floor lights were all still on. He pressed the door intercom.

'Who is it?'

The unmistakable French accent of the town's reporter issued mechanically from the weathered speaker.

'DI Corstorphine and DC Frankie McKenzie. Can we come in?'

A harsh buzz from the door lock was sufficient invitation for Frankie to push ahead, and they ascended the narrow stairway to find Josephine waiting for them in the small reception area.

'I'm sorry to hear about Shamila and Phoebe,' Josephine began. 'I can't begin to imagine how terrible that must be for you.'

Corstorphine bowed his head in acknowledgement. He couldn't dwell on how he felt. That way lay sheer panic.

'The parcel you had delivered. When did you receive it? Did they talk to you, say anything? Did you see who they were or a vehicle they might have used?'

He was aware the questions had come too fast and deliberately slowed his breathing in an attempt to calm his nerves. Josephine seemed not to have noticed.

'At 4 p.m. The intercom sounded, but nobody responded. It's usually deliveries, so I went down and saw this had been put through the letterbox. There wasn't a name on the package and it didn't look as if it had come from a courier or the mail, so I went out into the street. There wasn't anything unusual to be seen – no car driving off from the kerb, no one acting strangely.'

'Why didn't you contact me immediately!' He heard the edge of anger in his own voice, told himself to get a grip on his emotions.

'I didn't know what it was, to start with. Phoebe's ID, a gold ring and the handwritten note. It looked like a windup at first, so I didn't want to waste your time. I tried the vets, but they didn't sound too concerned – said Phoebe hadn't returned after her lunch but thanks for letting them know about her lanyard.' She turned to Frankie. 'You'd be surprised how many times people post cryptic notes through our door. They want publicity for something or other but won't pay for advertising.'

Her focus returned to the DI. 'I was puzzling over whether to take it seriously and call Robb McCoach when I saw your PC Phil Lamb walking down the high street, so I asked him to collect the parcel if he thought it was anything serious.'

'And he told you.' Corstorphine had already made his judgement on Phil Lamb.

'No. He refused to say anything.'

She must have noticed the disbelief in his expression as she hurriedly continued.

'Phil's exact words when I asked him if Shamila and Phoebe were in any sort of trouble was to state that he couldn't say anything. And then he raced off back to the station.'

Corstorphine began to revise his opinion of the young PC just as heavy footsteps and the sound of an unhealthy wheezing issued from the stairwell, resolving into the portly figure of Jack Hammond – *The Courier*'s editor and de facto owner.

'James.' A hot, sweaty palm extended his way. Corstorphine shook the proffered limp object with a distinct lack of enthusiasm.

'I've just come from your wife's clinic. Would you like to tell me what's going on?'

Corstorphine felt the pressure of both reporters' eyes bearing down on him and made a quick decision. Jack Hammond gave every impression of being a dead weight, a wheezing heart attack in waiting, but he had a sharp mind – and they'd all had dealings with his French reporter before. A story this size couldn't be contained for long. Odds were they'd already put most of it together in the last hour if Jack had left the comfort of his office to investigate for himself.

'Shamila was abducted from her clinic after 2 p.m. this afternoon. Whoever has taken her may also have taken Phoebe McCoach.' He saw the two reporters exchanging a meaningful glance and carried on. 'Shamila's receptionist was left bound and gagged, it's only because we were acting on other information that we discovered her. Robb McCoach had separately been in touch a little earlier with his concerns about Phoebe. She'd not returned to her work at the vets after lunch. Now that we have the note that was left at your offices, it appears these two events may be connected.'

He was aware of Josephine's pen scratching shorthand across her pad and Frankie's shocked expression at his indiscretion. It didn't matter. The sooner the news hit the streets, the greater the chances of someone getting in touch about something they might have seen or heard. Whatever it took to find Shamila and bring her home.

'And how is this connected to the body dressed as a scarecrow on William Haddow's field?' Jack Hammond's attention was firmly fixed on Corstorphine.

'We don't know. There may not be any connection.' The lie came easily to him. The link to Carstairs State Hospital, the missing staff member and Shamila's previous job were all too clearly associated in his mind. If that information came to light, it would dominate the headlines and risk turning the search for Shamila and Phoebe into a sideshow.

One look at Jack's cynical expression was enough for Corstorphine to know he'd only managed to delay that news getting out. Both reporters were like bloodhounds, they'd not rest now they had the scent of something.

'Then do you have any leads in that case?' Jack pushed for more information.

Corstorphine heard his radio call sign with a sense of relief.

'Charlie six-four.' He held his breath to hear what came next. Beside him, three other people listened intently.

'Forensics have arrived here at the station, sir.

Corstorphine cut him off before the reporters heard anything else.

'On our way, over.'

'Good luck with your search, James. We'll do anything we can to help, you have my word.'

Corstorphine looked again at Jack Hammond, seeing past the cynical newspaper reporter in his unhealthy body and for the first time understanding he was dealing with someone who genuinely wanted to help.

'Thanks, Jack. Josephine. We'll need all the help we can get.'

FORTY-FOUR
MIT

Corstorphine entered the police station office to find PCs Lamb and McAdam waiting by the crazy board. One look at their worried faces was enough to tell him they were all still in the dark.

'OK, everyone, this is what we know.' He stood with his back to the wall and forced his racing mind into coherence.

'The body we found has been identified as a pharmaceutical nurse employed at Carstairs State Hospital – Richard Bryce. He went missing some time after leaving work on the evening of Friday 24th.' He indicated the name on the crazy wall behind him. 'Time of death is estimated to be anytime between last Friday and Saturday.'

Corstorphine turned back to face his team.

'In addition, fingerprints belonging to a recent inmate of the hospital – Duncan Lewis – were found at Richard Bryce's address. The Lanark police have been unable to find Lewis and have raised an arrest warrant.' Corstorphine's finger shook as he pointed to the mugshot. 'You have all been issued with his details.'

He breathed heavily as his emotions threatened to take over. He could sense his team's disquiet as he struggled so publicly in front of them: shifting positions; nervous coughs; exchanged glances.

'And today, Shamila was taken from her clinic after 2 p.m. by someone claiming to be a Mr Samson. Her receptionist was bound and gagged, but other than being badly shaken hasn't been hurt. The address on file for Mr Samson turned out to be false, as is most likely his name.'

He glanced at the plastic bag containing a black wig that had been left on Frankie's desk.

'There's also reason to suppose that the physical description we have for Mr Samson is false. Lamb found a black hairpiece abandoned in a wastebin by the high school.'

Corstorphine had to pause it there. His throat threatened to dry out and he swallowed repeatedly before Frankie passed him a water bottle. He nodded gratefully, taking a deep drink before feeling able to continue.

Bill McAdam spoke up in the silence. 'I've taken a formal statement from Kira, sir. She stated Mr Samson's beard felt artificial and confirmed the wig was very similar to Mr Samson's hair.'

'Good work, Bill. You've taken Kira home?'

'She wanted to walk, sir. Said she needed some air and didn't want to waste any more police time.'

Corstorphine nodded in acknowledgement before continuing.

'Finally, Phoebe McCoach has also gone missing. Her brother called us at 3:45 p.m. to say she hadn't returned to her job at the vets.'

This was the most difficult part of what he had to say. Corstorphine willed himself to keep it together.

'Finally, *The Courier* were given this parcel,' he indicated the brown wrapping on Frankie's desk. 'They didn't see who posted it through the letterbox, but it contains Phoebe's ID, Shamila's wedding ring... and a note stating that the kidnapper has Shamila and Phoebe and will be in touch with instructions.'

'Is this a kidnapping for money, sir?' Frankie asked. 'He mentions that Phoebe's family are the richest in town.'

Corstorphine knew there was more to it than that.

'If it wasn't for the dead body and the link Shamila has to

Carstairs, then I'd be prepared to work on that assumption. When I told her that we'd found a body dressed in a scarecrow's clothes, Shamila admitted it was her one phobia.'

Internally, Corstorphine's anger had turned on himself. The link was painfully obvious. Why hadn't he acted on his intuition and made sure she was kept safe? It was only Shamila's certainty that Duncan Lewis was harmless that had stopped him.

'So, we should be looking at the other scarecrow thefts as well, sir?' Lamb piped up.

'I've already been to Glenarty village and talked to the owner of the second missing scarecrow there. For which we have some video,' he added. 'Not that it shows enough detail, but there's clearly one person taking it away from the front porch. Frankie, you've talked to Mart McKeown?'

'Sir. Yes, I saw Mart McKeown on Monday evening. His scarecrow is quite distinctive.' She walked over to her desk, retrieved an A4 sheet with a print of the waxwork faced figure and guitar case and pinned it to the board beside Corstorphine's stick figure. 'He's put a reward up for information. Again, nobody saw anything, but both Glenarty scarecrows were taken the same night that William Haddow's scarecrow went missing. I think we can assume they were taken by the same person.'

'In the case of the second Glenarty theft we can be specific on the time.' Corstorphine checked his notebook, hoping the tremor in his hands wasn't as obvious to the team as it was to him. 'Tabitha Richardson's scarecrow was untied from her porch and the activity logged by her doorbell camera at 23:24 Sunday night.'

'Do you think it's this Duncan Lewis, sir?' Bill McAdam spoke for them all.

'He's the most likely suspect, Bill. He's had previous; he knows Shamila. His is the only name that can be linked to the individuals involved in the case as it stands.'

They all turned to face the office door as it opened, and three men marched in as if they owned the place.

'DI Corstorphine?' The leader of the group was holding up a

warrant card, his gaze sweeping over them all and settling on the DI.

'Aye.' He already knew who they were and what their arrival meant.

'DI Brown. These are DCs Robbins and Knight. We're from the Major Investigations Team, Glasgow.'

FORTY-FIVE
DAEMON ATICUS

Corstorphine left the station after having run through the entire briefing again with the MIT, after which the lead DI took him to one side and informed him he was off the case. He'd tried arguing against it, but he'd known it was coming. There wasn't a snowball's chance in hell they'd let him stay – not with his own wife being involved.

'We'll keep you fully informed of every development, James,' DI Brown had assured him. 'But for now you have to leave us to get on with the job. Shamila and Phoebe McCoach stand a better chance without your emotional involvement.'

Only Frankie had the courage to meet his eye as he packed up and made for the door, raising her fist which he interpreted as a message to stay strong. The two constables lowered their gaze to the floor, not knowing what else to do.

'Give them your full support. I'm counting on you.' His words raised an acknowledgement from the team as they finally looked at him directly.

'Whatever it takes, sir,' McAdam spoke out.

'Same, sir,' Lamb echoed.

He nodded to them and left the police station, his mind spinning. Somewhere out there in the gathering darkness, Shamila was relying on him to find and rescue her. He had no idea where she and Phoebe had been taken; no one apart from Kira witnessed her abduction; and the only suspect they had was Duncan Lewis who was a psychotic killer.

Corstorphine couldn't face going home, not when the house reminded him so much of her. Instead, he drove aimlessly around the town hoping against hope to see Shamila. How could he work without the small, loyal police team and manage the case on his own? It was an impossible ask – yet he had to do something.

Against his better judgement, he drove back to Shamila's clinic. Blue and white police tape sealed off the doorway. He walked around the small industrial estate, searching for CCTV cameras. Nothing. The SOC team would have already covered that angle, he was wasting valuable time. The western filled with ragged clouds shredded by Atlantic winds meeting the Scottish mountains. At any other time, he'd drink in the breathtaking beauty of the scene but not tonight. This would be the first night without her since their marriage, and the realisation twisted a dagger in his heart.

Corstorphine drove home, dreading his return to an empty house. He parked in the driveway, staring at the dark windows and trying not to visualise the black and empty sockets Richard Bryce's ruined face had presented to the crows. He didn't dare imagine that such a fate awaited Shamila or Phoebe.

Corstorphine turned the key and pushed open the door, fingers automatically pressing the numbers on the alarm panel. He pushed it closed behind him to stand in the darkened hall, breathing in Shamila's scent that still hung on the air and held his head in his hands. All the stored grief and emotion that he'd bottled up was released in body-shaking shudders as he slid to the floor.

He might have sat there for hours if it wasn't for the dawning realisation that a package was pressing into his side, digging into his ribs. His fingers searched until he felt a parcel similar to the one left at *The Courier*'s offices and he froze. The message left in that parcel had said the kidnapper would be in touch. This had to be the ransom demand!

Corstorphine climbed back to his feet, switching on the hall lights and saw the brown paper parcel lying innocuously on the floor. He'd already handled it – a fatal error whenever evidence was made available. There were latex gloves in the kitchen. Corstorphine rushed to pull them on, returning to pick up the parcel and carry it through to the kitchen counter.

The procedure at this point was to call the station and have the MIT deal with it. Corstorphine dismissed the thought and started to carefully unwrap the parcel. Shamila depended on him and even a few minutes delay could mean the difference between finding her alive or... He refused to follow that line of thought any further.

As the last of the brown paper was peeled back, Corstorphine was astonished to find a paperback book. He lifted it, searching the brown paper for anything else. There were no more personal items, no scribbled notes, only the book. He turned the book over to look at the cover, seeing an illustration of a man tied to railway lines with a train heading towards him. It was only artwork, done in cartoonlike style, but the similarities to how Richard Bryce had died were only too clear.

The book's title was *Done With Crying*; the author was Daemon Aticus.

Corstorphine's blood turned to ice. Daemon Aticus was the pseudonym for Duncan Lewis. There was now no longer any doubt that Shamila was being held by him. The knowledge of how he'd dismembered his wife was still fresh in his memory after reading part of *Outgrave* last night – the book that had contained the clues leading to where her body parts had been buried.

Was this what he held? Another storybook containing clues set by a madman but this time they described where Shamila and Phoebe were imprisoned? Corstorphine couldn't allow himself to even imagine that they may already be dead.

He carried the book over to a chair, turned on the light and began to read.

FORTY-SIX

SOUL KITCHEN

Frankie had been tasked with searching through video feeds from the few traffic cams that covered the main roads in and out of town. Most of the footage was of such low quality that even recognising number plates was problematic, never mind attempting to judge if passengers were being held against their will. The MIT team leader had sent his two DCs off to try and find any cameras covering the industrial estate or general locality, before making himself at home in Corstorphine's office.

She looked up from her screen, more to give her eyes a rest from the poor resolution video and viewed DI Brown with resentment. He'd had little choice but to ask Corstorphine to leave yet to take her boss away from the search for his own wife seemed cruel beyond belief. Frankie sighed at the injustice of it, imagining Corstorphine waiting alone in his home, desperate for any information and being powerless to help.

PCs Lamb and McAdam had volunteered to work on into the night. They'd been given the task of running spot checks on vehicles they came across and generally looking out for any suspicious behaviour. It was a fool's errand in her view – Duncan Lewis was hardly likely to advertise the fact that he was holding two people captive. Trying to find his vehicle was worse than looking for a needle in a haystack.

Where would he have taken them? The question gnawed away at her mind. In the absence of any tangible leads, they only had their own intuition to fall back on. Shamila must be locked up somewhere remote, otherwise surely someone would have heard screaming or seen something? The thought wasn't encouraging. They were surrounded by some of the most remote areas in Scotland. Even from the police station window she could gaze out over lochs, forests and mountains – except now they were all cloaked in darkness.

How long had Duncan Lewis been planning this? He'd been released a year ago according to the briefing notes she'd read from Lanark police. If he'd spent that time working out where he could imprison Shamila, then it could be anywhere. Phoebe was most likely just an opportunistic victim. Had he been keeping tabs on the clinic and seen her visit for one of her sessions? Who knew what was going on in his mind?

'DC McKenzie!'

Frankie jerked her head towards Corstorphine's office in response to her name being shouted.

'Come in here, will you.' DI Brown held the dividing office door open in invitation.

'Sir.' She stood uncertainly as he settled himself back in the DI's favourite chair.

'This Robb McCoach. Phoebe's brother. The note made mention of him being the richest man in the town. Is there any basis to that?'

'Robb's family own the distillery, sir. I don't think there's any doubt that he is considerably better off financially than anyone else here.'

DI Brown observed her closely from under furrowed brows. His nails tapped a repetitive pattern on Corstorphine's desk. She focussed in on them, seeing nicotine stains on the index and middle fingers and could smell the unmistakable odour of tobacco smoke permeating the room.

'This note that was left with the local newspaper – *The Courier*. It suggests our kidnapper is going to be back in touch to ask for a ransom. Is that the interpretation you and DI Corstorphine came to?'

'Yes, sir. Robb is fiercely protective of his young sister. He'd do anything to have her back safely.'

Maybe Duncan Lewis had planned to take Phoebe as well for the money. The thought gave her little comfort. He'd killed before and if he was having another psychotic episode then... she couldn't bear to finish that thought.

'Can you go and visit this Robb McCoach? We need to ensure that any communication he might have from the kidnapper is relayed directly back to us. The last thing we need is for him to take himself off like an idiot with a suitcase full of money.'

'Yes, sir. I'll go and see him now.'

'Impress upon him the need to keep us in the loop, McKenzie.' He looked distractedly at his jacket hanging up by the door and his fingers abruptly stopped their drumming.

Frankie had the impression he needed another hit of nicotine.

'I've tried calling on this number I have for him,' the DI continued, 'but he's not picking up. Are you OK with going on your own?'

'Yes, thank you, sir. I've the radio in case I require backup.'

'OK then, well, off you go. I don't think we're going to have much luck tonight unless something turns up. I'll see you back here.'

'Will do, sir.' Frankie went to grab her coat. Now that it was properly dark outside, the temperature had dropped to a few degrees centigrade. She saw DI Brown leaving Corstorphine's desk and his hand delving into his jacket pocket, coming back into sight holding a packet of cigarettes. As she reversed out of the parking space, DI Brown stood watching her from the shelter of the porch, his face briefly illuminated by the glow from a struck match. The glowing tip of his cigarette was like a single, malevolent eye in her mirror as she drove off to Robb McCoach's Victorian mansion perched on the edge of town.

FORTY-SEVEN
ROOKERY

You don't see me. Have you turned me into a wraith with your cruelty? I stand here, dressed in rags with no fear of the cold or of winter to come. Why should I, now that you have stopped my heart? They will take my eyes first and I will see the world one last time. See what I see; feel what I feel; follow me into a new dawn and then think of me one last time.

Corstorphine visualised Richard Bryce's dismembered body, sagging on its makeshift crucifix in William Haddow's field. He had no doubt the reference was deliberate. Duncan was playing the same elaborate game – hiding clues in his novel. But this time it was personal. He had taken Shamila and made sure that the clues were in his hand.

How long did he have? It took countless readers to decipher the clues in *Outgrave*. He couldn't do this by himself, but neither could he pass the book onto the MIT team without at least trying. There were 300 pages. He flattened the first page and raised his phone; he turned the page and repeated until the end before contacting the station.

'DI Brown? This is James Corstorphine. I've had a parcel delivered which has come from Duncan Lewis. You need to see it.'

'When was it delivered? Did you see anyone?'

'It had already been put through the letterbox when I arrived home. I didn't notice it at first. It's a book – like the one he wrote with the clues to where his wife's body parts had been buried.'

'*Outgrave*? Shit!' DI Brown's outburst echoed down the line. 'Stay there, I'll send one of the boys to collect it. Have you handled it?'

'What do you think?' Corstorphine retorted. 'I wore gloves,' he added in a more conciliatory tone.

He slumped down in his chair, feeling the world closing in on him. Why was this happening? They'd only been married a couple of weeks and already someone was out to destroy everything he held dear. Shamila had been so certain that Duncan Lewis was no longer any threat, how could she have been so wrong? Nothing about this made any sense. It had been a year since she'd been instrumental in his release. Why would he want to harm her – and why did he have the strong impression that this was personal? Duncan Lewis wanted him to suffer as well.

It's not just me, he reminded himself. Robb McCoach would be dealing with Phoebe's disappearance; Richard Bryce would have family and friends who now had to deal with his murder.

Corstorphine forced himself to quieten the maelstrom in his mind and to think clearly and logically. Duncan Lewis had somehow managed to overpower Richard Bryce and transport his body. Gyles Lambert was out of reach and on leave until next week. Shamila and Phoebe – he couldn't face the idea that they might already be dead. That meant they were being held somewhere isolated.

He almost lost all hope at that stage. Their small police station covered some of the remotest areas in Scotland. How in hell's name were they meant to find the missing hostages? The only clue as to their whereabouts lay in the arcane writings of a psychotic.

A knock at the door made him jump. Corstorphine reached for his baton before checking through the side window. It was one of the DCs from the Major Investigation Team.

'Evening, sir. You have some evidence for us?'

He beckoned the DC in without being able to place his name. The DC produced an evidence bag, carefully placed both book and wrapping paper inside with gloved hands.

'Is this everything, sir?'

'Aye. Have you heard anything? Any developments?' Corstorphine couldn't help but ask even though he could see from the DC's demeanour they had nothing yet.

'Sorry, sir. We'll let you know as soon as we have anything.' The DC searched for words of comfort and failed.

'Just do the best you can.' Corstorphine held the door open for the flustered DC, not hearing his response.

The house felt like a tomb now he was on his own again. Corstorphine flicked to the first page of the book, spreading his fingers to magnify the small text on his iPhone screen.

They will take my eyes first

Daemon Aticus would have known that crows would make for the easy pickings.

follow me into a new dawn

Was the scarecrow facing east? He swiped through the crime scene snaps he'd taken on his phone, seeing the angle the decapitated head sat at. If that had been deliberately placed, where was the scarecrow looking?

Corstorphine rushed to his bookcase, pulled out a map of the area and smoothed it down on the kitchen table. He placed a salt cellar down on William Haddow's farm, centred on the location they'd found the body and then tried to work out in which direction the head faced. After several minutes he realised it was impossible. He had a general direction, except it covered such a wide angle that he'd need accurate forensics SOC photographs. But Corstorphine knew they'd not have taken account of where the corpse was looking – why would they?

He swept a ruler across the best guess arc he could manage. The scarecrow had been orientated roughly north south and facing east. Was this to signify the rebirth of the day, an end to the endless night of death?

See what I see; feel what I feel.

Corstorphine tried to put himself in the scarecrow's position. What had the scarecrow seen?

Daemon Aticus had referred to the eyes. *I will see the world one last time.*

What if he was describing the last journey taken by the scarecrow's eyes. Tasty morsels taken in strong, grey beaks or settling in corvid stomachs as they flew back to the nest?

There was a circular wooded hill four kilometres due east. The sort of spot crows might select for a rookery. He couldn't stay here, waiting. Corstorphine grabbed a torch, radio and baton, sealing the map into an inside pocket of his weatherproof jacket. Chasing wild hunches was infinitely better to sitting in an empty house waiting for the worst possible news.

FORTY-EIGHT
RANSOM

Frankie headed up the long, tree-lined drive to Robb McCoach's mansion set high above the town. Had it only been a year since she and Phil Lamb had first visited the house? So much had happened in the intervening months that it felt to her like another age. There were no lights showing, apart from the automatic floods that had thrown the driveway into sharp relief as she drew to a halt.

She raised the doorknocker, hesitated then rapped it sharply a few times. The sound echoed from inside the cavernous hallway and an internal light came on, followed by Robb's cautious face appearing as he opened the door.

'What is it? Have you found her?' His eagerness to hear good news was evident in his face, lit up with hope and expectation. He must have read the truth of it in her expression as his features fell into despair.

'I'm sorry, Robb. I don't have any news for you.'

His shoulders visibly slumped in response.

'I was hoping that you might be able to help us in our search.' She began. 'Have you had any contact with whoever has taken her? Any demands for money or instructions?'

He instantly appeared ill at ease, shifting from foot to foot.

'I can't talk to you, I'm sorry. You have to leave. Now!' The last word was issued as a command.

Frankie had to put her foot in the way of the door before it closed on her.

'He's been in touch, hasn't he?'

'I can't talk. You shouldn't have come here. What if...' Robb abruptly stopped as if he'd already said too much. 'Please, just leave me alone.'

Frankie read the situation as best as she could.

'Are you alone?' she all but whispered as she attempted to see around him and into the hall.

'Yes, I'm on my fucking own. He's taken Phoebe!'

'I'm trying to help, Robb. But I need you to help me. Has someone been in touch about Phoebe?'

Robb McCoach shook his head. 'No. Can you go now?'

It was an unconvincing denial.

'If the kidnapper has contacted you, then we need to know so we can help. This isn't the first time the police have had to deal with a kidnapping. You have to trust us.' *It's the first time I've had to deal with a kidnapping,* Frankie's internal voice unhelpfully advised.

'I can't,' he said simply. 'I can't risk Phoebe's life.'

'Someone has threatened to kill her if you speak to us, is that right?'

'Why don't you listen to me? Just fuck off and leave me alone!'

This time the door was pushed with enough pressure to risk her foot being crushed if she didn't move it out of the way.

'It's not just Phoebe.'

The pressure on her foot reduced.

'What do you mean?'

'I said it's not just Phoebe. Whoever has taken her has DI Corstorphine's wife, Shamila as well.'

Robb's shocked face expressed disbelief. 'Why? Jim would tell me if that were true.'

'DI Corstorphine has been taken off the case. There's another team been brought in – it's standard procedure when an officer has a personal involvement in a case. Nobody can function to the best of their ability when they're put under that sort of pressure. He's been sent home to wait.'

She thought of her boss sat inactive at his home whilst someone had Shamila. He'd be going out of his mind with worry and needing to do anything he could to find her.

'Shamila was taken just after lunch today. We believe Phoebe and Shamila were taken by the same person,' Frankie added. She held back about Farmer Haddow's scarecrow. There was no point in worrying him any more.

'This is to do with the body you found, isn't it?'

Shit! Of course he'd seen the newspaper.

'Look, can I come in and talk?' Frankie was tired of speaking through a gap in the door.

'You'd better come in.' Robb anxiously glanced left and right out of the door before admitting her into the hallway. 'Come through to the lounge at the back, no one can see us there.'

She followed him into the cavernous interior.

'Take a seat,' Robb motioned vaguely in the direction of some chairs. She took the smallest. He had his back to her, face bent down towards something he concealed in his hands. When he turned to face her, she saw a familiar brown paper parcel.

'Here. You'd better take a look at this.' Robb handed it over and she hunted in her pockets in vain for forensic gloves. 'Just look at it!' he snapped at her in his impatience.

Frankie ignored protocol, turning the parcel around in her hands to read the note printed inside.

£1 million in large denomination used notes by tomorrow or she dies. I'll tell you where and how. Involve the police and you'll never see Phoebe alive again.

'When did you get this?'

Robb had taken to pacing back and forth. She noticed a whisky bottle and half-filled glass next to the chair he must have recently sat in, the indentation of his weight still evident in the cushion.

'It must have been sometime earlier this evening. I've been going in and out of the front door, looking for her – hoping she'd just turn up.' He stopped pacing and reached for the glass, swallowing the contents in one gulp. 'Phoebe's been through too much already, I can't let anything happen to her.' He looked at her pleadingly. 'Do you understand?'

Frankie understood. His sister had been imprisoned most of her life in an upstairs bedroom, sedated and under the charge of nurses from the family's own private health centre. A mistaken diagnosis of psychosis from an early age. If it hadn't been for Corstorphine calling in Shamila, then Phoebe would probably still be under a chemical cosh. No wonder Robb felt responsible for her – he was as guilty as the rest of her family for how she'd been treated.

'Have you access to that amount of cash?'

'What do you think?' Robb swung from pleading to anger. 'People say we're rich, but the money's tied up in the distillery or stocks. There's no way I can put my hands on a million pounds in cash and even if I could, the banks are all closed until tomorrow. It will take days to release that kind of money. I don't know what to do!'

Frankie watched as he filled the glass up again. At this rate he wasn't going to be able to stand, never mind help his sister in any meaningful way. She stood up, placed a hand on the glass before he raised it to his lips.

'Listen to me, Robb. You have to work with us. It's the only chance you have for seeing Phoebe again, but you have to do exactly as we say.'

Corstorphine parked as close to the wooded hill as he could, pulling off the single-track road at the nearest gate. Was he wasting his time? A sliver of moon teased with passing clouds, casting the merest hint of silver light across rough pasture towards his target destination. There wasn't enough moonlight to see by, he'd need his torch. Somewhere in the distance he could hear an owl hoot a desultory cry as if in warning.

He'd read random selections from the book before handing it in, snippets of disjointed text that at first gave the impression of being coherent but containing nothing of any real substance. They were all written in the same peculiar style that *Outgrave* was known for – heavy in imagery and allegory but lacking in rational or emotional content. It worked for that book, especially when readers discovered the clues that pointed to where he'd buried his wife's remains. Reviewers had referred to it as a cryptic novel without realising how accurate a description that had been.

But something about *Done With Crying* didn't ring true. For a start, how could he have had the time to write an entire novel? Even if he'd been writing it in the year since his release, no amount of planning would be capable of detailing the kidnapping and loca- tion of his hostages. It had been different for *Outgrave*. That had been created concurrent with the murder and disposal of his wife's body. The whole novel had screamed insanity once that truth was understood.

He flicked to a random page on his phone, read the content.

Light of Lucifer, blinded by hate, consumed by evil. This is a land of ancient rock and bone, borne on restless tides and carried across the mantle of the earth. Walk the road towards a black sun and your tears will fill the footsteps of those gone before you.

Nowhere in the text had he seen anything that could lead him to find Shamila. He could spend years with these impenetrable words, seemingly so full of meaning yet ultimately empty. But it had been left with him on purpose and at no small risk, so there must be some message hidden inside. Duncan Lewis, or rather Daemon Aticus would know that the first few pages would be read in detail and the rest merely skimmed. Time constraints alone would preclude the idea that he'd read the book from cover to cover. Hence the opening had to be the message, in his view, and the rest discounted for the time being. Corstorphine had the suspicion that all the book had been written by AI except for the first pages.

The walk across to the tree-clad hill took almost an hour. On the map, he'd estimated at most two kilometres from his parking place, but the ground was crossed with barbed wire fences and when the land dipped, he found himself knee-deep in concealed bog – all proving more challenging than he'd expected when relying on a handheld torch for illumination. The hillock itself was fenced, then the trees so closely packed that he had to feel his way upwards towards the summit. Fallen trees and branches threatened to trip him, and briars clung onto his jacket whenever he staggered into them. When Corstorphine finally reached the clearing at the top, he had to pause and catch his breath.

Above his head, branches rubbed squeakily together in a slight evening breeze; crows cawed their displeasure at an intruder underfoot and the rustle of leaves sounded like he was being circled by someone just out of view. The torch beam leapt erratically from tree to tree, catching threatening shadows and turning them back into twisted branches and contorted trunks.

Corstorphine relaxed slightly. He'd half expected to find someone here waiting for him. Maybe he was completely wrong with his interpretation of the opening paragraph. If the book *had* been written with the help of AI, then the first words may have no hidden meaning at all. In which case, why leave him the book?

He was here now. If this was where Daemon Aticus had wanted him to come, then there should be something for him to find. Corstorphine began exploring, shining his torch at his feet and kicking at the fallen leaves to see if anything lay covered on the ground. All his efforts managed to uncover was damp loam – the rotten remnants of many autumns.

Corstorphine began to lose hope. This was the only lead he had, tenuous as it was. Had he hiked all this way in the pitch darkness for nothing? Filled with a sudden renewal of urgency, he aimed his torch at the surrounding tree trunks, searching for any message or clue that might have been left for him to find. He hoped to hell that DI Brown was having a better time of the investigation than he was.

A glint of reflected light from one of the trees caught his attention and he swung the torch beam back and forth in an attempt to find what had caught his eye. There, tied just above head height. Corstorphine took a few steps towards the object, aiming the torch directly at a trail camera. It was one of those camouflaged units which are commonly used for the remote observation of wild game, using infra-red illumination to send a real-time video over the mobile phone network. Was he being observed now or was the camera looking towards something of importance? He followed the line of sight, seeing something wrapped in plastic that hadn't been visible until he'd reached this spot.

It was a sheet of paper, wrapped in a clear plastic wallet and tacked onto a tree. Corstorphine reached up to tear it down, aware that his every move was likely being viewed remotely. If this was Duncan Lewis, then he'd know Corstorphine was coming for him. He held the plastic, angled his torch down to see what the sheet contained.

There was a single word in capitals: *SMILE*. That wasn't what made his heart leap into his throat – it was the photograph of Shamila, bound and gagged staring defiantly at him that had shaken him to the core. He turned back to look at the trail camera, then moved decisively to take it down.

There were no clues here, just the twisted game of a madman. Corstorphine pocketed both items and started back towards his car. The trail camera would have a SIM card. It was the only chance he had to find where the camera's feed was being viewed.

FIFTY
LOYALTIES

Frankie returned to the police station after visiting Robb McCoach. The two DCs had taken over Lamb's and McAdam's desks and were punching keyboards with two-fingered aggression. They looked up as she entered, gave the slightest nod of acknowledgement and bent down to their staccato tasks. She knocked on the door to Corstorphine's office, DI Brown waved her in.

'How's Robb McCoach coping? Is he going to keep us in the loop? I don't want him going rogue on us – he's the best shot we have of finding them before anything else happens.'

Frankie thought of the whisky bottle in Robb's hand. He was coping as best as he could.

'He's sound, sir. He knows it's in his sister's best interest if he keeps us informed.'

The DI brushed lank, black hair back from his forehead where it had adhered to beads of sweat. She could see where hair dye had stained his skin an unnatural shade. She handed him the ransom note, waited for him to pull on latex gloves before handling it. He whistled in surprise when he read the amount.

'A million! Does he have access to that sort of money?'

She noted his failure to comment on the threat to Phoebe's life.

'He said it would take a few days, sir.'

'And how was the note delivered? Did he see anyone?'

Frankie shook her head. 'Same brown paper parcel as the other one, sir. It was left in the letterbox. He didn't see who delivered it.'

The DI grunted in response.

'He's not tried phoning Robb or trying to contact any other way?'

'No, sir. But he made it clear that if Robb tried contacting the police, it would end badly for his sister.'

DI Brown stared into her eyes. 'Do you think you were seen?'

The same question had occupied Frankie's thoughts since leaving Robb's house.

'I don't think so. I told Robb we know what we're doing, sir.'

'Then we'd better hope you're right.'

He placed the ransom note inside a clear plastic evidence bag, sealed and wrote on it whilst she stood in front of him. DI Brown glanced up from his task, seemingly surprised to find her still standing there.

'You may as well go home, constable. We'll be finishing in the next half hour. There's nothing else we can do until forensics come back in the morning – or Robb is contacted by the kidnapper. I've already sent the other two constables home...' He glanced down at the desk, searching for names.

'Lamb and McAdam, sir,' she prompted.

'Aye. Lamb and McAdam. None of you are any use to me if you don't have a good sleep. I'll see you in the morning.'

Frankie stood there after his dismissal and waited until he looked up from his paperwork in surprise.

'Just one thing, sir. Has anyone been in touch with DI Corstorphine?'

He shook his head in response. 'Until we have anything for him, he's best left out of it. That applies to you too, constable.'

'Sir.' Frankie turned sharply on her heel and marched out. DI Brown hadn't actually told her not to see Corstorphine. Not unequivocally. She knew where her loyalty lay, and it wasn't with the MIT.

FIFTY-ONE
TRUDI

Trudi McKeown read through her notes, shuffling them back into order and replacing them on her desk next to the laptop. A well-thumbed copy of *Outgrave* lay within easy reach and she turned the book over so the author's face stared back at her. She didn't need to refresh her memory – his features had been a constant presence in her mind ever since she'd decided to write about him.

A glance at the clock made her jump out of her seat. She'd arranged to meet him in the village at nine and it was almost that already. She picked up her phone, and a copy of the letter she'd been asked to have him sign – then grabbed a pen in case he hadn't thought to bring one himself.

Her dad was downstairs, strumming away on one of his guitars and searching for the inspiration to start on another song.

'*Do you want me, now that I'm ancient. Do you want me, now that I'm old.*

My world is so empty, but I have plenty. Love to give and stories untold.'

Trudi's expression soured as she listened. More and more his lyrics turned to self-pity and railing against the injustice of life. Why couldn't he just grow old gracefully? He could see how the press treated his geriatric contemporaries with their never-ending farewell tours.

'I'm popping out for a bit, Dad. Won't be long.'

'Hang on.' The sound of a guitar being laid non too gently down sounded from what he termed 'the studio'. Mart's head poked around the door.

'Who is it you're seeing again?'

She considered him thoughtfully through half-closed eyelids. His memory lapses were becoming more obvious.

'I've already told you, Dad. Duncan Lewis, the author. My publisher needs him to sign this before they'll consider making a firm offer on the book.'

She waved a sheet of paper in the air in emphasis.

Mart took a step into the hall, his Botoxed features attempting to express concern.

'Are you sure he's OK? I mean, he was locked away in a mental hospital for years. Do you want to invite him here – or I could go with you?'

'No, Dad. He wanted a quick meet in the village so he can drive in and out. Didn't want to bother with coming here.'

She could see even through his fixed expression that her dad remained unconvinced.

'Look. It's fine. He's been out in the community for years like a regular person. They wouldn't have done that if there was any chance that he was a danger, would they?'

Trudi sounded more convinced than she felt. Everything she said was true, but a nagging doubt remained. He'd responded quite differently in his last email exchange – almost to the point where she worried that his alter ego might be making a reappearance. Duncan Lewis was one thing – meeting Daemon Aticus on a dark night alone was something completely different.

'Well, if you're sure...' her father said doubtfully.

'Yes, Dad. It's fine. I'm only down the road and then I'll be back again. Maybe I can persuade him to come back for a cuppa?'

'Just be careful. I'm not sure about this at all.'

'Don't be such a fusspot. I can look after myself. What's the worst that can happen?'

Trudi blew him a kiss and shut the door. She'd give Duncan Lewis ten minutes to show up, then she'd go back home. The evening air had cooled, an involuntary shiver ran down her back. An owl hooted once in the distance, and she listened in vain for a melancholy response, but the night remained quiet. Once the drive gates swung shut behind her, Trudi began to have second thoughts.

She banished the feeling of disquiet, told herself she could handle any problems. A fox slinked across the road in front of her, the sudden movement making her heart leap into her mouth. It froze on the spot, swinging its pointed muzzle towards her and she wondered which one of them was the most scared. This time of night the villagers would all be safely tucked up in their homes, the central heating banishing the chill she felt entering her bones. She was, to all intents and purposes, completely alone.

A few streetlights did little to illuminate the pavement, but Trudi knew the way so well she could have walked it blindfolded. There was a car parked by the public telephone box, and a figure leaning on the bonnet. She picked up her pace, relieved that he'd made the rendezvous.

'Duncan Lewis?' Trudi extended a hand towards the man as he straightened up. It was only as his face entered the light spilling from the phone box that she felt the first real doubts, but by then it was already too late. His gloved hands were around her throat before she could react, pulling her into the shadows.

FIFTY-TWO
DONE WITH CRYING

Corstorphine drove back home. He needed to see if any more messages had been delivered before taking the trail camera and photograph to the station. A single light showed in the hallway. The rest of the windows remained in darkness – a reminder, as if one was needed, that the house remained empty.

There were no brown paper parcels waiting for him in the hallway and Corstorphine shut the door with a feeling of helplessness. Duncan Lewis had Shamila, of that he was certain, and for reasons that he couldn't understand had decided to play this game with him.

He laid the trail camera and printed photograph of Shamila on the kitchen table, trying not to meet the eyes staring back at him. He'd felt strangely hollowed out when he'd realised Duncan Lewis had taken her, and now that empty space was being filled with fury. At least she was still alive. He held onto that thought like a talisman against his fears, ignoring the voice in his head that advised him the photograph must have been taken hours ago. A knock at the door made him freeze to the spot.

Corstorphine reached for his baton, edging silently towards the front window. It was Frankie.

He noticed Frankie eying his baton, still held ready to strike out. 'Sorry,' he apologised. 'Didn't know who it might be.'

'I'd do the same,' Frankie admitted.

He led her into the kitchen. 'Any developments?'

'Robb has had a ransom demand for Phoebe. A million in high denomination used notes. Delivered in the same brown paper packaging *The Courier* had. He's going to notify us once he has been contacted again.'

'How long has he got? To raise the money?' Corstorphine couldn't help but equate Shamila's situation to Phoebe's, but there hadn't been any demand for money in his delivery.

'Tomorrow. We're going to try and extend the timescale. Robb said he couldn't raise that money overnight. It will take time to liquify assets.'

'He's planning on paying the demand?'

She grimaced acceptance. 'He doesn't have much choice until we have a lead.'

'There's been nothing else?'

'No. Sorry, sir.'

Corstorphine sank down into a seat, holding his head in his hands. He raised his chin with effort to look at her, seeing her concern.

'What are those?' Frankie was pointing at Shamila's photograph and the trail camera.

'I've just come back. The book he left for me – I think he's pulling the same trick he did with *Outgrove*. The first paragraph was written as a clue, steering us towards a rookery east of where we found Richard Bryce's body. I found the trail camera aimed at Shamila's photo.' The stored emotion was released in anger. 'He's playing with us!'

Frankie stared at him in confusion.

'Did you see the book? One of the MIT squad collected it and took it back to the station for forensics to look at.'

'I don't know anything about any book, sir. DI Brown sent me out to see Robb and when I came back, he said they're calling it a night and to go home and get some sleep. He never mentioned anything about it.'

Corstorphine updated her, sharing the pages he'd saved to his phone. 'Most of it seems like total gibberish, but I figured there must be something in it, otherwise why risk delivering the book here?'

Frankie's focus was on her screen, her finger swiping from one screenshot to the next.

'Is this the title, *Done With Crying*?' She held the screen to face him, showing the cover picture of a scarecrow.

'Aye. He must have planned how the body was going to be displayed before having the book printed.' Corstorphine paused, there was something niggling him about the cover.

'That's the song that made Mart McKeown famous. I was looking at the gold disk in his house. Why would Duncan Lewis reference his song and steal his scarecrow – unless it's coincidental?'

Corstorphine's view on coincidences was well known.

'Have the MIT left the station?' He was reaching for his car keys.

'I think so. They were about to leave when I left.'

'I think we should pay a visit to Mart McKeown. Don't you?'

'DI Brown more or less told me not to contact you, sir...' She paused, her tone apologetic.

Corstorphine held up the photograph of Shamila, gagged and desperate to be found. 'Shamila and Phoebe need our help *now*, Frankie! They can't wait for the MIT boys to finish their breakfast or forensics to pull their fingers out.'

'That's why I'm here,' Frankie replied.

FIFTY-THREE
FIND A FRIEND

They drove in silence to Glenarty. Corstorphine's mind kept circling back to the picture of Shamila – her pleading eyes. Was Duncan Lewis deliberately taunting him by leaving this clue, and if so, why? His behaviour suggested he had a personal grudge against Corstorphine in particular – yet he'd never met the man, never had any dealings in the case. Shamila had been the lead clinician, instrumental in his release. Something didn't add up – even if the man was suffering from psychosis.

In the passenger seat, Frankie kept her own counsel. She was going against orders even being there with him, but he was grateful for her company. Corstorphine wouldn't have been able to cope with remaining at home on his own.

The village was quiet when they arrived. Minimal street lighting cast the assorted scary figures into theatrical life like some abandoned film set from a horror movie. Those windows that hadn't drawn curtains showed scenes of domestic tranquillity: a cat perched on a windowsill; a family watching a huge TV; a figure bent over a silent piano.

Mart McKeown's house was obscured by the tree-lined drive. He stopped at the gate and Frankie opened her door to reach the intercom. A metallic rasp sounded as she pushed the button, then a voice issued from the speaker.

'Who is it?'

'DC Frankie McKenzie. I was here Monday evening – about your missing scarecrow?'

'What time is it? You know it's gone 10 p.m.? Isn't it a bit late for you to be coming round? Have you found Rufus?'

Frankie waited for the flood of questions to finish. 'No, I'm sorry. We've not found Rufus. I'm here with DI James Corstorphine. Could we come in and ask you a few questions?'

'What? At this time of night? What sort of questions?'

Corstorphine's patience was at an end. He leaned over Frankie to shout into the intercom.

'Can you open the gates so we can talk? We won't take much of your time, but you may have information that will assist with an urgent enquiry.'

A buzz announced the gates were about to swing open.

'Thank you.' Frankie's response was lost as Corstorphine accelerated up the drive.

They parked in front of the house, floodlights casting their surroundings into harsh relief. The front door opened before they reached it and Mart McKeown stood on the doorstep, his fixed expression focussed on the two police officers.

'How can I help?'

Corstorphine took the lead. 'Do you happen to know a Duncan Lewis?'

Mart McKeown's features weren't capable of expressing surprise, but they had a reasonable attempt. His eyebrows raised a few millimetres and his eyes widened imperceptibly.

'Duncan Lewis?' Mart McKeown repeated. 'The madman who chopped up his wife and then wrote a book about it?'

It was a succinct summary.

Corstorphine nodded. 'He's written another book which I believe is meant to contain a message, specifically for me. I need to know where he is.'

'I see,' Mart McKeown began slowly. 'No, I don't. What's this to do with me and my missing scarecrow?'

'The book's title is *Done With Crying*.'

Corstorphine watched him closely for a reaction. It was like trying to read a blank page.

'My song?' Mart McKeown's eyebrows had reached the limit of their extent, a full 3mm higher than their normal fixed position. 'What's that got to do with anything?'

Corstorphine could sense Frankie's restlessness beside him. He'd hoped for some breakthrough – an insight into why an anodyne pop song from the Nineties had been selected as the title of the second book by Daemon Aticus. That hope was fading.

'You've never had any contact with Duncan Lewis?' Frankie took over. 'Never made use of his book *Outgrave* for lyrics?'

Mart turned towards Frankie, his disconcertingly fixed expression giving Corstorphine the impression they were dealing with a robot.

'No. Why would I?'

'What about your daughter, Trudi? Has she ever had any contact with him?' Frankie tried what must surely be the last attempt to gain anything useful from the visit.

Mart McKeown looked uncomfortable. Without the natural ability to change expression, he gave himself away by his eyes flicking between them, his fingers flexing nervously.

'You'd have to speak to Trudi.'

'Is your daughter at home, Mr McKeown?' Corstorphine shared an ability with other apex predators – seeing a weakness and knowing when to strike.

'She's gone out.' He consulted his watch, and the first sign of doubt showed. 'She should be back by now.'

'Do you know where she is, Mr McKeown? It's urgent that we speak to her tonight. Even the slightest thing she can tell us could mean the difference between life or death.'

Corstorphine waited as Mart McKeown processed his request.

'Why are you looking for Duncan Lewis?'

Corstorphine had nothing to lose. 'There are reasonable grounds to suspect him of kidnap and murder. The sooner we can find him the better.'

'Oh God!' Fear flashed across his face. 'I was told he was sane. He'd been released from hospital and now he's completely normal.'

'We think he may have stopped taking his antipsychotic drugs. He's an extremely dangerous man, Mr McKeown. If you know anything, then you have to tell us.'

Even Mart McKeown's Botox failed to contain the look of shock that crossed his face.

'Trudi's writing a biography about him. She said he'd agreed to meet her this evening!'

'Where?' Corstorphine's urgent tone cut through Mart McKeown's sudden panic.

'I don't know. She didn't say. Just in the village. Oh my God, not Trudi!'

'Do you have her on Find My on your phone?' Frankie asked. 'We can track her, make sure she's safe.'

Mart McKeown fumbled in his pockets, his fingers lacking musical dexterity in his rush to find his daughter. He activated the app, turned the screen towards them in hopelessness.

'She doesn't like me knowing where she is,' his voice broke in helplessness. 'I can't track her.'

FIFTY-FOUR
PHOEBE

Something felt wrong. The driver had shut Shamila in the back, then purposely locked the doors before moving off. She'd twisted her head around to say hello to Shamila only to be met with a silent shake of the head in response.

'You said you'd let her go.' Shamila's words only added to Phoebe's confusion.

Why would he let her go? They were going home to see Robb, weren't they? Phoebe frowned as she saw they were going in the wrong direction. The taxi driver hadn't responded, keeping his eyes fixed on the road ahead.

'You promised me.' Shamila's voice was tight with anger.

Phoebe glanced at the man driving them, his attention leaving the road ahead to catch Shamila in the rear-view mirror.

'You keep quiet or I'll kill her.'

Her blood ran cold.

'She's just a kid. Please, whatever this is about it doesn't involve her.'

'I said shut the fuck up!'

His sudden anger made her jump.

'Phoebe's brother is rich – he'll pay anything to have her back safely.' Shamila spoke softly from the back seat.

He spared a sidewise glance as if making an evaluation.

'Not another word. I mean it.'

They travelled in silence as the road twisted alongside Loch Lochy. Robb had taken her this way many times before. She loved seeing the mountains mirrored and the way clouds seemed to scud across the surface of the water. But not today. She feared this may be the last time she'd live to see anything ever again.

The taxi driver was too big to fight. He gave the impression of being ready to explode into violence at any minute. Shamila's ready acceptance of his demands was proof enough that she took his threats seriously. Phoebe didn't dare turn around again in case he made good on his warning to kill her.

They turned off after a few miles, driving down an overgrown lane. Unkempt hedges brushed the windows and the car kept lurching as the wheels dropped into potholes and ruts. They came to a halt beside an abandoned church. Was he going to kill them here? Phoebe's heart began to race. Instead, he left Shamila locked in the back and forced her into a small room at the rear of the church.

White paint had fallen to the floor in large flakes, exposing rough stones underneath. One high window let in a subdued light through grimy glass. There was a small heap of water bottles and packets of sandwiches, together with a sleeping bag and a bucket.

'Stay here. Keep quiet and maybe you'll see your brother. It doesn't matter to me either way.'

He left, shutting the single door and securing it from the outside with a padlock. She listened as the car door slammed again, then the sound of another door opening into what must be the church behind her. Shamila could be heard trying to reason with their abductor until he forced her into the church, shouting at her to do what he told her. The walls were too thick to hear anything else after that, no matter how hard she strained.

Phoebe looked around her, searching for a way out. The door was solid and wouldn't budge; the window too high for her to reach and too small to climb through. The floors were made of solid timber planks and too heavy to lift even if she had a tool to prise them up with.

She sat on the sleeping bag and tried to make sense of it all. The one thing she wouldn't do is to give in to despair or cry. Being locked in a small room was something she knew she could cope with; she'd dealt with isolation for most of her short life. The only thing for her to do was wait.

The car door slammed again after a while, and the engine noise faded away into the distance. It sounded as if the man had left them alone. She wanted to shout out in case Shamila could hear her, but the taxi driver's threat remained clear in her mind. Phoebe pressed her ear to the cold wall dividing her space to the church and heard nothing.

Above her head, a small rectangle of light made slow progress towards the roof until the sun no longer reached the window. Phoebe's stone cell immediately darkened and she shivered with the onset of night as the room began to chill.

She climbed into the sleeping bag and prepared to face the first night of her captivity alone.

FIFTY-FIVE

DEFIBRILLATE

'When did Trudi leave?' Corstorphine asked urgently.

Mart McKeown had lost the ability to speak – his facial features retained the same immovable expression with which he'd greeted them at the door.

'Think, man! You have to know when she left the house.' Corstorphine's shouts managed to break through Mart McKeown's paralysis.

He sagged against the door, a hand raising to hold his chest.

'An hour, maybe longer. She said she was meeting him in the village. Oh God! I need to sit down.'

'Help me take him inside, Frankie.'

They took an arm each and manoeuvred the rock star back down the hallway. Corstorphine spotted a chair, and they half carried, half dragged Mart until lowering him down.

'Can we fetch you water?' Frankie asked with concern.

Like him, she viewed the aging rock star with the distinct possibility that Mart was having a heart attack.

'Do you have a pain in your chest?' Corstorphine desperately tried to remember if he'd seen a defibrillator in the village. He motioned for Frankie to bring a glass of water, and she ran out of the room, heading deeper into the house.

'No, at least, I don't think so. It's the shock. I never imagined. Trudi never said. Oh God. Is she going to be alright?' His words came in short bursts. His eyes pleaded for Corstorphine to say everything was going to be fine.

He'd seen that look a hundred times before.

'The best chance for us getting Trudi safely back is for you to tell us everything you know about her dealings with Duncan Lewis. Did she say exactly where she was meeting him?'

A shake of the head put an end to that hope. 'She just said in the village. I don't know why she didn't say to come to the house. I didn't think anything of it.'

'How long has Trudi been in touch with him? Is this all fairly recent?'

Frankie returned with a glass of water which Mart took gratefully in both hands, slurping noisily as the glass shook.

'She had the idea a year ago. She's tried writing various things – crime fiction, romance, historical. None of the publishers wanted her work. She did English at university.' He added this in wonder, as if an English degree gave an automatic entrance to the world of publishing.

Corstorphine willed him to get to the point.

'Then she pitched the idea of writing a biography on Duncan Lewis, exploring the dark side of his character and the book he wrote.'

'*Outgrave?*' Corstorphine prompted.

'Aye, that was it. She'd pitched it as a true-life Dr Jekyll and Mr Hyde and had an agent almost immediately. Next thing she had an offer from a publisher. She was over the moon.'

Frankie interrupted before Trudi's life story was laid out in front of them. 'How long has she been in contact with Duncan Lewis and writing this book?'

'Well, only a month or so. She couldn't find any contact details and the hospital and local police were no help. Thing is, she'd already written a chunk of it so she could get the publishing contract.'

Corstorphine struggled to make sense of what he was hearing. 'How do you mean, she'd already written a chunk of it? This is before she'd had any contact with him?'

Mart nodded unhappily. 'She said it was being creative. That's what they wanted. But when she was offered the deal, it was on the basis that the book was written with Duncan Lewis's help and approval.'

'So, she managed to find him? Has she met him previously?'

'No, they've just exchanged emails. He didn't like to talk on the phone or video. That's why she was so excited to meet him tonight.' His glance swept to take in a wall-mounted clock as it struck eleven.

'She should have come home by now.' His hand returned to his chest, fingers clutching at his shirt. Mart groaned and stretched rigid in his chair, looking more like a waxwork than ever – except no waxwork face wore such an expression of pain.

'Frankie! Down the road. The public telephone box. I'm sure I saw a defibrillator sign as we drove past. I'll call for an ambulance.'

He returned his attention to Mart McKeown as Frankie hurried out, hastily punching out the emergency number on his mobile even as Mart's lips started to turn blue.

FIFTY-SIX

JEKYLL OR HYDE

Frankie jumped into Corstorphine's car. The wheels spun uselessly, spitting out gravel until gaining purchase and then leapt forward causing her to grab at the steering and wrench the front wheels to aim back down the drive. She had to slow as the gates swung ponderously open, then accelerated into the village. The phone box was somewhere in the centre, she remembered seeing it.

A red telephone box sheltered underneath a beech hedge, a rectangular cut providing a niche for the box to settle into. She screeched to a halt, ran to wrench open the door and stopped in her tracks at the sight of another scarecrow slumped against the defibrillator cabinet. Frankie's first thought was how thoughtless to place a scarecrow so it blocked access to the medical aid. She pulled at an arm to throw it out of the way and felt an unexpected weight. She was face to face with the hessian sack that she remembered seeing on Farmer Haddow's photograph. That leer wasn't easily forgotten. But what had really caught her attention was how realistic the arm had felt under her hand.

She patted the scarecrow on the chest and felt a human body. Frankie recoiled in shock. With mounting horror she pulled at the hessian face, revealing Trudi's silent scream underneath. Willing her fingers not to tremble, she reached two fingers under the line of the jaw and beside the windpipe, aiming for the carotid artery. Frankie willed a pulse to show, but Trudi's heart had stopped. The bruising on her neck was sufficient to show she'd been strangled. Her skin still retained warmth — she'd only been recently murdered.

Frankie had to prioritize. Mart needed the defibrillator now, or there was the very real possibility that another body would be lying in the morgue tomorrow. Corstorphine would have already called for an ambulance, but she couldn't risk having Mart taken to hospital with his daughter's dead body. She called DI Brown, letting the phone ring as she pulled the defibrillator out of its box on the wall.

'DI Brown.' His voice issued curtly from her phone.

She tried to still the panic rising in her voice. 'This is DC Frankie McKenzie. I'm at the public telephone box in Glenarty village. There's the body of a young woman, I believe to be Trudi McKeown. Her father lives here and has just had a heart attack. I have to leave the body unattended whilst I deal with her father.'

'Have you called for medical assistance?'

She felt relieved that the detective coped well under pressure. 'DI Corstorphine has called for an ambulance, but we can't risk him travelling with his daughter's body.'

'Corstorphine...? Leave it. We'll talk about this later. I'll call in forensics, you deal with the father. What a fucking mess!'

Frankie could only agree with the DI's summing-up. Mart McKeown was dying and his daughter's body lay dumped in a phone box. She slammed her palm on the steering wheel as Corstorphine struggled to work the electric gates.

Finally, they swung open with frustratingly slow progress and she raced back up the drive.

Corstorphine grabbed the unit out of her hands and ran back to Mart's prostrate body.

'I've been giving him CPR,' he explained breathlessly, ripping

Mart's shirt open to expose the skin. Two adhesive paddles were pressed onto bare flesh diagonally across the heart as the defibrillator box began issuing mechanical instructions.

'See if you can find Trudi's room. See if there's anything about this meeting or any notes she's made. There may be something we can use to help us find them.'

'*Evaluating heart rhythm. Stand by. Preparing to shock. Everyone clear. Do not touch patient.*'

Frankie couldn't choose her moment. Mart was unconscious, it had to be now.

'Trudi's dead, sir. Her body was in the phone box. Looks like she's been strangled.'

'*Delivering shock.*' The electronic unit issued a warbling cry of distress as Mart's body arched. Corstorphine's expression obeyed the mechanical voice's instructions.

'*Shock delivered. Provide chest compressions and rescue breaths.*'

'Search her room!' Corstorphine returned both palms to Mart's chest, compressing the heart in an effort to keep him alive.

The Bee Gees song 'Staying Alive' played inappropriately in her mind to the rhythm of Corstorphine's compressions as she ran past the wall display of gold discs. Frankie flew up the sweeping staircase to the first floor, opening door after door to find Trudi's room. The makeup desk and paraphernalia gave it away – that and the clothes left strewn carelessly across the floor. There was a desk against a window with pads and pens covering its surface. An Apple Mac screen lit up as she touched the keys, requesting she enter a password. *Outgrave* lay open, multicoloured page markers inserted throughout. Downstairs the mechanical voice issued further instructions to Corstorphine, followed by another electronic warble as further shocks were applied.

'Jesus! Not another death!' Frankie's plea was for herself and Mart McKeown.

She opened the top pad, swiftly scanning the neat cursive script for anything they could use. It was mostly a synopsis of

Outgrave, descriptive passages that had been decoded like a cryptic crossword to provide the locations for his wife's body. She flicked through to the most recent entry, reading Trudi's last words.

Jekyll's emails show a change from our first exchanges. The way he words things. Could this be a result of having had a split personality? A duality of spirit? Or does this signify something darker – a return of Hyde that is no longer hidden? I need to ask him to agree to the book, otherwise the publisher won't take it. He wants to meet tonight, in the village. He's being a bit mysterious, not like Duncan at all. Says I'll know him when I see him. I hope he's not dangerous!!!

Corstorphine's rhythmic grunts told her that Mart McKeown's life still held in the balance. She snatched up Trudi's papers and the laptop. They'd need to access her emails and soon. In the meanwhile, her dead body lay slumped in the telephone box waiting for forensics.

It was close to midnight when DI Brown and his two DCs finally decided to call it a day. They'd arrived within thirty minutes of Corstorphine's call, the smell of alcohol and cigarettes surrounding them like a tribute to Glaswegian detectives of old. Mart McKeown was being stretchered out at the same time. Two paramedics were checking his pulse and holding an intravenous drip high above his head as they wheeled him into the ambulance.

'Is he going to make it?' DI Brown watched the ambulance make an awkward three-point turn around the crowded driveway.

'Aye. I think so.' Corstorphine felt the ache in his arms from performing CPR. He rubbed the muscles absent-mindedly, attempting to relieve the pain before it settled into place.

'And the girl?' He aimed this at Frankie.

'Forensics confirm strangulation is the likely cause of death. They've taken the body back to Inverness for an autopsy.'

'Did anyone see anything? What about the telephone box, anything there for us to work with?' DI Brown's voice veered towards exasperation.

'There's a technician working the SOC now, sir,' Frankie volunteered. 'The phone box is almost completely obscured by a beech hedge. No houses overlook the location. We can do a door to door first thing tomorrow?'

The DI gave her a look that implied he didn't like being told how to run an investigation.

'That doesn't explain what you're doing here at the exact same time as a lassie is strangled in a telephone box and her father almost dies of a heart attack.'

Corstorphine had never felt so tired in his life. The events of the last twenty-four hours had finally caught up with him. He'd thought he'd not stop until Shamila had been found, but all he wanted was to close his eyes and rest, just for a few minutes.

'That was me, sir.' Frankie spoke beside him. 'When DI Corstorphine described the book he'd had delivered, I immediately related the title to a song by Mart McKeown – "Done With Crying". Mr McKeown had only recently reported having his scarecrow stolen and it was too much of a coincidence to ignore.'

Corstorphine interrupted before Frankie could incriminate herself for going to see him when he was meant to be kept out of the investigation.

'I'd talked to Frankie on the phone, just to see if there had been any updates, and she made the connection to the book straight away.' The white lie made, he caught Frankie's eye then continued. 'She offered to come with me as she'd seen Mr McKeown just a few days ago and thought it would make a late evening call less stressful for him.'

'That worked out well!' DC Robbins' Glaswegian accent delivered his caustic verdict on proceedings, only to be met with a glare from DI Brown.

'Mart McKeown said that his daughter...' Corstorphine began.

'Trudi?' DI Brown sought confirmation as DC Robbins started writing in his notebook.

'Aye, Trudi, is writing a biography on Duncan Lewis and had arranged to meet him this evening.'

The three detectives exchanged a knowing look. The evidence against Duncan was overwhelming.

'When I informed Mr McKeown that Duncan was believed to be a dangerous man and was being sought for murder and kidnapping, he had a heart attack.'

DI Brown looked like he needed another cigarette. 'What contact has Trudi had with Duncan Lewis?'

'This was the first time she'd met him. Everything else has been by email. Frankie has the laptop and notes from her bedroom.' Corstorphine pointed vaguely upstairs.

'Collect everything that might be of use,' DI Brown commanded. 'We'll have to have forensics here too. And see if you can raise IT to access her computer.'

'I'll show you where her room is.' Frankie led the two DCs back into the house, leaving the two inspectors alone.

'I'll have to say you were involved with all this, despite being relieved of duty. I don't have any choice.' DI Brown spoke quietly enough not to be overheard.

'I know. It doesn't matter what happens as long as I have her back.'

'We'll do everything we can, James. You have my word. We'll catch this bastard.' He checked his watch. 'It's well past midnight. Take yourself home and get some rest, man. You're no use to her if you can't think straight. Alright?'

He laid a hand on Corstorphine's shoulder. 'I'll keep you up to date – besides which I need your local knowledge and you've made more progress on your own than the three of us have managed since we got here.'

'I can work the case?' Corstorphine said hopefully.

'Not officially.' DI Brown didn't need to say anything else.

Frankie and the two other DCs came back down the stairs. They added *Done With Crying* to the laptop and notebooks.

'Put it all in the car,' DI Brown directed.

Corstorphine took advantage of having DI Brown to himself. 'I followed up on a hunch from Daemon Aticus's book earlier this evening. There's another SOC you need to look at – it's the

Rookery a few kilometres east of Haddow's farm. I've a trail camera and photograph of Shamila that I found there...'

'You've been tramping around another SOC?' DI Brown said angrily.

Corstorphine saw the MIT DCs returning and felt their eyes on him.

'I thought Daemon Aticus might have been re-creating *Outgrave* – leaving clues in this new book where he might have taken Shamila...' Corstorphine found his throat closing up at her name and it took an effort of will for him to continue. He swallowed noisily and gathered himself together. 'Shamila and Phoebe.' He hurried to continue before his emotions could get the better of him.

'The first pages were about a scarecrow. Where it was looking. I thought there was a possibility that he was directing us to look at the hill where a rookery is.'

The incredulity in the three detectives' expressions suggested he'd better speed up his synopsis.

'I found a recent photograph of Shamila. She's bound and gagged. There was also a trail camera which I believe had been placed there to catch us searching the area. I have both items at home awaiting further investigation.'

'It sounds to me that the words "you're off the case" didn't get through to you?' DI Brown's words were delivered as a threat.

Corstorphine knew he could be subject to disciplinary procedures. This might even be the end of his career. He was beyond caring.

'Shamila is my wife,' he said quietly. 'What the fuck do you expect me to do? Sit at home with a mug of cocoa and have an early night?'

DI Brown locked eyes with him, then nodded acceptance.

'We'd all do the same.' The two stooges took their cue and nodded alongside their boss.

'Frankie, take DI Corstorphine home and collect those items

for evidence. Then get some sleep yourself. We'll all be needing our wits about us tomorrow.'

FIFTY-EIGHT
COMPLETE IDIOTS

Frankie arrived at the police station early. She'd barely slept. It seemed strange not to have Hamish's dour greeting waiting for her; his absence was just another reminder that everything was falling apart. She spared a thought for him and Molly, returning to their wee home after being told news they already suspected. Another layer of worry and puzzlement to add to an already confusing world.

The MIT team were all at work in the main office. Lamb and McAdam must have just arrived as they were making the first coffee of the day. She called a greeting to the two DCs, then caught DI Brown looking at her through the glass windows of Corstorphine's inner office before he looked down again, speaking to someone on the phone.

'Do you know what's happened?' Bill McAdam urgently asked her. 'Was that a photo of Corstorphine's wife I saw you put on your desk?'

'I was out with him last night. There's been some developments, but as far as I know we're no closer to finding Shamila or Phoebe.' Frankie added another mug to the two already waiting and Lamb spooned instant for her, adding hot water and milk.

'Thanks.' She sipped gratefully at the hot liquid, willing the caffeine to work its magic on her lethargic mind.

'Did you see the news?' Bill McAdam asked.

Frankie caught Lamb's guilty expression out of the corner of her eye. 'No, I was out until gone midnight then went straight to bed.'

'Our PC Lamb's a film star,' Bill McAdam added cryptically. 'That French reporter, the one who works for *The Courier*, she took a photo of the body we found – minus its head. Lamb was right in the frame pulling his best stop traffic move.'

'I thought I'd stopped her from using her phone,' Phil began defending himself only to stop as DI Brown stepped out of Corstorphine's office.

'Right, everyone. Gather round.' He stood in front of the crazy wall, still displaying Corstorphine's first tentative attempts at linking the scarecrow body to suspects.

Frankie stood alongside Lamb and McAdam. The two MIT DCs stood slightly apart from them, two tribes on the same side.

'This is where we are.' DI Brown pinned the copy of Shamila's photograph to the crazy wall. Her pleading eyes seemed to stare directly into Frankie's soul, the gag in her mouth holding back a scream.

'DI Corstorphine had a package delivered to his home some time yesterday. We don't yet have any witnesses who saw the package being delivered. PC Lamb, I want you to ask door to door on Corstorphine's street just in case there's a witness.'

'Sir.' Lamb almost saluted beside her.

'The package consisted of a book. I don't have it to show you as forensics are working on it as we speak, but the author purports to be Daemon Aticus – who you all should be aware by now is the pseudonym for Duncan Lewis. Corstorphine was able to decipher a clue in the first few pages which led him to a hill not far from the location of the scarecrow body. There he found this photograph and a trail camera which he believes was being used to notify Duncan Lewis when someone discovered the location.'

DI Brown turned to face the crazy wall, added Rookery Hill as a location and attached red thread between Richard Bryce and Duncan Lewis connecting to the hill.

'The Anacapa chart connects Duncan Lewis to all these events. Accordingly, we have to make his arrest the highest priority.'

Frankie waited until DI Brown's intense gaze returned to the crazy wall before exchanging a querying look with the two PCs. Their expressions confirmed they'd never heard of an Anacapa chart either.

'You all have Duncan Lewis's photograph. Show it to everyone you talk to. Just one person could give us the break we need. It goes without saying that Duncan Lewis is a dangerous man. We have to apprehend him before any more people are killed.'

The dry marker pen squeaked as DI Brown added another name to the death tally at the top of the board.

'Trudi McKeown's body was found in the Glenarty public call box by DC Frankie McKenzie last evening at 23:21. Forensics are still working on the cause of death, but initial findings suggest she had been strangled around 10 p.m. – almost immediately after she had left her home.'

He turned to face them, a grim expression etched on his face. 'Her father, Mart McKeown, said that she had arranged to meet Duncan Lewis in the village to discuss a book she was writing about him.' DI Brown took the red thread and linked Trudi to Duncan Lewis.

Frankie saw the crazy wall turning into a giant red web in front of her eyes, with Duncan Lewis's photograph sat like a bald spider in the centre.

'DCs Robbins and Knight. I want you to talk to every single person in Glenarty. Someone will have seen or heard something. Frankie.' DI Brown's attention switched to her. 'We need someone with local knowledge to go through this book, *Done With Crying*. Forensics have sent an electronic copy which I'll forward onto you.

Look for clues as to where he's holding the hostages. He's wanting to play a game. Our job is to make damn sure we win it.'

PC Bill McAdam shifted beside her. He was the only one who hadn't yet been given a task.

'PC McAdam. We're spread thinly here; I may have to request additional manpower. I want you to revisit this hill.' A finger tapped at the crazy wall. 'DI Corstorphine went there in the middle of the night. There's a good chance that he missed something. Forensics can't spare anyone until this afternoon for a SOC visit, so it will have to be you. Are you able to inspect the site without trampling over evidence?'

'Yes, sir,' McAdam answered with an edge to his voice.

Frankie couldn't blame him. The DI was treating the three of them as complete idiots.

'I've asked for an expert to try and trace what device the trail camera has been accessed from in case that gives us a lead, but the likelihood is that Duncan has covered his tracks, so we have to rely on good old-fashioned policing. Has anyone any questions?'

He was met with silence.

'Right then. Let's get to it!'

The DI marched back into Corstorphine's office and shut the door. It was their cue to set to work.

Corstorphine hadn't slept. Trudi McKeown's callous murder played over repeatedly in his mind, and he struggled not to imagine Shamila suffering the same fate. Duncan Lewis had no concerns about murdering a young woman in public, knowing full well how soon her body would be found. He'd have even less compunction in disposing of his other hostages in some hidden location. Corstorphine had no doubt the murder was premeditated – the way Frankie had described Trudi's face being obscured with the sacking features of Farmer Haddow's scarecrow was proof enough that Duncan had planned how she'd be discovered.

DI Brown had promised to keep him up to date with the investigation. It wasn't enough. He needed to be in the office and piecing together every single clue as they came in. That was what he was good at – seeing patterns where others saw chaos; spotting links where others saw random events, discovering the causality that underpinned an investigation. Without that flow he was effectively working the case blind.

Shamila had been missing for almost twenty hours. He didn't need to refer to previous cases to know that her chances of survival were diminishing by the minute. The 'Golden Hour' had come and gone – those first three hours after a kidnapping when evidence crucial to finding a victim is of most use. All they had managed to discover was a discarded wig which forensics still hadn't reported on – as far as he knew. If nothing more was found in the next four hours, then he knew he had to prepare for the worst.

Forensics now had the two parcels, the photograph and the trail camera from Rookery Hill. He had little hope any of those items were going to provide a breakthrough. Duncan Lewis wouldn't be so stupid as to keep the camera feed live once it had been discovered, so they'd have to apply to work on cellular records which he could guarantee would lead to a burner phone within a wide mast triangulation area.

Corstorphine had to work with the little he did have. The book, *Done With Crying*, and the motive. He'd been pouring over the book throughout the long night. Searching the obscure text for more clues. They had to be there, but his mind was clouded with exhaustion and stress. Nothing had presented itself to him as a possible location for the hostages.

All he had left to work with was motive. At first, it had seemed obvious to him – a return of Duncan's psychosis. For all they knew, he saw Shamila and the others as dangerous supernatural creatures that he had to destroy – the same way that he had killed and then butchered his own wife. But why murder Richard Bryce in such a brutal manner, and why did he feel the need to kill Trudi?

Corstorphine cleared the kitchen table, reached for a packet of fluorescent-coloured sticky notes and began re-creating the crazy board on its surface. At the top went the names of the missing and dead. Richard Bryce – he added *scarecrow* underneath – Shamila, Phoebe and Trudi McKeown.

The common link to them all was Duncan Lewis. Corstorphine wrote his name on a bright red sticky note and laid it down underneath the top row of names. After a moment's hesitation, he added another red note with the name Daemon Aticus and placed it beside Duncan Lewis. Maybe he needed to see his psychosis as two separate people? Motivation, behaviour, every thought process had to be completely differentiated between the two personalities. In effect, he was chasing two people. Two green sticky notes were placed underneath Daemon Aticus with the titles of his books, *Outgrave* and *Done With Crying*.

Corstorphine stood back to view his handywork, then rushed off to raid Shamila's sewing box, returning with red wool and drawing pins. He began linking the top row of names to Duncan Lewis, then moved them to have the red woollen threads attach to Daemon Aticus instead.

He traced the first thread, Richard Bryce to Daemon Aticus. Why would the pharmaceutical nurse be the first to die, and what was the significance of the manner of his death and the way the body had been presented? Corstorphine picked up his mobile, swiped through to recent calls and touched his finger to the screen on DI Anderson's name, Lanark CID.

'DI Anderson.' The detective's curt voice sounded loud in the empty house.

'This is DI James Corstorphine. Have you made any progress?' He hoped the detective hadn't yet been advised that he was off the case.

'We've confirmed Duncan Lewis was definitely at Richard Bryce's house as his fingerprints were found on other items, and forensics have since found his DNA there, but there's no evidence that they met regularly for any reason. As far as we know, he only saw Gyles Lambert and Richard Bryce at Carstairs Hospital as an outpatient. Bryce for the anti-psychotic drugs he was on and Lambert for psychological assessments.'

Corstorphine listened with disappointment. He'd been hoping for more – anything that could help explain Duncan's motivation.

'We have found the spot where Richard Bryce was murdered,' DI Anderson added.

Corstorphine's head jerked up. 'What have you got?'

'We'd put out some feelers with the rail network, asking if train drivers had run into anything or rail workers had seen anything suspicious and had a response back. A train driver reported hitting a deer just before the Cleghorn level crossing on Saturday night. Didn't think much of it at the time – it's a regular occurrence on that stretch.'

Corstorphine interrupted. 'Cleghorn – where's that?'

'Sorry, it's a road crossing some 100m from Richard Bryce's house.'

The proximity to the missing nurse's address made DI Anderson's next words redundant.

'He was concentrating on the road junction ahead, said the lights are so bright on the road that he never saw the deer until the last minute, but it looked as if it was already dead. We had a look ourselves, soon as we heard, and found a deer carcass near the spot. There was evidence of blood there. Normally, we'd assume it was the deer bleeding out, but we had a sample checked. It matches Richard Bryce's genetic markers.'

Corstorphine paid little attention to the DI's words. His mind raced as he pictured Duncan Lewis overpowering the nurse before tying him to the tracks. How long had he been planning this? More importantly, what was he intending to do next?

There was a pause before DI Anderson continued in more suspicious tones. 'Hasn't DI Brown from the MIT briefed you?'

'Not yet,' Corstorphine answered truthfully. 'I'll wait for him to distribute the full report. I was just trying to see if there was any other connection other than professional between Duncan Lewis and any other Carstairs staff.'

'Right. No, it's the first angle we tried for. I wouldn't spend too long on analysing the man's motive. He's psychotic. That's all you need to know.' The gruff policeman's tone softened as he remembered Corstorphine's personal involvement in the case.

'I'm sorry I can't be of more assistance. I hope you find him – and your wife.'

'I hope so too. Thanks.'

Corstorphine laid his mobile down on the table next to Daemon Aticus.

Lanark CID might have given up on trying to work out motive. In the absence of any hard data pointing to Shamila's whereabouts, it was the only thing Corstorphine had left to deal with.

SIXTY

MADMAN

Corstorphine's mobile vibrated on the table, alerting him to an incoming call. DI Brown's name was displayed on the screen.

'Corstorphine?' DI Brown's Glaswegian accent made everything sound like a threat.

'Aye. This is me. Where are you with the investigation?' he asked without much hope of any new breakthrough being announced.

'I've just briefed the team. We're not much further forward. I'm sorry, I know you wanted to have better news.'

Corstorphine waited. He didn't trust himself to comment diplomatically to that statement.

'We've found where Richard Bryce was murdered. Traces of his blood were found near Cleghorn level crossing. It's close to his house. We're working on the assumption that he walked there with Duncan before being tied to the tracks.'

'How could he do that? Surely Bryce would have fought back, shouted?'

'We have a few hypotheses. He may have been attacked when they reached the level crossing – maybe he was knocked unconscious or drugged. Forensics haven't come back with a definitive answer. They may not be able to do so, given the state of the body and time since he died.'

'When did he die?'

'Forensics put his time of death between 36 and 60 hours before you discovered his body. That matches with a train driver reporting hitting what he thought was a deer on Saturday 25th October at 9:42 p.m. They found the deer's body beside the tracks but called us in because of the blood. Forensics have confirmed it matches Richard Bryce's DNA. We're going door to door in Glenarty in case anyone saw or heard anything last night, and I've sent McAdam to Rookery Hill in case there's any more evidence up there he can find in daylight. Lamb's presently talking to your neighbours in case they saw your parcel being delivered, and I've asked Frankie McKenzie to search through your book in case she can spot any other clues he might have left for us. As soon as I hear back from forensics, or anything else, I'll be in touch.'

'OK. Thanks for the update. One thing – there's at least one Ring video doorbell in Glenarty. Tabitha Richardson, Treasury Cottage. It's her video on file for one of the scarecrow thefts in the village.'

'I'll pass that on. Thanks. And we'll have a closer look at that video. It could be our man!'

The call ended on what DI Brown must have fondly imagined was a positive note. Corstorphine added the date and time of death to Richard Bryce's sticky note, then after a moment's consideration added a pink sticky note with the single word 'Why?'.

Had Duncan Lewis/Daemon Aticus positioned Richard's decapitated body for when he and Shamila had returned from their honeymoon, knowing it was bound to be discovered the same day they returned? Somehow Duncan knew of Shamila's unusual phobia, making her his focus and target.

In that case, why kill Richard Bryce? Was he just in the wrong place at the wrong time? God knows, they had enough experience as police for that to be a common enough rationale. He'd needed a body for the scarecrow and Richard Bryce was on hand. Or was there an ulterior motive? He had access to drugs, was that something to investigate?

He wrote 'Drugs' on another sticky note, placed it next to Richard's name. Carstairs Hospital would have a system in place to ensure drugs didn't go missing, and they'd have flagged any such discrepancies with the Lanark police. As the hospital's clinical pharmacologist, Richard Bryce would monitor Duncan Lewis's medication. Did he suspect or know Duncan had stopped taking his anti-psychotics? Was he becoming aware of the symptoms? It made sense then for him to be murdered if the psychosis was already well-developed. Duncan wasn't stupid and would have known that Richard was a threat. The same went for the clinical psychologist, Gyles Lambert, who'd picked the worst time to go on holiday. If he had detected symptoms of Duncan's psychosis returning, then he'd have known he'd be put straight back inside the State Hospital.

Corstorphine now had a possible motive for why Richard Bryce had been killed that fitted in with the Daemon Aticus persona having returned. It also went some way to explain why Shamila had been targeted, if he still saw her as a threat rather than his alter ego's reason for being set free. Maybe Gyles Lambert would have been targeted too if he'd still been there.

There were problems with his speculative analysis. Firstly, Shamila was so convinced of Duncan Lewis's recovery that she'd refused to consider that he might be a threat. That meant she was either a poor clinician or Duncan Lewis had pulled the wool over her eyes. Or, Corstorphine considered, for reasons best known to himself, he'd stopped taking his medication.

The second problem he faced was Trudi McKeown. If Duncan was truly suffering from psychosis, would he have had regular email exchanges with the young woman wanting to write his biography only to strangle her on their first and only meeting?

Corstorphine tapped the sticky note with Daemon Aticus

written on it as if encouraging it to speak. If he wanted to find Shamila, he had to get inside the mind of her abductor – the mind of a madman.

SIXTY-ONE
BORROWED RAGS

Frankie found it difficult to concentrate on the text displayed across her screen. *Done With Crying* was a dense, barely coherent outpouring of grief, hate, love and pseudo-philosophical observations on life. It didn't help that Daemon Aticus used the most cryptic comments in which to hide his clues. *Outgrave* might have provided a diversion for retired crossword enthusiasts with a penchant for finding the location of body parts, but when she needed to find Shamila and Phoebe before he harmed them...

She couldn't face the idea that they were already probably dead. Not when she knew them both as friends. If it was Shamila's dead body they found at the end of all this, it would destroy Corstorphine. That she knew for a stone cold fact.

DI Brown was bent over his laptop in Corstorphine's office. He conformed to the role of detective inspector, leading the investigation more like a conductor with an orchestra. Staying in his office, working the phones and radio, collating emails and evidence. Corstorphine could never stay in one place all day – he'd take every excuse to be out on the hills or driving the Land Rover around the lochs and mountains he loved so much. *But not as much as he loves Shamila.* Frankie spared a thought for her boss, waiting in an empty house which had only recently been brought back to life. The MIT were pissed with him for following the lead last night, even if they didn't make it clear. He'd been told to stay out of the investigation, but what did they expect?

It was thanks to Corstorphine that they had the first break-through – and discovered Trudi McKeown's body only hours after she'd been strangled. They could only just have missed Duncan Lewis by an hour or so. She knew he'd be working on the case even now. A glance at the clock told her it was 9:38 a.m. The DCs and two constables hadn't returned or called in – which implied they'd found nothing. Frankie couldn't bear to imagine how Shamila and Phoebe were coping after being held for twenty hours. Where had he hidden them? She refused to consider the most likely scenario where they were already dead.

The impenetrable text displayed across her screen. This is all they had to work with, in the absence of any hard evidence. She leaned forward, eyes scanning another chapter from *Done With Crying*.

When the unholy trinity face the fire, then they will burn with a fragment of the passion I held for you. Then you'll understand how deeply I loved you. In borrowed rags you'll end your life, surrounded by the things you fear the most.

Frankie sighed with feeling. This was what a commissioning editor must feel like as they waded through the slush pile. How was she meant to look for hidden meanings in prose as dense as this? She plodded into the small kitchen to make herself a coffee hoping that would get her through it. Trudi's slack face appeared unbidden in her memory, revealed as the crude sacking mask peeled away. Frankie banished the image as soon as it appeared, but it gave her fresh impetus to find Shamila. Outside the office windows the sun played peekaboo with fluffy yellow clouds, their reflections scudding across the loch's ruffled surface like impressionist yachts.

Her mind played back the paragraph she'd just read as the

kettle wheezed towards boiling. *Unholy trinity.* Was Daemon Aticus referring to religion, had he used a church to hide them away? There were plenty of abandoned chapels and churches scattered around the area their small police station had to cover, now that they lived in a mostly secular society. She decided to run a search on abandoned churches with the word trinity in the name.

Or he could be describing himself and the two people he held captive: Shamila, and Phoebe? Frankie sat at her desk and re-read the last paragraph. The focus was on one person, a person he loved. Was that Shamila he referred to?

Her brows drew down in concentration as she thought it through. Shamila had treated Duncan Lewis for a number of years before deciding he was safe to be released. During that time, could he have developed feelings for her which she wasn't aware of? She jotted *Stockholm Syndrome* on her pad. It hardly seemed likely, yet this passage was as much a declaration of unrequited love as anything. Frankie considered herself an expert in that branch of human frailty if nothing else.

Then the title, *Done With Crying,* Mart McKeown's only real hit and played over and over again by lovelorn teenagers who could personally identify with rejection and loss. Was this what it was all about? A love spurned, ignored and not even given the closure of a rejection? That would hurt anyone's sensitivities, and this wouldn't be the first time rejection had turned so easily from love to vengeful hatred. Add that to a man whose mind already teetered on the edge of madness and was only kept sane with regular medication...

Frankie added notes on the pad next to her. *Church with Trinity in name, love affair?* Then the mention of fire. It implied he'd already chosen the method with which he was going to kill the hostages. *Fire* was added to her notes and underlined. She hoped this interpretation was wrong – it would mean Duncan Lewis never had the intention of releasing them. But then he'd been in touch with Robb McCoach for a ransom, so maybe Phoebe hadn't figured in his original plan and was just an opportunistic attempt to make some money?

She followed that line of reasoning. Phoebe was the odd one out in all of this with no connection to Carstairs State Hospital. There was a certain logic that his clinicians would figure in his twisted desire for retribution. The only connection Phoebe had was as one of Shamila's original patients when she'd first moved here. Perhaps he'd seen her as easy to take? A young woman who wouldn't be able to fight back and could be used as bait to get Shamila. According to Kira, the receptionist at Shamila's clinic, she went willingly with Duncan Lewis when she was taken. From what she knew of Shamila, that's precisely how she'd behave when faced with a dangerous psychopath who was holding a young woman hostage. The more she thought about it; the more convinced Frankie became that she was right.

But this book was written prior to the events of the last few days. Who then was the third person he described in the trinity? Trudi was murdered last night and left in the phone box. That didn't have the feel of a premeditated crime – Duncan Lewis couldn't have known she'd try and meet him that night, and he certainly wouldn't have predicted that her father would have needed the defibrillator! If it hadn't been for her going to see Corstorphine and mentioning the book title was a famous song by Mart McKeown, they'd have never gone to see him that late in the evening. Which made Trudi's death all the stranger.

Frankie returned to the text. *Borrowed rags* – he'd dressed Richard Bryce in Farmer Haddow's scarecrow clothes. Was he planning on doing the same with his hostages?

Surrounded by things you fear the most. Corstorphine had mentioned that Shamila had a phobia of scarecrows. If Duncan really wanted her to suffer, he couldn't have devised a worse way for her to die than to be surrounded by scarecrows. Frankie added *Scarecrows* to her list. It was all supposition and guesswork at best, yet she had to present it to DI Brown as a potential lead. She took a deep breath and started typing a message to Corstorphine's private phone.

SIXTY-TWO

ANALYSIS

There was a knock at the door. Corstorphine's concentration faltered – he'd felt he was following a line of investigation that was leading somewhere. He pressed a palm to his forehead in an attempt to clear the fog that was settling on his brain and went to check who was waiting on the doorstep. It was PC Lamb.

'Morning, sir.' Lamb stood to attention like he was still in training.

'Morning, Phil. What have you got?' He waited with the diminishing hope that the constable had arrived at his door for a purpose, maybe even to provide an update on the search. One look at his face was enough for him to know that Lamb was paying a courtesy call.

'I've just been around your neighbours, sir. To see if anyone had seen anything yesterday when your parcel was delivered.'

'And had they?' Corstorphine's eagerness must have shown in his voice, because the PC's expression turned to regret.

'No, sir. Nobody can remember seeing anything out of the ordinary.' He paused to clear his throat and shifted awkwardly from foot to foot. 'But I was passing, so I thought I'd just see how you are. If there's anything I can do to help?'

Corstorphine could see he was trying his best, like a child

playing at being an adult. He dismissed that thought as being unkind. Lamb might be the most juvenile member of his team, but his heart was in the right place.

'That's good of you, Phil. No, there's not much you can do apart from what you're doing now. What's the latest?'

'Bill McAdam is at Rookery Hill, sir.'

Corstorphine held his hand up before Phil Lamb continued. 'Where?'

'Rookery Hill. Sorry, the place where you found the camera and the, eh, photograph.' Phil looked at his feet, momentarily embarrassed to have mentioned the picture of Shamila bound and gagged when she was still missing. 'He's checking the site in case there's something you might have missed last night. Forensics are visiting later today.' He drew a breath. 'The two DCs, Knight and eh...'

'Robbins,' Corstorphine prompted.

'Aye, thank you, sir. Knight and Robbins are going door to door in Glenarty. And Frankie's staying at the station, looking into that book for clues.'

'OK. Thanks, Phil. Sounds like you're covering all the angles.' The PC didn't look as if he knew how to leave. 'Best get on, lad. DI Brown will be needing you at the station.'

'Yes, sir. Sorry, sir.' He turned awkwardly, stopped and looked back over his shoulder. 'I am sorry, sir. I'm really sorry. We're all working as hard as we can to find her, find them.'

'I know, Phil. Thanks for dropping by.'

His phone chirped a notification as he shut the door on the young constable. It was a message from Frankie and a screenshot from her work laptop. He recognised the text, a section from the book he'd been given. Corstorphine read the message with the mounting hope that she'd spotted a clue that he'd missed.

Read this section. Couple of things. Is he referring to a church with Trinity in the name, maybe one no longer used in a remote location? The mention of fire suggests he's not harmed them, so there's still hope we can find them. Borrowed rags sounds like a reference to Haddow's scarecrow and he mentions things you fear the most – Shamila's phobia? Finally, the whole book and title implies he's breaking up with someone. The song Done With Crying is all about the end of a love affair. Was Duncan in love with Shamila? Some form of patient/doctor Stockholm Syndrome?

Corstorphine returned to his kitchen table with Frankie's observations whirling around his mind. What had been his line of thought before Lamb's knock had spoilt his concentration? He'd been trying to think like Daemon Aticus, seeing Shamila as a threat. And trying to understand the rationale for murdering Trudi.

If Duncan had fallen in love with Shamila during the course of his treatment, then surely she would have known? She'd never mentioned anything that suggested there was more than a clinician/patient relationship, yet there were aspects to this that gave weight to Frankie's idea. The delay until their honeymoon was over before presenting the body in that bizarre manner. The use of the scarecrow motif to scare her.

He could have been planning this ever since being released a year ago; or had her leaving Carstairs six months ago and the announcement that she planned to marry pushed him over the edge? It provided motive. There were so many instances when domestics turned into serious injury or death. Some of the most harrowing murders occurred due to the breakdown of a relationship – some partners made it their mission to extract the ultimate revenge for a perceived slight.

The more he thought about it, the more convincing Frankie's analysis became. The first murder was just to set the scene. Perhaps Richard Bryce had picked up on Duncan Lewis's change of mood and realised he'd stopped taking the drugs that he needed to keep him sane. Duncan was no fool and would have noticed when Richard started doubting his sanity.

That also explained why Corstorphine had been given the book of clues; it was a means of taunting him. Extracting revenge for taking what Duncan loved the most. Shamila had mentioned the risk of transference when treating her patients – could Duncan have redirected childlike notions of love and dependency onto her? And Frankie's observation that the whole book was Duncan Lewis railing against the injustice of Shamila loving someone other than himself. It all made horrific sense.

Corstorphine was filled with a sudden burst of newfound energy. Finally, he had something to work with. He put Frankie's comment about fire to one side. He began to look for every church within a thirty-mile radius that incorporated trinity in its name. Whatever Duncan had planned for Shamila, he had to be found before he could finish what he had started.

SIXTY-THREE
SNACK VAN

Frankie drew a blank in her search for a church incorporating the word trinity in its name. The nearest she could find was in Pitlochry, over seventy-five miles away. Wherever Duncan Lewis was using as his base, she felt it had to be closer than that.

She ran a web search on the definition of the *unholy trinity* and found a description from the Book of Revelations: the dragon (Satan); the beast from the sea (the Antichrist); and the false prophet – represented as a parody of the Holy Trinity (Father, Son, and Holy Spirit). Religious studies had never been her strongest subject and this was getting her nowhere. It was easier to imagine he was referring to the two people he'd kidnapped except he'd now taken four and killed two of them.

What if he'd only planned on taking three and the others were mistakes? Carstairs State Hospital was the common factor. That meant the three people he was describing as an unholy trinity could be Richard Bryce, Shamila Mallick and one other. Frankie followed her logic to see where it would lead. The two mistakes: Phoebe McCoach and Trudi McKeown. Why take them and expose himself to unnecessary risk? She already had a suspicion that Phoebe had been taken following surveillance at Shamila's clinic. A young woman made an easy target and gave him something he could use to pressure Shamila into leaving with him. He hadn't used force, according to the receptionist – just an initial struggle in her office before she left quietly.

The more she imagined the scene in Shamila's clinic, the more convinced she was that this explained how Duncan Lewis was able to take her without a fight. Shamila wouldn't have wanted to put Phoebe in any more risk if she'd thought he had her held captive. But that only posed another question – how had Duncan snatched Phoebe off a busy street at lunchtime as she went to grab food near the veterinary surgeons?

She opened a map on her screen, traced the route Phoebe would have taken from her part-time job to the takeaway on the High Street. It was a ten-minute walk at most, on busy roads. Nobody had reported seeing a young woman being coerced into a vehicle. It was as if Phoebe had just disappeared in plain sight. She cursed the lack of CCTV in the town centre. It was unlikely that Phoebe would have been snatched off the pavement – there would have been too much pedestrian traffic at that time, and someone would have come forward by now, especially with the news interest.

She looked up from her screen as PC Lamb entered the office.

'Did anyone see the parcel being delivered to the DI's house?' She asked more out of hope than anything. Phil had lost the spring in his step. He was acting more like she was feeling – a full day gone by and they were no closer to finding Shamila or the others.

A negative shake of his head was all she needed to confirm her suspicions.

'No. Nothing. You'd have thought someone would have seen something.' He slumped down dejectedly at his desk. 'I looked in on the DI. He's not doing too well. Doesn't look as if he's slept at all.'

Frankie wasn't surprised. If she knew her boss, he'd have spent every second going over the little evidence they had in an effort to work out where Shamila was being held. Like her, he knew the significance of finding a kidnap victim within the first twenty-four hours. She checked the clock – 11:34 a.m. Shamila had been missing now for almost twenty-two hours.

DI Brown banged on the glass divide to his internal office and beckoned Lamb in for a debrief. She felt a flash of anger at the way the MIT DI behaved – staying put at Corstorphine's desk instead of out searching with everyone else, but then she relented. His was the right course of action, pulling in all the evidence, sending the team out to find new leads. Every fibre of her being urged her to go out of the office and look for them, but where could she start?

It made perfect sense for Duncan to take Phoebe as a form of blackmail to ensure Shamila's compliance, and then once he found out her family were millionaires, he'd have had the motive to ask for a ransom. But why kill Trudi McKeown?

If Phoebe's abduction was the result of his surveillance of the clinic, then Trudi's murder must have had a completely separate motive. There had to be a reason that Duncan Lewis risked leaving his captives to drive to Glenarty and meet with Trudi. Frankie refused to believe that he'd only left his captives because they were already dead, not if he hoped to make a million by returning Phoebe to her brother.

Trudi was hoping to write his life story. If he simply hadn't wanted her to write about him, he wouldn't have arranged to meet her – especially given the risk. Frankie was missing a clue that was right in front of her nose, she was certain of it.

Lamb came out of the DI's office and sat dejectedly at his desk.

'What's he got you doing now?' Frankie asked.

'Nothing.' Phil glanced towards the inner office, checking he couldn't be heard. 'I don't think he rates me, to be honest.'

Frankie thought back to her imagined scenario where Duncan Lewis had the clinic under surveillance.

'You'd been to keep an eye on Shamila's clinic, hadn't you? Before she was abducted?'

'Aye. Sat outside the place in a patrol car for a while.'

'Is there any way the other industrial units could have seen someone waiting around? You know, if Duncan had been keeping an eye on her clinic for a few days before taking her?'

Phil's brows creased in concentration. 'Don't think so. We've asked all the units already and none of them have a clear view over the car park. Every bloody reception desk faces the other way.'

Frankie lost the one glimmer of hope she'd briefly raised.

'But there's the snack van!' Phil exclaimed. 'He's only there sometimes, but I grabbed an egg roll when I was there yesterday morning. We haven't asked him if he saw anything – he'd left by the time Shamila was taken.'

Frankie grabbed her jacket, rapped on the inner office door.

'There's a snack van, parks up at the industrial estate where Shamila's clinic is. He's not been seen as a potential witness to her abduction. I'm taking PC Lamb to track him down if that's alright, sir?'

'Aye. We need every lead we can get. Be quick about it.'

'Sir.' She closed the door, motioned to Phil to get up.

'Come on, Phil. We need to find this snack van. Any ideas where he'd be?'

He nodded enthusiastically in response. 'Bill and me know his usual places. This time of day he should be at Shamila's business park.'

She raced out of the police station followed by the sound of PC Lamb's boots hurrying to catch up.

SIXTY-FOUR
EMERALDS

Corstorphine had given up on searching for churches incorporating the word trinity in their title. He'd never felt so useless. The sticky notes spread over his kitchen table mocked him with their inability to provide even the slightest hint of a lead to where Shamila was being held. He'd had no word from the MIT team which meant they weren't making any progress either. The kitchen walls felt like they were pressing in on him and he had an urgent need to get out of the house. If only he was doing something, anything but waiting impotently to hear if Shamila was still alive.

There was only the one card left to play – Robb McCoach and his ransom demand. Duncan Lewis would still be trying for his million pounds and had said he'd be back in contact. Corstorphine climbed into his car and set off for Robb's mansion. Outside, the sun was shining, but he only had eyes for the man who'd taken Shamila, scanning every driver, every pedestrian as he drove the short distance to the outskirts of town.

Robb answered the door and wordlessly invited Corstorphine inside. They walked side by side through the silent building, dark wooden panelling echoing their footsteps back at them and adding to the sombre mood. He could see that Robb hadn't slept well either, his hand distractedly pushing hair away from a face covered in stubble.

'You've heard nothing, from the kidnapper?' Corstorphine broke the unnatural silence as they entered the brighter surroundings of the kitchen.

Robb's hand stopped pulling at his hair and went to a pocket, pulling out a phone as if he'd been doing nothing else but check for messages every few minutes.

'Nothing. Where the fuck is she?' Robb slammed his phone down on the table in disgust.

'Everyone's doing their best, Robb. We just need a break.' Corstorphine's voice dried up. He was caught between impotent rage and wanting to break down in tears. The lump forming in his throat made the latter option more likely.

'I'm sorry, Jim. I know you'll be wanting Shamila back too.'

Robb's kindness almost pushed him over the edge.

'How's it going, with the ransom money?' Corstorphine concentrated on doing his job – this wasn't the time to grieve, not whilst there was still hope of finding them alive.

'There's not a hope in hell of my raising that amount overnight.' Robb reached up to a biscuit tin on a kitchen shelf and withdrew a pouch, placing it down in front of the detective.

'What's this?'

'See for yourself.'

Corstorphine picked up the cloth pouch, felt the weight of something inside and turned it up to empty the contents onto his upturned palm. He saw two large, vivid green emeralds first. They caught the overhead lights and shone as if they were lit from inside. He was holding a pair of earrings, the emeralds clasped in diamond-studded silver.

'My mother's,' Robb said simply. 'They're the most expensive present my father ever gave her. They cost close to a million years ago, worth more than that now.'

Corstorphine replaced them in the pouch, handing it back to Robb. 'And you keep them here, in a biscuit tin?'

'No. In the bank vault. The insurance wouldn't cover them being held in the house.'

Corstorphine nodded.

'Phoebe's worth more,' Robb stated as a simple fact.

He couldn't argue. Phoebe was as priceless to Robb as Shamila was to him. He tried not to think about how many of the few hundred kidnappings each year resulted in death.

Robb's phone vibrated on the table, a single chime announcing a message had been received. They looked at one another in shared shock before Robb opened the message and read it out loud.

Do you have the money?

'What should I do?' Robb's panic was contagious.

'Answer. Say you haven't had time to obtain that amount of cash, but you have the emeralds which are worth more.'

Robb's fingers shakily relayed the message back. They waited in silence for a response. After twenty seconds Robb looked enquiringly at the DI. 'Shall I send it again?'

'Wait.' Corstorphine had to remind himself to breathe as the seconds dragged by, when all he wanted to do was grab the phone and ask how Shamila was.

Send photo of goods.

Corstorphine nodded in response and Robb emptied the earrings onto the table, sending the photograph he'd taken as an attachment. There followed another anxious wait.

Proof of value.

'I was expecting that,' Robb spoke to himself. He opened a drawer, flattened out a sheet of paper until Corstorphine could read an invoice from a London jeweller, and sent a copy in response.

Again, they had to endure a wait before the phone chirped another message had arrived.

> If you want to see the girl alive, take the goods to the top of Cow Hill. Come alone. No police. Be there at 2 p.m. exactly today. I'll send further instructions.

'Ask him for proof that Phoebe's still alive!' Corstorphine's urgent demand was as much for Shamila.

Robb typed for confirmation.

The phone chirped and Robb opened the attached photograph. Phoebe's frightened face stared back at them, her mouth taped over. A copy of that morning's *Courier* headline could be seen at the bottom of the shot.

Corstorphine grabbed the phone out of Robb's hands, searching the picture for anything that might provide a clue of their whereabouts. Phoebe's face filled most of the screen, a flash making her skin appear pale and leaving the background in darkness.

'Cow Hill?' Corstorphine wondered. 'He can be seen from miles around. How's he expecting to get away from meeting you there?'

'I don't care, as long as I have Phoebe.' Robb shoved the earrings back in their pouch and reached for a waterproof jacket.

'Hold on, Robb. We have to tell the Major Investigations Team.' Corstorphine reached out to rest his hand on Robb's arm.

He shook off Corstorphine's hand. 'He said no police! I can't risk it.'

'Don't be daft, son. You can't guarantee he'll give Phoebe back once he has the jewels. You have to involve the police if you want to see Phoebe again. It's the only way.'

Corstorphine could see the battle going on in Robb's mind. 'Trust me. They've had to deal with things like this before.'

Robb let out a long, drawn-out sigh. 'Alright. Tell me what I have to do.'

PC Bill McAdam straightened his back from surveying the leaf litter at the top of Rookery Hill, feeling his muscles complain at the unnatural posture they'd been subject to for the last few hours. Above his head, crows laughed derisibly at his failed attempts to find anything of use to the investigation, their harsh caws echoing from tree to tree.

He gave up and returned to his parked patrol car, scraped the worst of the mud off his boots and used his radio to call through to the station. DI Brown's Glaswegian accent tersely responded to his update.

'Aye, well. Make your way back to the station. We'll have another update at twelve-thirty once everyone's back and take it from there. Over.'

Bill headed back towards town, his thoughts on his own wife and her imminent childbirth. He couldn't imagine what he'd be like if she'd been the one taken. All he knew for sure is that whoever did it would pay, policeman or not. He had a sudden urge to call her and check if she was alright. There was no reason she wouldn't be, but with everything going on nothing felt as certain as it used to.

'Hi love, just checking in on you.'

Caitlin's amused voice answered back. 'You think I'm having an affair or something?'

That was one concern he didn't have to worry about. 'No, I was just seeing if you're alright.'

'Due date's not for a week. Don't worry, you'll be the first to know when I feel a contraction!'

Her ability to deal so calmly with the whole childbirth scenario was a constant amazement to him. Their life was about to be turned upside down, she was going to have their first baby, yet Caitlin treated it all like it was simply an everyday event.

'Any news on Shamila? Have you found the Carstairs patient?'

'No. Everyone's out looking for him and the people he's holding hostage.' Everyone except the sergeant, he reminded himself. He pictured Molly sitting in the office after Lamb had brought her in, that vacant stare into her own diminishing future.

'What about that Suzie girl? Is she being looked after? I worry about her now I'm not at work. I think sometimes I'm the only one who knows she exists!'

'I'll swing by on the way back to the station.' Bill changed direction to take a detour towards the flats. 'I had to leave her with the locksmith. I'll see if everything's alright. You take it easy and stop worrying about anyone else – you have enough going on in your own life.'

He made for Suzie's block of flats after ending the call.

Flat 5D sported a shiny new lock. Bill rapped on the door and listened.

'Who is it?'

He stood back to afford Suzie a full view of him in his uniform. 'PC Bill McAdam, Suzie. Remember I took you to the station and sorted out new keys for you?'

She opened the door, and he was relieved to see a security chain fitted. The locksmith must have taken her under his wing and added that for free.

'How are you doing?'

'I'm fine, thank you.' The chain remained in place.

'Has that boy been back to bother you?'

Suzie shook her head in response.

'That's good. Is there anything you need, anything I can help with?' Bill stood there feeling useless. This was a job for the social workers, not the police.

'No. I've got a key and a spare.' Suzie held up a key and gave him a smile.

She didn't seem to be in any danger.

'Well, you mind you keep it safe. If that boy comes back, don't let him in. Call the police – do you know how to do that?'

She nodded enthusiastically. '999!'

'That's right. You call us and we'll make sure you're safe. OK?'

'OK.'

Bill left it at that. He'd done all he could – and had a locksmith bill to pay. He hesitated at the lift door, then continued until he reached the stairs, climbing down from the fifth floor to ground level. There was someone coming up, their steps at first confident then beginning to falter as they drew closer. When Bill turned the corner towards the second floor, he was face to face with the youth he'd pursued yesterday lunchtime. He grabbed him before he had the chance to turn and run.

'Wait there.' His grip on the boy's shoulder made any other option impossible. 'I want words with you.'

He wanted more than words, and here in the stairwell away from prying eyes, it would be easy for the boy to 'have an accident'.

'I haven't done anything!' His voice was shrill with panic.

'We'll see about that. What were you doing in Suzie's flat?'

'I was helping her out, see. Thought she needed help.' The bravado returned as the lies came fluently.

Bill merely held him more tightly until the boy began wincing in pain.

'You're hurting me!'

'I'll do more than that. You were keeping Suzie locked in her flat. Do you know how long in prison you'll get for that?'

'I wasn't! I just took a key. She was letting me stay, like.'

'You can tell that to the court. You're coming with me.'

'No, I haven't done anything. You can't arrest me.'

Bill was beginning to feel his day was improving. He reached for the handcuffs with his spare hand, allowing a smile to cross his face.

'Can't I now?'

The boy was panic-stricken, attempting to wrench himself free of the PC's grip. Bill increased the pressure beyond what he needed to simply hold the boy, seeing his knees starting to give way under the pain inflicted on his shoulder.

'Stop! You're breaking my shoulder. Look, I can help you.' An air of desperation had entered his voice as Bill calmly clipped one wrist into the cuffs. He reached for the other arm, pulling the boy's hands together.

'You really want to add attempting to bribe a police officer to the list, son?' The second wrist secured with a satisfying click.

'No, it's not that. I can tell you where one of the scarecrows is. The one in today's newspaper.'

Bill's eyes narrowed dangerously as he looked the boy up and down. 'What do you know about the scarecrows?'

'You'll have to let me go first.'

'Nice try, son. Come on, you're coming with me to the station. If you've anything useful to tell us, you can talk to the inspector.'

Bill checked the cuffs were secure and grabbed the back of the boy's jacket to march him down the remaining stairs. He couldn't resist being a little over forceful at each corner as the boy was slammed into the walls.

'Watch where you're going, son.' Bill felt his smile would likely stay in place all the way to the station.

The snack van was open for business and a small queue of workmen waited in line for an early lunch. Their ubiquitous white vehicles circled it like wagons. As Frankie left the patrol car with Lamb, the line turned as one to gawp, spotting the uniform and then a flicker of interest as they concentrated on her. She ignored them, leaving Phil to exchange banter with those he recognised, and made straight for the jovial character flipping burgers inside his food truck. The smell of frying bacon made her realise she'd not eaten since yesterday.

'I was hoping you may be able to help.' Frankie stared down the painter at the head of the queue, his mouth closing as he thought better of arguing. This was not the day to start anything, her patience was stretched thin as it was.

'What do you want, love?'

Frankie held back her anger. She wasn't anyone's love, not today.

'There was an abduction around 2 p.m. yesterday, from the clinic opposite.' She pointed towards Shamila's office, the door still covered in police tape. 'We have reason to believe the suspect had been keeping the place under observation for a few days. Can you remember seeing anything unusual, anyone sat in their car who may have been keeping an eye on the units opposite?'

He expertly flipped the burger onto a roll, added lettuce and tomato as he thought.

'Can't say I have. Too busy to spend time looking around.' He raised his attention from the task at hand to call to the painter. 'Here's your burger, want sauce with that?'

The middle-aged man in paint-spattered overalls reached for his burger and began emptying the contents of a proffered tomato sauce bottle into his roll.

'So, nobody new here – someone who's not one of your regulars?' Frankie persisted.

The snack van owner made a show of thinking, staring up at the greasy ceiling in search of inspiration. He began scratching his chin to add to the pantomime of concentration.

'There's the guy with the beard. Haven't seen him before.' The words issued messily through a half-eaten burger.

Frankie turned her attention to the painter, trying not to see the tomato sauce covering his double chin.

'What guy?'

The painter suddenly had an attentive audience as the queue quietened. Even the snack van owner managed to look interested and leaned on the greasy counter to hear more clearly.

'You know.' He cast around the line for support. 'The beard. And long hair.'

Frankie's heart began to race. 'What about him? Did you see his vehicle?'

Almost the entire queue spoke as one.

'Taxi!'

'Make, model, registration?' Frankie optimistically reached for her notebook.

'Dunno. Taxi.' The painter wiped his hands clean on his overalls, adding a line of ketchup to his Jackson Pollock white canvas.

The queue all shrugged now the distraction was over and moved forward in line as the next order was called out.

'Come on, Phil.' She called out to the PC who was in animated conversation.

As she climbed into the patrol car, the radio crackled with her call sign. She recognised DI Brown's nasal tone straight away.

'You find anything?'

'People using the snack van report seeing a man with a beard and long hair. He drove off in a taxi. We don't have any further details.'

'We'll check the local firms.' The DI's terse voice responded. 'There's a briefing at twelve-thirty, you can update us all on your findings then. In the meanwhile, call in on the hospital – see if this McKeown character is able to give us anything on what his daughter was working on.'

Frankie's heart sank. She knew what was coming.

'And you'd better tell him his daughter's dead – unless that finishes him off.'

Phil had climbed into the passenger seat and heard every word. Neither commented on the DI's callous wording – they all coped with passing on the worst news in their own way. His was to cover the emotion with a thick layer of Glasgow hard man. Hers was to disassociate from the task and make-believe she was acting the part. Each time it still left an emotional scar.

She turned out of the industrial park and made for the hospital.

'Maybe he'll know something about his daughter that can help us find this fucking madman.' Phil voiced his frustration out loud.

'Maybe.' It was all she could bring herself to say.

When they arrived at the hospital, Frankie put an arm out to stop Lamb from leaving the car.

'Best just one of us goes, Phil.'

The young PC couldn't hide the look of relief that flooded his face. Frankie drew a deep breath and prepared to give Mart McKeown the worst news.

The reception staff recognised her as soon as she entered the building.

'Frankie, have you found them?'

She puzzled over how news of Shamila and Phoebe's abduction was so widely known before seeing *The Courier*'s headlines. The newspapers were displayed in front of the small retail unit in the open reception area. The paper's front page displaying *Police Inspector's Wife Missing* in the largest print they could fit on the page.

She shook her head, processing the fact that the entire town now had details of the kidnapping. Once the shock of seeing it spread across the front page had lessened, Frankie had the hope that this might bring in witnesses who could help.

'I'm here to see Mart McKeown. We were with him last night.'

'Of course. He's in ward 2B, just up the corridor and second right.' The receptionist switched into professional mode. 'He's made a good recovery.'

'Thank you.' Frankie gave a tight smile and made for the ward. The corridor smelt of antiseptic, white-coated doctors and nurses stared silently at her as she passed them.

Mart McKeown was sat up in a hospital bed, a drip attached to one arm and a fingertip pulse oximeter clipped onto one finger. A reassuring steady beep accompanied his pulse, quickening as he caught Frankie approaching his bed.

'Have you found her?' Mart's voice trembled with anxiety.

She cursed silently. How was she going to tell a man who'd just had a heart attack that his only child was dead?

SIXTY-SEVEN

BRIEFING

The police station office was fuller than normal. Three members of
the MIT team stood close to the evidence wall, DI Brown
surveying his audience with serious eyes. Corstorphine stood to
one side, part of the team yet excluded operationally. He couldn't
shake off the impression that he was having a bad nightmare, a
state of mind not helped by his lack of sleep. Robb McCoach had
joined Bill McAdam, Frankie and Phil Lamb to complete the set.

'Right!' DI Brown started decisively. 'This is what we have.'

He turned to face the evidence wall, began adding details
whilst talking.

'Frankie has confirmed the sighting of someone meeting the
description of the abductor at the clinic. He drives a taxi – we don't
have any further description apart from an observation that he had
a beard and long hair. DC Knight has checked with the local taxi
firm. Their only driver has an alibi for every hour of the working
day.

Corstorphine interrupted DI Brown as he stopped to take a
breath.

'The description we have is most likely a disguise. We've found
a wig matching the long hair – the beard could be equally false.

The taxi is too obvious – keep in mind he could have fitted a taxi sign to almost any vehicle.'

DI Brown turned slowly to fix Corstorphine in his sights like a gunslinger.

'Thank you, DI Corstorphine.' His expression suggested he didn't appreciate the interruption. 'As DI Corstorphine says, we should treat the description of the taxi driver with caution.'

His gaze settled on each of them in turn, daring anyone else to speak out without invitation before continuing.

'Nobody recalls seeing anyone deliver the parcels to either DI Corstorphine or the Courier offices. In Glenarty we've gone door to door and again, nobody saw anything on the night of Trudi McKeown's murder.' He turned to face them.

'What we *do* have is video footage of the character stealing a scarecrow from Treasury Cottage. This is the best enhancement we can come up with.' He held up a grainy black and white image of a man carrying a scarecrow. No details were discernible.

'Forensics have confirmed that traces of blood found on Trudi McKeown's clothing correspond to Duncan Lewis's DNA. They've obtained another match from the items DI Corstorphine found on Rookery Hill and on the packaging sent to *The Courier*, Robb McCoach and Corstorphine's homes. There's now no doubt that Duncan Lewis is our man.'

He pointed a dry marker pen towards Robb McCoach. 'I've taken the unusual step of asking both DI Corstorphine and Robb McCoach to join us for this briefing because they have critical information. Robb has agreed to pay a ransom for the safe return of his sister. This is happening at Cow Hill at 2 p.m. today. He's asked us to follow the kidnapper's instructions and stay away from the location.'

'I just want Phoebe back,' Robb interjected. 'I don't care how it's done as long as she's not harmed.'

There was a collective rumble of disapproval from the group. DI Brown held up both palms to quieten them down.

'I know. It goes against everything we do, but Cow Hill is an exposed location. There's no possibility of us being able to conceal ourselves and we can't put Phoebe or the other hostages in any more danger. But when Duncan Lewis makes an appearance to collect the jewels Mr McCoach has arranged to exchange, we've got him. There's no way anyone can make their way off that hill without us being able to apprehend them. I've asked for a helicopter to supply additional cover, but it's unlikely they can divert that resource in the time we have available. Do you want to take over at this point?'

He stood aside for Corstorphine to take his place.

The DI stood in front of the crazy wall, the focus of a sea of faces.

'Cow Hill can only be accessed easily from these locations.'

Behind his back, DI Brown was pinning an Ordnance Survey map onto the wall. Corstorphine reached for a red marker.

'Here, at the edge of the new housing at the top of the town.' He stabbed at a location where new housing had colonised the last available building land. Beyond that point, a steep gradient and rocky outcrops made further development unprofitable.

'And here, at the leisure centre.' Another red blob was added to the map. 'There's a footpath up the hill running from both locations. His only other option is to hike across the hills from the north or east and he hasn't the time to do that.'

DI Brown took over. 'He's only given us an hour to prepare for this, and we have to assume Duncan Lewis will be watching out for any signs of police activity. I'm going to base myself at the leisure centre which is the most likely place he'll be starting from. DCs Robbins and Knight, you're with me. None of us are going to be recognised by the locals and we're in plain clothes so we stand the best chance of remaining incognito. DC McKenzie, PC McAdam – you take the other location but park well away and out of sight. PC Lamb, you take a patrol car here, out of view of the main road in case he makes it to a vehicle. Wait at least twenty minutes before leaving the station – I don't want Duncan Lewis spooked by the sight of a police car.' DI Brown fixed them with a steely look. 'This may be our only chance at catching him. Don't fuck it up!'

'Sir?' PC McAdam held up a hand.

'What is it, McAdam?'

DI Brown had a way with words, Corstorphine thought, talking to McAdam as if he was beneath contempt.

'I've got this lad in custody. He says he knows where one of the missing scarecrows is.'

'We haven't time for that. We need to move. Now!'

DI Brown turned to face Corstorphine. 'You have to stay out of this, Corstorphine. If there was any way of keeping you involved, I would do so, but you know the score.'

'I'll mind the shop whilst you try and catch the bastard. I can at least make myself useful looking after the lad in custody.'

'Aye, good point. Don't want him committing suicide whilst the station unattended. Let's go – and try not to be obvious. Have we enough unmarked cars?'

Frankie responded first. 'I've my own car here, sir. I'll take Bill up to our location.'

'Let's do this. Keep radio silence, he's clever enough to be listening in on us with a scanner. Just don't let Duncan Lewis get away!'

Corstorphine watched them leave, wishing he could be with them and doing something more useful than babysitting some kid Bill McAdam had brought in. He held on to the small glimmer of hope that Duncan had allowed greed to affect his judgement. The location was remote enough to make his escape almost impossible, but the worry remained that they were dealing with a resourceful and intelligent adversary. What if he managed to evade capture?

SIXTY-EIGHT
LEGOLAND

Frankie parked at her destination. Identical houses clung to the hill, lining both sides of the street and making her feel like she'd entered Legoland.

'What do you think?' Bill McAdam spoke for the first time since they'd left the station. 'This Duncan Lewis – think he's stupid enough to arrange a meet here?'

The same question that had been worrying Corstorphine circled her head like a raptor searching for easy meat.

'I don't know, Bill. He'll be exposed on the hill. Easy to spot and there's nowhere to hide.'

'Well, he's not in his right mind so...'

That's an understatement! They were dealing with a man whose mental health issues had caused him to kill his wife and leave her body parts hidden around the Scottish Highlands. The trouble was, even if Duncan's psychosis had returned, he remained a cunning and dangerous criminal no matter which personality he manifested.

'I just hope we catch him – and he tells us what he's done with the hostages.'

'Do you think Shamila and Phoebe McCoach are even still alive?' Bill's voice had dropped even though they were both alone.

It was a question they all had at the front of their minds, not least Corstorphine and Robb McCoach. Frankie couldn't begin to imagine the stress they must both be under. But she refused to consider that option.

'He's asked for a ransom. I think he's keeping them alive, for whatever reason. We just have to find him before he changes his mind.' Frankie winced internally after using that expression for someone suffering from dissociative identity disorder or psychosis. Whatever the eventual diagnosis, Duncan Lewis was criminally insane and his actions impossible to predict.

'What's the story with the lad you brought in?' Frankie purposively changed the subject.

'Wee scrote had tried taking over this poor woman's flat. She has a learning disability and lives on her own. No carers or social visits as far as I could see.'

Frankie picked up on his careful use of language. Those training courses were having an effect.

'Why would he do that?' she asked for her own benefit.

'Dunno. Maybe cuckooing for drug distribution – but I didn't see any sign of it. Probably caught him before he got started.'

'You said he knew something about the scarecrows?'

'Aye. Once I'd collared him, he started trying to bargain with me. He said he knew where the scarecrows were being kept. The ones he'd seen in the paper.'

Frankie cursed. She'd not had time to pick up a copy of *The Courier*. This wouldn't be the first time that reporter was ahead of the police investigation.

'Which scarecrows?'

'I dunno. I don't read the rag. Suppose it's the two missing from Glenarty. The McKeown lookalike and whatever was taken from that woman's house on the video.'

'Shit! We should have heard what he had to say. If he knows where they are, then the hostages may be nearby.'

'Shall I radio through to the DI?' Bill reached for his radio.

Her hand stopped him before he began broadcasting. 'No. DI Brown said to keep radio silence, remember? I've a better idea.'

Frankie pulled out her mobile, selected Corstorphine's name and pressed the call button.

'Corstorphine.' His voice was so full of hope that her heart sank. 'Have you found something?'

'No. We're just waiting in the car for Duncan Lewis to make an appearance. Robb's started up Cow Hill from the Leisure Centre path. That youth that Bill brought in...'

'Michael McKay, your man Alex's boy. What about him?'

Frankie stopped in shock. 'Mikey? That's Alex's son we're holding?'

'I thought you knew? I've just booked him in and given him a cup of tea. I can't really do anything else as officially I shouldn't even be here.'

'No, I wasn't there when he was brought in.'

Bill interrupted the conversation. 'That's Alex's boy? I'm sorry, Frankie. I wouldn't have gone in so hard if I'd known.'

She held up a hand to stop him. 'It's OK, Bill, you were right to bring him in. Alex has been worried sick about him.'

She returned to talking to Corstorphine. 'Have a word with the boy. Bill says he knows where the missing scarecrows are being stored. Shamila and the others may be close. We're on radio silence in case Duncan has a scanner and can't leave the area.'

'Understood. I'll talk to him now.'

The phone abruptly cut off, leaving Frankie to her thoughts. If Mikey was involved with drugs, this wasn't going to go well for him, much less help with her relationship with his dad.

'I can see him!' Bill handed over the binoculars he'd taken from the station.

Frankie followed the line of his finger and found the lone figure of Robb McCoach making his way up the mountain path. She swept the hillside searching for another figure. So far, Robb was on his own.

SIXTY-NINE
ALONE

Corstorphine raced to the cells after talking with Frankie. Mikey sat on the single cot, his head raised from a contemplation of the cell floor at the sound of the DI's hurried approach. Corstorphine unlocked the door and impatiently motioned for him to follow.

'Out of there, lad, follow me.'

He waited until they were in the interview room and told him to sit. PC Lamb looked on with undisguised curiosity as they marched past him, reaching for his cap in preparation to taking the patrol car out.

'Hang on for a minute, Phil. I want you to witness this.' The PC joined Corstorphine in the interview room as he read the boy his rights and reminded him how important it was to tell the truth.

'We'll get to the reasons why you forcibly occupied that young woman's flat against her will, but for now I want you to tell me everything you know about the missing scarecrows.'

'It was just a laugh. We did it for a joke.' Mikey gave every indication that he was close to tears.

'Who's we?' Corstorphine asked.

Mikey looked even more uncomfortable. 'I'm not grassing on anyone.' He sounded like a bad actor playing a role he was totally unsuited for.

Corstorphine had no time for games. 'Tell me where the scare-crows are or you're going to be facing a year in a young offenders' prison.'

The boy's face paled. 'You can't do that. I wanted to join the police!' His attempt at bravado evaporated in front of the DI's stern face.

'Just tell me what you know, lad. We'll deal with everything else later. My wife is one of the people that are missing, so I don't have time to waste.' Corstorphine glanced at the clock on the inter-view room wall, showing 13:30. In another thirty minutes, Shamila would have been missing for twenty-four hours. He knew it was only a number but couldn't shake off the importance of finding her within that time.

'Olly said it would be a laugh if we stole one and left it some-where for the polis to find. Then we saw the news, about the body being found on the farm. He said we'd better keep quiet. In case you lot thought we were something to do with it.'

'Olly who?' Corstorphine shook his head at the stupidity of the boy sat opposite.

A look of surprise crossed Mikey's face, swiftly followed by the understanding that he'd just given away part of his accomplice's identity.

'Not saying,' he said miserably.

'Where did you take it from?' The DI tried to contain his impa-tience. Any hope that the boy might have had something of any use to the investigation was fading with every word he uttered.

'Went to Glenarty. The place is full of them.'

'Where in Glenarty?'

'I dunno. One of the houses on the street. Had a scarecrow held up on the pillars outside the door. We untied it and stuck it in Olly's car.'

'Olly's car?' the DI repeated.

'Aye. Then we dumped it in the bus shelter. Thought the bus would stop for him.' He smiled hopefully in case the DI shared the joke.

'Which bus shelter?'

'I dunno. The first one outside Glenarty. I dunno what the place is called. There's like only three or four houses there. Don't even know why they have a bus shelter.'

Corstorphine felt the last grains of hope slip through his fingers. All they had now was the hope of catching Duncan Lewis on Cow Hill.

'What about the other scarecrow?'

Mikey looked blankly at him.

'What other scarecrow?'

'You told the constable you knew where the scarecrows were being stored. Scarecrows. Plural.' Corstorphine spelt it out for him.

'We only took one. That's what Olly said would happen – we'd get accused of taking the one from the farm as well. It wasn't us!' Mikey's voice squeaked in desperation.

Corstorphine knew he was wasting his time. The boy didn't have the ability to lie as convincingly as this.

'Can I go now?' Mikey had reverted from swaggering man to small boy during the course of his interview.

'Why were you in that woman's flat, Mikey?' The DI managed to keep his tone neutral despite the helpless rage building inside him.

'Had a row with my dad. I needed somewhere to sleep and she'd wrecked my bike. Thought she wouldn't mind having a lodger for a day or two. I wanted to teach my dad a lesson – show him I can look after myself like. I didn't mean anything by it. I bought her some food,' he added hopefully.

Corstorphine wasn't a catholic, but he identified with the priest in his confessional box at that moment.

'We'll see if the woman wants to press charges. In the meantime, I suggest you go straight home and apologise to your dad.' His tired tone altered to more of a bark as Mikey stood up. 'I've not finished with you yet!'

Mikey collapsed back into his seat.

'You're quite likely to be facing criminal charges, in which case you can forget about a career in the police. There's also the small matter of apologising to the young woman you terrified and an apology to the Glenarty family whose scarecrow you took. Wait here.'

He turned to Phil. 'One more minute, Phil – and then you'd better take the patrol car to wait for further instructions.'

Corstorphine pulled the enhanced picture from Treasury Cottage video footage, compared it to the boy sat in the interview room and placed it down on the table in front of Mikey.

'This you?'

An unhappy nod gave him his answer.

'I need you to speak, for the recording,' Corstorphine advised.

'Yes.'

'OK. You're free to leave. Interview terminated at 13:45.'

Corstorphine watched the boy's departure with mixed emotions. There went another hope for finding Shamila. Mikey had wasted valuable time.

'I'll be off, sir.' PC Lamb stood in the open doorway, unsure of what else to say.

'I'll stay here, for the time being.'

The police station door closed leaving him feeling more alone than he'd ever been in his life.

Robb McCoach approached the top of Cow Hill. It was almost 2 p.m., only a few minutes before his rendezvous with the man who'd taken his sister. The earrings sat heavily in his pocket, but it was the fear that Phoebe might have been harmed that weighed down every step he took. It was one of those autumnal days when the wind held its cold breath, giving the sun's heat a chance to be felt on bare skin. From his elevated vantage point, Robb could see for miles. The sun wasn't warm enough to raise a blue haze so even the most distant mountains appeared in high definition. On a day such as this he loved nothing more than to be out on the hills – but not today.

He stopped on the summit, shielding his eyes from the sun's glare as he swept a 360-degree turn. There wasn't anyone else on the hill or he'd have spotted them. The realisation that Duncan Lewis wasn't going to show hit him like a sledgehammer blow to his heart. What did it mean? Was Phoebe going to be released? He reached in a pocket for the radio DI Brown had issued him, but the warning not to break radio silence stopped his hand.

Then a new sound entered the landscape. A harsh buzzing as if someone was driving up the path on a trail bike. Robb tried to identify the direction of the sound, turning his head back and forth until he locked onto the source. It didn't originate from the ground.

At first, he thought there must be a light plane. Even though the sky was mostly free of clouds, it took him a few minutes to spot the small dot making towards his position. As it drew closer and hovered high above his head, he realised he was being observed by a drone.

The drone operator must have been satisfied that he was on his own as it swooped down to within touching distance. Robb didn't know what he was expected to do and began shouting at it in frustration.

'What do you want? Where's Phoebe?'

The drone didn't respond, remaining within arm's length as if to taunt him further. Then he saw a small bag slung underneath on a cord. His attention was caught by a curl of paper protruding from the bag and vibrating in the rotor downdraft. He reached out and the drone lowered the bag into his hand, allowing the message to be retrieved before lifting up and out of reach.

If you want to see Phoebe alive, put the earrings in the bag and seal it. When I have confirmed they are what you say, then I'll tell you where your sister is.

Robb was acutely aware of the drone's single glass eye observing him. He didn't have any choice – the police weren't going to be able to follow the drone. He nodded acceptance and the drone lowered within reach so he could transfer the jewels from his pocket into the suspended bag. Robb cursed inwardly, belatedly realising that no one had thought to attach a tracking device as he watched the drone head back towards town.

His radio crackled, DI Brown's urgent voice issuing tinnily from the speaker.

'What's happened? Was that a drone?'

'Aye. I had to put the ransom in it. He left a message saying Phoebe would be released once he'd checked the jewels.'

'Which direction did it go?'

'Back towards the town. I lost sight of it.'

'Fuck's sake!' The DI lost all attempts at keeping calm under pressure.

He could hear urgent shouts as DI Brown told his two DCs to go outside and look for the drone before the radio returned to silence. Up on Cow Hill, the first breath of wind announced a change in the weather. A line of dark clouds lined the western mountains like a smudge. Robb started back down the path. He'd done everything that was asked of him. Why then did he feel that he'd failed his sister?

DI Brown was apoplectic. Why hadn't he considered Duncan Lewis might use a drone? The location and gentle weather made it an obvious choice – visibility was excellent for the drone operator, the hilltop an easy target and he'd have known they'd place units at all the usual access points. He'd been made a fool of, and that sat very uncomfortably on his wide shoulders.

'Get out there and look for the bloody thing!'

His two DCs moved with alacrity. They knew him too well not to get out of his way when his blood was up.

The DI followed them outside, searching the blue sky for a vanishing dot. Somewhere at the edge of his hearing he thought he could hear the fading bluebottle sound of the drone's rotors, but it was already too late to follow.

'Fuck!' Duncan had outplayed them all. How in God's name was he going to find the hostages now? The fact that a fellow offi-cer's wife had been taken made the whole thing that more personal. He called Frankie over the radio.

'Foxtrot Kilo. Foxtrot Kilo from DI Brown, over.'

'Foxtrot Kilo receiving, over.'

'Have you sight of a drone, should be overhead travelling from the top of Cow Hill towards your location? Over.'

'Heard something a minute ago but no sign of it now, sir. Over.'

'You didn't see where it went?'

'Sorry, sir. Over.'

'Tell PC Lamb to drive to this location and wait for McCoach to come down off the hill, then meet us all back at the station. Over.' He stopped transmitting and glowered at his two DCs.

'Get back in the car. We'll never find the drone now.'

The drive to the police station was completed in total silence. DI Brown tried not to imagine how Corstorphine was going to react to the news.

DI Corstorphine overheard the entire exchange over the radio. Of course Duncan Lewis wouldn't have walked into such an obvious trap. He'd selected Cow Hill knowing they'd stake out the area and had outwitted them so easily it was almost embarrassing. Even the timing, leaving them little option but to respond in the way that they had. It was too predictable. If they wanted to catch Duncan, then they had to outthink him.

He glanced at the clock. It was now over twenty-four hours since Shamila and Phoebe had been taken, and they were still no closer to finding them. He tried not to imagine any outcome other than finding the hostages safe and well, but the images of William Haddow's scarecrow kept intruding into his memory.

Corstorphine entered his office. The room had developed an underlying smell of stale tobacco, so he propped the door open before sitting at his desk. Shamila's photograph had been pushed to one side and with a flash of anger he moved it back so it regained pride of place beside his computer screen. It was only when her picture started to blur that he realised tears were forming in his eyes. He brushed them away with the back of his hand, feeling the salty wetness on his skin.

The sound of DI Brown and his two shadows entering the

main office caught him off guard. Corstorphine hastily reached for his handkerchief to make a show of blowing his nose, using the distraction to dry any tears still adhering to his cheeks.

'Not good news I'm afraid.' DI Brown strode into the office, stopping dead when he saw Corstorphine had taken his seat.

'I heard. On the radio,' Corstorphine explained. He vacated his chair, and the two DIs performed an awkward ballet as they swapped positions.

'We're struggling here, Jim. I don't know how else to put it. Somehow Duncan is managing to stay off the radar and is playing us for fools. The only hope we have now is for him to slip up when he hands Phoebe McCoach over now that her brother has paid the ransom.'

Corstorphine knew how much of a long shot that hope was. Now that Duncan had the jewels, he could renege on the agreement – he'd only be risking his own capture by letting Phoebe go.

'I interviewed the lad in custody. Mikey McKay. DC McKenzie said he had information about the missing scarecrows. The interview's on the recorder. He's admitted to taking the one from Glenarty. It's him on the doorcam video, not Duncan Lewis.'

'Fuck! Did he own up to taking the other one as well? The pop star?'

'Mart McKeown,' Corstorphine added. 'No. He said they only took the one and I believe him.'

'They?'

'He was with one of his mates. Just youthful high spirits. They thought it would be fun until they saw *The Courier*'s news.'

DI Brown looked up sharply at the mention of *The Courier*. 'That paper knows a damn sight more about this case than they should do!'

'I'll deal with that,' Corstorphine asserted.

DI Brown's combative stance slackened. 'It's your team,' he said dismissively.

'Are you following any other lines of enquiry?' Corstorphine already knew the answer but still hoped that the MIT had something else to go on.

One look at DI Brown's expression told Corstorphine the truth of it.

'Forensics have confirmed Duncan Lewis's DNA on the brown paper packaging left at *The Courier*'s offices and your home address, as well as the items found at Rookery Hill. For an intelligent man he's being careless spreading his DNA around. They've identified his hairs and blood samples on everything he's handled, as well as his prints left at Richard Bryce's home. He can't hope to hide Shamila and Phoebe for much longer. It's only a matter of time before we find him.'

DI Brown's words were meant as a comfort, Corstorphine knew that, but he felt them as the final nails being hammered into Shamila's coffin.

'Look.' DI Brown's features softened. 'There's nothing you can do here, James, and you look as if you didn't get much sleep last night. Let me have one of the constables drive you home and we'll be in touch the very instant I have something for you.'

'I'll take myself home,' Corstorphine countered. He walked through the main office, his gaze sweeping over the crazy wall as he left. The two remaining MIT officers made no comment as he shut the door behind him, their silence a tacit expectation that the outcome they all now expected was the worst possible scenario.

Frankie and Bill McAdam pulled into the police station car park as Corstorphine triggered his door lock open. She made directly for him.

'Hello, sir. Bad news I'm afraid.'

He stopped her there. 'It's OK, Frankie. I listened in on the radio and DI Brown's provided me with an update. I talked with young Mikey – he's the character in the doorbell footage nicking the scarecrow in Glenarty. I've informed DI Brown.'

Frankie's face fell. Corstorphine could sympathise even through his own concerns. She had enough on her shoulders without having Alex's boy in trouble as well.

'Is he still in the cells, sir?'

Corstorphine shook his head. 'I told him to go back home and apologise to Alex. He's a distraction none of us need at the moment.'

Bill shuffled awkwardly beside her. 'What's the course of action now, sir?'

'You two are working for DI Brown now. I'm not even meant to be here.' He pulled his car door open and then hesitated. 'How's it been left with Robb McCoach and the ransom?'

Frankie made a deliberate effort to talk up the events on Cow Hill. 'Lamb's waiting for him to come back off the hill. Duncan Lewis has taken the ransom. We're just waiting to hear where Phoebe is so she can be reunited with her brother. Hopefully, she'll be able to give us some idea where the others are being held.'

Corstorphine saw right through her. He knew they shared the same thoughts about how the ransom exchange had been handled, and the likelihood that Phoebe would be released.

'Keep in touch. I'm going home. Didn't manage to sleep at all last night and I'm no bloody use to anyone if I can't think straight.'

'We'll catch him, sir, and bring Shamila back.' Bill McAdam called a final message before he shut the car door.

Corstorphine forced a smile and pulled away, even though he felt his heart was being squeezed by a vice. They had nothing. No leads, no ideas, no hope. It would take a miracle to find Shamila, and he had no faith any divine intervention would be forthcoming. All he had was his mind, and he felt as if he was losing that.

SEVENTY-TWO
PREMONITION

Corstorphine hadn't slept since Wednesday. He glanced at the clock, still ticking steadily on the mantlepiece and keeping better time than it ever had. It reminded him of his previous wife; her death to cancer and the woman who left a message inscribed on the back. The time was 16:30. A colourful autumnal sunset shone through the windows in stark contrast to the shadow on his soul. The last thing he wanted to do was sleep, yet his mind was muddled when more than anything he needed clarity.

He'd left the police station with the weight of despair heavy on his shoulders. Corstorphine had nothing more he could give them, and it was with an air of utter dejection that he collapsed onto his bed. Sleep remained elusive, as he knew it would. How could he even contemplate closing his eyes when Shamila was still missing? Daemon Aticus's book remained on his phone. He propped himself up on pillows, opened the photo App and began skimming through the text hunting for anything that might lead him closer to Shamila.

Gather your souls, for tonight we unite with the ones we have lost. You cast me aside at Beltane. I endured Litha, Lughnasa and Mabon without

you. Only Samhain can bring us together. Your soul forged to mine in the
flame. So mote it be!

Corstorphine felt his eyelids dropping. The text was impenetrably obscure. Even with his mind unclouded by exhaustion, he'd struggle to make sense of any of it – far less discover clues that might lead him to Shamila.

When he forced his eyes open, it was light outside. His phone had slipped from his hand, laying screen down on the bedcovers. It had been the vibration that had woken him, and he fumbled to reach for it even as it fell silent. For a few seconds, his fingers remained numb, and he felt his muscles complaining as he attempted to swing his legs off the bed. When he finally managed to stand, the room swayed alarmingly in his vision, causing him to sit back down before he fell. He forced his eyes to focus on the screen as he searched for the time. It was 8:12 on the 31st October. He'd slept through the night!

In a panic, Corstorphine searched for missed calls and hit Frankie's number.

'Morning, sir. I was trying to reach you.'

'Aye, I didn't get to the phone in time.' Corstorphine felt guilty for having slept at all, never mind for sleeping close to twelve hours straight. 'What have we got?' He scarcely dared to breathe as he waited for Frankie's update.

'Phoebe McCoach has been released. She called us from the Glenarty shop just a few minutes ago. DCs Robbins and Knight are on their way now to pick her up.'

'Is she OK?'

'She sounded alright. A bit shaken up, but as far as I know, she's unharmed.'

'What about Shamila?'

There was a pause and Corstorphine's fists clenched in anticipation of news he never wanted to hear.

'We still haven't made any progress, sir. We were all working late last night until DI Brown called it a day. We're hoping Phoebe will be able to provide us with details that will help us find the others. I'll call you as soon as I have anything else.'

Corstorphine stared blankly at the bedroom wall.

The house retained an unnatural silence, a reminder of how it felt until Shamila had come into his life. The silence was so loud that he could feel the pressure of it on his eardrums – an oppressive force pressing in on all sides. Corstorphine worried that he was losing his mind. Above everything he felt an oppressive premonition that something was about to happen that would destroy his world, and he was powerless to stop it.

SEVENTY-THREE
PRIZE

Frankie glanced guiltily at DI Brown in his office. It was a risk talking to Corstorphine, but he needed to know what was happening, and this was a good chance whilst the two MIT DCs were out of the office. Bill McAdam gave her a conspiratorial look from over the top of his screen. She smiled in return.

They operated as two separate tribes, the MIT and existing staff, and DI Brown's overbearing attitude was only making that divide stronger. Frankie bent down to her screen again but took nothing in. Like the rest of them, they were waiting to see what Phoebe had to say. She was their only lead now.

They'd finished at eight o'clock yesterday evening after the debacle on Cow Hill. Duncan Lewis had played them like idiots, knowing full well that they'd have the site under surveillance. Now he'd taken Robb's ransom, and they were still none the wiser where he was hiding out or keeping his two hostages. One hostage, Frankie corrected herself. Only Shamila remained unaccounted for now he'd released Phoebe.

The call from Glenarty stores had galvanised the entire team. Same as Frankie, no one expected Duncan Lewis to make good on his exchange. This was the first mistake he'd made. All the same, a nagging doubt remained in Frankie's mind – why would he let

Phoebe go when he knew full well that the police would make use of everything she could give them?

Her screen came back into focus, the book by Daemon Aticus displayed two pages at a time. She read the same paragraph again and again in the hope that she'd see something that would lead them to him.

When the unholy trinity face the fire, then they will burn with a fragment of the passion I held for you. Then you'll understand how deeply I loved you. In borrowed rags you'll end your life, surrounded by the things you fear the most.

She had thought that he was referring to three hostages, but Phoebe's kidnapping was spur of the moment. Did that mean he planned on taking another two people? Phoebe's kidnap gave every impression of being opportunistic, a method for ensuring Shamila came quietly. That was reinforced by his surprising willingness to let her go now he had the ransom. In which case, was he planning on burning his hostages?

Frankie dismissed that thought. To start with, he'd left Richard Bryce's body at William Haddow's farm to be found, so his unholy trinity was missing at least one body.

She began making notes on a spare pad of paper. Corstorphine had accepted the possibility that this was a crime of passion. The entirety of *Done With Crying* was a tirade against the perceived injustice done to a spurned lover. Was it that far-fetched that Duncan Lewis had nursed feelings for Shamila during the years she'd treated him, and these had poisoned his mind when she left?

Corstorphine was the only one she could run these ideas past, but he was non-communicado and under the threat of a disciplinary if she ignored that order. There was also the difficulty of talking over these ideas when his wife was at the centre of it all.

Who would Duncan Lewis take to make his unholy trinity? Was Corstorphine in danger? If her instincts were correct, then he'd be the focus of Duncan's rage as the man who taken her away from him. He'd certainly want him punished, one way or another.

The arrival of DCs Robbins and Knight broke her concentration. Phoebe walked in between them like a prize nobody ever expected to win. She recognised Frankie and gave her a shy wave before being ushered into the DI's office.

All they could do now was wait.

SEVENTY-FOUR
PHOEBE'S STORY

Phoebe listened to the cross-sounding man with half her attention as he asked if she'd been hurt.

'What can you tell us about where you were being held?' The man they called DI Brown was asking her a question.

He was trying to be kind, she perceived that. Lowering and softening his harsh voice, but his eyes held the truth of it. She pictured the room she'd been put in.

'I was in a white room. There was a sleeping bag on the floor but no heating or windows. It smelt of damp and the paint was flaking off the walls. He'd put bottles of water and a pile of sand-wiches on a plate, but all the labels were missing.'

'Can you describe the outside of the building?' DI Brown's frown accompanied his words.

Phobe looked over his head and avoided his eyes. They made her feel uncomfortable.

'An old church. It was down a small road, almost hidden in trees. There were crows in the trees – I like crows. He drove us there in a taxi.'

The DI and his two constables were all writing furiously in paper notebooks.

'A taxi?' DI Brown asked in surprise.

'Yes. I thought Robb had hired it for me. He said Robb had sent him to take me home, but we had to collect Shamila first.'

The DI exchanged a look with one of the other policemen.

'Can you describe the taxi driver for me?'

'Long, dark hair, big beard.'

'Check taxi companies further afield. Bring in any driver matching that description.'

One of the officers left in a hurry. DI Brown turned his attention back to Phoebe.

'How far away is this church? Is that where he took you and Shamila?'

'Yes. Shamila didn't want to go. She was arguing with him until he said...'

'What did he say, Phoebe?'

She remembered when she had first felt frightened. When everything had gone wrong.

'He threatened to kill me,' she answered quietly. 'Then Shamila said Robb would pay anything to have me back.'

'I understand, Phoebe. That must have been very frightening for you. You're doing very well. Can you tell us how long the taxi took to reach the church?'

Phoebe tilted her head to one side as she considered. 'About an hour. I recognised the road, by Loch Lochy, and then we turned off to the right and the church was down a small road. It's all overgrown.'

She could feel the tension building in the small office.

'Was there anyone else there? Anyone in the church or helping the man who took you?'

'I don't know. He put me in the white room on my own. I don't know where Shamila went. I think he put her in the church – I couldn't hear anything through the walls.'

DI Brown produced a photograph of Duncan Lewis and laid it down on the desk. 'Is this the man who took you?'

Phoebe studied the picture. It didn't look anything like the taxi driver. 'No,' she said simply and shook her head from side to side in emphasis.

'What if he was wearing a long, black wig and had a false beard?' The DI encouraged.

She tilted her head, imagining the bald man with long black hair and his chin concealed in a beard. 'I don't think so,' she said hesitantly.

'OK. Tell me exactly what happened this morning. How did you get to Glenarty village?'

She brightened. This was easier.

'He told me to climb into the back of the taxi and he'd take me home to Robb.'

'Did he still have the long hair?'

'I don't know. He made me put a black bag over my head and lie down on the back seat. He told me to stay down if I wanted to see Robb.'

The DI scowled. 'You didn't see him, or Shamila or anyone else?'

'No.'

The only sound she could hear were pens scratching urgently across paper.

'Didn't you see the driver when he let you go? In Glenarty?'

'He said to wait for five minutes and then take my hood off. Once he'd let me out.'

DI Brown appeared puzzled. 'You didn't see him drive off?'

'No. I'm sorry.'

'OK, Phoebe, you've been a great help. I'm going to ask one of the constables to take you to the hospital for a check-up and I'll let Robb know you're safe.'

He opened the small office door and called to Frankie.

'Take Phoebe to the hospital for a check-up. She's had food and water and appears to be physically unharmed. We'll inform her brother and have him meet her there.'

Frankie came towards her and offered a hand. 'Come on, Phoebe. Let's get you home.'

Phoebe was glad to leave the men in the office. Their eyes were unkind and they stank of cigarettes. Not like the man who had kidnapped her. He smelt of cedarwood.

SEVENTY-FIVE
PROGNOSIS

Frankie waited in the hospital reception once a doctor and nurse had taken Phoebe away for a check-up. Her mind raced with the information she'd been able to get from Phobe during the short trip. Either the taxi driver was complicit in the kidnapping or Duncan Lewis had pulled another ruse to waste their time. One of DI Brown's DCs was busy with taxi companies which left precious few of the remaining team to find the church she said she'd been held in.

Frankie called Corstorphine to give him an update.

'You have her! Thank God! And she's unharmed?'

'Looks that way, sir. I'm with her at the hospital and they're giving her a quick check over now.'

'What's he playing at? He knows the church will be easy to find?'

The same thought had occurred to her. One of the MIT team were tasked with finding the taxi driver. The rest of them, including McAdam and Lamb, would all be heading towards Loch Lochy to find the church.

'Could be he's made a mistake, sir?'

The silence on the other end of the line expressed Corstorphine's doubt more than any comment he could have made.

'He's deliberately sent them there. I bet he's moved Shamila already. Phoebe never heard anything after he shut her in the church?'

'That's what she told me. She was on her own in a small room inside the church. She said she never heard anyone else all the time she was there.' Frankie didn't dare voice the thought that Shamila had already been killed. It was the only logical conclusion she could draw to the silence Phoebe reported.

'Fuck! I need to go there.'

'Then they'll know I've spoken to you, sir.' Frankie sought for anything that would provide him some comfort. 'DI Brown is bound to give you an update soon. If they find the church and Shamila, you'll know before anyone else.'

'Aye.' Corstorphine's reply lacked conviction.

'I'll get back to you as soon as I have something for you. I just need to make sure Phoebe's safe with Robb.'

'Of course. I'll wait here. Something's not adding up. I need time to think. Thanks again, Frankie.'

'Don't be daft, sir. I'll be in touch.'

Frankie had a few more minutes before Robb would arrive. She called Alex and was gratified that this time he picked up straight away.

'Hi, Frankie. Have you found them yet?'

'We've got Phoebe back – and a location where she was being held. I'm hoping we find Shamila there.'

'That's great news! What a relief for you all.'

Frankie couldn't bring herself to celebrate along with him. Not yet.

'I was calling to see how Mikey is. Whether he's made up with you for running off like that.'

'Aye. We've had words.' Alex's voice lost all enthusiasm. 'I can't believe he pulled a stunt like this. What's going to happen with this young woman he threatened?'

Frankie sighed. 'Very much depends how she wants to proceed

and whether she is treated as a reliable witness with her learning difficulties. His best outcome is a slap on the wrist.'

'What's the worst?'

She could hear the worry in his voice.

'He could get custodial. Depends on the procurator fiscal and who he's in front of in court.'

'Will it come to that, Frankie? Is there nothing you can do? Please say something on his behalf,' Alex pleaded.

'I'll do what I can, but it's out of my hands. You should know that.'

An awkward silence lay between them. Frankie broke first.

'Can I see you tonight, assuming this is all over today?'

'I can't.'

She couldn't help but hear the relief in his words.

'Why?'

'It's the Glenarty event tonight. We're always there as part of the parade and in case we're needed. You know, steam engines and—'

'Frankie! Where's Phoebe?' Robb McCoach rushed over to her in a panic.

'Have to go. I'll get back to you.' She ended the call with the sense that she had more problems than before.

'She's with the doctor.' She saw the look that crossed his face and added hurriedly, 'She's OK. It's just a routine check-up after being kidnapped. She's fine.'

Robb grabbed her in a bear hug and squeezed the air out of her lungs.

'Thank you, Frankie. Thank you for finding her.'

She didn't have the breath to explain that her part in Phoebe's return was insignificant. A white-coated doctor appeared from the treatment rooms, Phoebe trailing happily behind. She ran to hug Robb as the doctor made a decision as to who should be given the prognosis, turning his attention from one to the other before deciding to address them both.

'Phoebe's had a terrifying experience and will likely be needing some quiet time to process everything that has happened. Physically she's in good shape and hasn't been maltreated. Her vitals all come back normal and she's had food and drink over the last couple of days, so we have no concerns in that regard.'

The doctor smiled at Phoebe's obvious delight to be back with her brother, then his face turned to a more serious expression.

'Is there someone you have who can offer psychological counselling?'

Frankie answered for them both. 'Phoebe sees someone on a regular basis. She'll be best-placed to make that assessment.'

The doctor appeared satisfied with that and left in a swirl of his white coat.

Robb made to ask a question, but Frankie placed a finger to her lips behind Phoebe's back. This wasn't the time.

SEVENTY-SIX
SAMHAIN

Corstorphine couldn't settle. He'd been desperate for news about Shamila, yet fearful of what that news might be. Frankie's call left him in limbo – relieved that Phoebe had been released but tortured not to have the closure he needed. Frankie's words echoed in his mind. Why release Phoebe in Glenarty? Duncan Lewis was returning to the site of Trudi's murder. Why would he risk being recognised and discovered when he could have let her go anywhere?

He searched for the location of the church Frankie had mentioned, fingers tracing a map until pausing at a simple cross in a copse of trees. Streetview brought up a blurred image.

It looked like an estate church. There were similar examples dotted randomly around the Highlands. This one might even have been named after the Trinity on some ancient map. Now it was disused the building had been all but forgotten.

Corstorphine had no expectation that either Duncan Lewis or Shamila would be found there. He'd outwitted them every time and this was too obvious. By letting Phoebe have her freedom he was laying down a final challenge. Whatever Duncan had in mind, this had to be his endgame. Corstorphine clenched his fists so hard that the nails dug into the soft meat of his palm, leaving moon-shaped indentations in his flesh.

There were still clues waiting to be found in his *Done With Crying*, that was the one certainty he was still able to cling to. What would Daemon Aticus be thinking now? He'd killed the one man, dressed him up in scarecrow clothes so that he'd be found the day they returned from their honeymoon. Shamila's clinic had been under observation for however long – long enough for him to see the taxi driver dropping off and collecting Phoebe on a regular basis. She wouldn't have been suspicious if a taxi collected her in the town and she made the perfect bait to make Shamila go with them. Now Phoebe had served her purpose he had let her go – and made a small fortune in the process. That was his one straw to cling to – Duncan Lewis was still behaving rationally enough to let Phoebe go. But why give away his location?

Even now, DI Brown and the rest of the local force would be arriving at the old church. He might delay until an armed response team could be brought in, but from what he'd seen of the DI, he was more likely to attempt a rescue without risking giving Duncan further time alone with his hostage. In that hopeless situation even a madman would know there's no way out and he'd already killed before.

Corstorphine reined back from following that logic, concentrating instead on the likelihood that the church would be empty. Duncan Lewis wanted them to focus on the church – was that to leave him free to finish whatever this was?

The passage he had read last night remained fresh in his memory. Daemon Aticus had written of Beltane. Litha, Lughnasa, Mabon and Samhain. He knew Beltane was a fire festival celebrated in various parts of the Celtic nations, but what were the others?

Corstorphine typed into a search bar, pulled out information relating these words to Sabbats in the Wiccan religion – Gaelic feasts spread over the year. *You cast me aside at Beltane.* Beltane occurs on 1st May. That was the last day Shamila worked at

Carstairs before joining him here. His pulse quickened as the other feasts took him up to today. *I endured Litha, Lughnasa and Mabon without you.*

Corstorphine knew he was right when he realised today was Samhain – the end of harvest and the beginning of the dark part of the year. He could feel ice forming around his heart as he recalled the last paragraph. *Only Samhain can bring us together. Your soul forged to mine in the flame. So mote it be!*

Duncan intended to die with Shamila. He grabbed his phone, swept through page after page of Daemon Aticus's text until he found the section he was looking for.

When the unholy trinity face the fire, then they will burn with a fragment of the passion I held for you. Then you'll understand how deeply I loved you. In borrowed rags you'll end your life, surrounded by the things you fear the most.

Shamila feared scarecrows – and by now she certainly feared Duncan. There was only the one place locally that he knew of where scarecrows and fire co-existed. His heart raced. Corstorphine now knew what Daemon Aticus had planned. If he was right, there was still another person Duncan Lewis intended to kill.

SEVENTY-SEVEN
BONFIRE

The road to Glenarty was busier than usual. The annual parade attracted growing numbers of people every year to the village's narrow streets. This year people were arriving early to grab the few parking places before the steampunk parade that was scheduled to begin at 2 p.m. Corstorphine cursed as he crawled along the crowded road, his siren and flashing lights having no effect on a slow-moving traffic jam.

He called Frankie on her mobile, stabbing at her number with a shaking hand.

'Hello, sir? Have you heard from DI Brown?'

'No. I haven't time for him. I know what Duncan Lewis has planned – at least, I hope I'm right.' The first doubt crept into his mind as he wondered if he was being played for a fool as well. He dismissed the thought as soon as it came. 'I'm coming into Glenarty. I think he's already here with Shamila.'

'In Glenarty, sir?'

'Aye. It's something he wrote in that book, about facing the fire and surrounded by the things you hate. The festival here ends with a fire, doesn't it?'

There was a stunned silence as Frankie processed his words.

'Aye. It's one of the biggest bonfires for miles. Alex will be there with the fire crew to keep an eye on it. Shit!'

Corstorphine was taking his four by four up the side of an embankment to pass a car that had frozen in the middle of the road, mesmerised into inactivity by the flashing lights.

'What is it?' he asked hurriedly as the Land Rover returned to an even keel. He'd made a few metres, that was all.

'On the bonfire, sir. They load it up with all the scarecrows! What if she's already on the bonfire? It would only take a match and the whole thing will go up!'

'Can you get hold of Alex? Tell him to make his way to the bonfire and make sure no one tries to light it. Explain Shamila might be dressed up as one of the scarecrows.'

'I'm on it, sir. I'll get there as soon as I can. And I'll try and reach the MIT in case there's nothing at the church.'

Corstorphine cut the call. He was shaking with adrenaline and crawling along at a few mph wasn't helping. There was a driveway ahead. He pulled in and abandoned the car. It was quicker by foot.

He ran as fast as he could, trying to pace himself so he didn't catch a stitch or double-up as he fought for breath. The village general store was ahead – he burst in, the bell ringing an urgent klaxon at his arrival. A familiar face poked up from over the counter in surprise.

'Oh, it's you. You gave me a shock coming in like that. Look – you've woken Pussykins!' The shopkeeper's voice expressed annoyance.

The cat stirring into some semblance of life was the last of his concerns.

'The bonfire! Which way is it?' He wheezed like the bellows of an abandoned forge.

'Bonfire?' The shopkeeper's surprised expression stared blankly back at him.

'I haven't time for this. Where is the bonfire? Which way do I have to go?'

'Well. There are ways of asking. To the end of the village and turn right after Mart McKeown's house. You can't miss it. There's a long line of Steampunk vehicles...'

Corstorphine raced out of the shop, the peeved shopkeeper's declaration of *what a rude man* left hanging in the air. He passed Mart McKeown's house to enter a narrow lane filled to capacity with bizarre vehicles. A fire engine had come to a halt faced with the impossibility of passing the array of belching, smoking creations. He recognised Alex hanging out of the passenger window and berating the closest vehicle – a cross between a giant lawnmower and mechanised dragon.

'Alex!' Corstorphine shouted with the last of his available breath. 'Did Frankie talk to you?'

'Hang on.' Alex climbed down from the cab giving Corstorphine a chance to recover. 'She said something about the bonfire, said Shamila might be on it?'

'It's possible. I don't know. I'm trying to make sense. Can you get through?' Corstorphine realised he was almost incoherent. He forced his breathing to slow down.

Alex looked at the line of vehicles blocking the road as if calculating whether the fire tender stood any chance of making progress.

'Not a hope.'

'I have to search the bonfire, just in case. Have you any extinguishers you can carry in case he tries lighting it?'

Alex nodded with understanding. 'Hang on.' He called out to the other occupants of the cab and they all joined him at the side of the tender, reaching for portable fire extinguishers. They started up the road where the top of a giant bonfire could be seen above the tallest Steampunk vehicle.

'There it is,' Alex shouted.

Corstorphine's heart was pounding fit to burst as he followed the fire crew up the road.

'It's on fire!' Sandy called from the front, his finger pointing towards an untidy heap of wood.

The first wisp of smoke curled languidly into the autumn sky from the top of an artificial volcano built of pallets and firewood. They had seconds before the whole thing would go up in flames.

SEVENTY-EIGHT
TENDER TRAP

When they reached the towering bonfire, the first flames were already showing. Alex and the other fire crew shouted commands and directed blasts of water and foam to limit the fire's growth.

Corstorphine gazed helplessly at the pile of firewood in front of him. Scarecrows were positioned all over the heap, some buried inside so only their heads showed. He didn't hesitate and began climbing up the unstable pile of pallets to reach the first stuffed figure, ignoring Alex's calls for caution.

One pull at the scarecrow was enough to confirm that it didn't contain a body and he moved onto the next. He ignored repeated calls for him to get down, scaling the side like a mountaineer to reach the next figure. This one was also straw, and the next. He began to doubt his hunch and both he and fire crew were risking their lives.

'It's too dangerous!' Alex shouted up at Corstorphine. As if to emphasise how dangerous it was a bright yellow flame erupted at his feet. Corstorphine spotted the other firefighters climbing up behind him, jets of foam spraying from their fire extinguishers as they attempted to slow the conflagration.

He moved up another level, away from the immediate danger.

There were more scarecrows here and he felt each one, encountering paper and straw before moving onto the next. He stopped in shock when he saw Mart McKeown's face staring at him from inside the bonfire, his features melting in front of his eyes. It took precious seconds for him to realise he was looking at a waxwork head turned into a candle, the wick burning rapidly as flames took hold. The musician's missing guitar case lay buried deeper in the bonfire where the flames hadn't yet reached. A strong smell of petrol issued from the case, encouraging him to redouble his efforts and stretch towards the next stuffed figure. When his hands felt soft flesh, he pulled the sacking off the head to reveal Shamila's face. She looked as if she was asleep.

'I've found her!' he shouted to the others, unwilling to believe the lack of any response to his voice could mean she was already dead. His shaking hand touched her skin and felt warmth. She was still alive!

Corstorphine pulled at her body, but it was held tight within a cocoon of rope, anchored to one of the large trunks forming the structural heart of the bonfire.

Alex responded to his shout and climbed up to join him, sawing away at the ropes holding her bound with a knife from his belt. The other fire crew joined them and they managed to lower her body to the ground and drag her a safe distance away from the growing fire just as the guitar case exploded in a ball of flame.

'There may be others.' Corstorphine bent down to check Shamila's breathing, seeing the worry etched on Alex's face.

Alex exchanged a look with his crew as the bonfire began to roar in earnest. The sound of wood splintering in the intense heat covered up any discussion.

'There's nothing we can do.' Alex glanced up at the fire as it took hold, shielding his eyes from smoke.

Corstorphine willed Shamila to respond, but her head flopped as loosely as a rag doll in his hands.

'Call an ambulance, she's been drugged or something.'

Jo put a hand on his shoulder, her gaze fixed on the growing fire.

'We'd better move. It's not safe to stay as close as this. The bonfire could fall over at any minute. We'll carry her between us.'

Corstorphine could only look on helplessly as the fire crew took over, hurrying Shamila's limp body away from danger. Behind his back he could feel the angry heat from the fire. If there were any more bodies concealed within the blaze, there was no hope of saving them now.

The unlikely procession of the fire crew and semi-conscious woman dressed as a scarecrow attracted the attention of a growing crowd. Phones raised in the air for a clearer view of the spectacle as they hurried towards the fire tender. Corstorphine punched the number for an ambulance as he followed, needing to be doing something.

Frankie's call came as they reached the relative quiet of the road.

'DI Brown has been trying to call you, sir. They've caught Duncan Lewis!'

'When was this?'

'Just a few minutes ago, sir. He was still at the church. His car's there as well with a taxi sign concealed in the boot. Have you found Shamila? There's no one else here at the church?'

Corstorphine hadn't taken his eyes off her.

'Aye. She's safe. I've called for an ambulance – she's drugged I think.'

'I'll pass that on. I'll meet you at the hospital, sir. Will she be alright?'

'I think so. I'd better go.'

He ended the call and reached for Shamila's hand.

'Shamila, I'm here. You're going to be alright.'

He bent towards her face, felt her breath on his cheek and kissed her gently on her lips.

'We'll take you to hospital. Get you looked at.' Corstorphine brushed the hair away from her face and leaned in to whisper in her ear. 'I love you so much.'

The hint of a smile played at the edges of her mouth and Corstorphine gripped her hand in response, ecstatic that she was conscious enough to hear him. He had Shamila back. Now he'd make sure Duncan Lewis would never be released again.

SEVENTY-NINE
HE'S THE ONE

Corstorphine sat in the hospital reception with his head bowed. Shamila had been taken into intensive care as the medical team tried to ascertain what drugs she'd been given. The entire fire crew were sat with him, each one suffering from various degrees of burns and smoke inhalation.

Frankie spotted them as she entered the hospital and made straight for Corstorphine.

'Is she going to be alright, sir?' She stood by his seat, her hands anxiously twisting around each other.

'I think so, Frankie. The doctor thinks she's been given a large dose of ketamine. They're still running tests. Did they find anything at the church?'

'His car was parked there, with a taxi sign in the boot. Duncan Lewis wasn't making much sense by all accounts, they weren't able to get much out of him. It sounds like his psychosis has returned. Carstairs are sending a team to collect him – he'll need to be dealt with by the staff there.' She hesitated, looking around her before adding quietly, 'Duncan left a suicide note. He meant to die with Shamila.'

'Figures,' Corstorphine responded. 'He knew we'd find the

church and his DNA over everything. He'll be spending the rest of his life in the state hospital.'

'But why stay at the church instead of getting away?' Frankie questioned.

Corstorphine shrugged. He had no interest in what happened to Duncan Lewis, apart from ensuring he was never released again. 'He's not in his right mind. Maybe Shamila's replacement will be able to get to the bottom of it. Main thing is they have him in custody.'

'How did you know where she was?'

Corstorphine could feel Frankie's eyes on him as she asked the question.

'It was a hunch. His *Done With Crying* talked about the trinity being consumed in the flames – being surrounded by the things you feared. When he let Phoebe go, then I realised he himself was a part of the trinity. He knew Shamila was frightened of scarecrows. There was only one location where I knew scarecrows and fire co-existed.'

'At the Glenarty Harvest Festival,' Frankie volunteered.

'Aye. The Celtic Samhain festival celebrating the harvest and beginning of winter.'

'Why a trinity, though? If it was only ever Duncan and Shamila?'

'I don't know. I initially thought maybe another body was on the fire, but now I suspect he meant himself as two separate people. If that makes sense?'

A doctor swept into the waiting area, looked around and made directly for Corstorphine.

'Your wife has regained consciousness, Inspector. You can have five minutes with her and then she needs to rest.'

Corstorphine followed the doctor through a maze of corridors until he stopped outside a private room.

'Her responses may be a little odd,' he warned. 'Until the drugs are out of her system. Don't worry too much if she doesn't make a lot of sense.' He opened the door and Corstorphine saw Shamila's head turn to face him. She smiled a welcome.

'How are you?' He felt for her hand and held it tightly in his, feeling her squeeze back in response.

'I'm sorry it took so long to find you. I was going out of my mind.' He stopped, knowing this was more to salve his own conscience than soothe her.

'Is Phoebe...?' Her voice faltered.

'Phoebe's fine. She's with Robb.'

Shamila's eyes closed. He wondered whether she'd slipped back into unconsciousness until her eyelids flickered open again.

'How's Duncan? Did you find him?'

Corstorphine felt the anger coursing through his veins at the mention of his name.

'We've got him. Don't worry – he'll not be able to threaten you ever again.'

Shamila's expression turned to puzzlement. 'No – you don't understand.'

He watched her with mounting concern as she tried to lever herself up to a sitting position. The steady background beep that provided the soundtrack to their conversation increased in frequency as a red light started to flash on the ceiling.

'Lie back down, love,' Corstorphine urged. 'Don't exert yourself.'

The white-coated doctor re-entered the room, sending Corstorphine a disapproving glare whilst gently pushing Shamila back down to a resting position.

'You'd better leave,' he advised.

Corstorphine reluctantly started for the door until Shamila's hand stopped him.

'It's not Duncan Lewis,' she said urgently. 'It's Gyles Lambert who kidnapped me. He's the one you need to stop!'

EIGHTY
LIKE A BOMB

Corstorphine ran back into the hospital reception area, shouting for Frankie to follow.

'We've been after the wrong man. It's Gyles Lambert who did all this. Call the MIT team, tell them to find what car he owns and put out a general alert – he'll not be expecting us to know he's responsible.'

'How...?' Frankie reached for her radio as she ran alongside him.

'Shamila told me. He planned for her to die. We'll take the Land Rover.'

Frankie hadn't strapped in before he accelerated out onto the main road. He could hear her repeating his accusation over the radio to a bemused DI Brown.

'He could only have left a short while ago.' Corstorphine thought rapidly as the heavy vehicle swung through the traffic. 'We need to know what he's driving. Tell them to make that a priority and then notify Road Traffic to keep a watch on the cameras. My guess is he'll be making leisurely progress back to Carstairs or wherever it is he lives.'

The memory of Mart McKeown's waxwork face dripping wax into the bonfire filled his mind – that and the unmistakable smell of petrol coming from the guitar case. How long would it have taken for the waxwork head to have burned down to the level he'd spotted – two, three hours?

'They're on it now, sir.' Frankie interrupted his thoughts.

'He's probably a few hours ahead of us. I think he used Mart McKeown's waxwork head as a slow burn fuse to set the fire going. Once it reached the petrol leaking from his guitar case, the whole thing went up like a bomb.' He stopped speaking, suddenly aware of how wafer-thin the margin had been between bringing Shamila to safety and losing her forever. If he'd been a few minutes later...

The radio crackled into life, DI Brown's Glaswegian accent made more obvious over the speaker.

'He drives a light blue Volkswagen camper van. Traffic Scotland have the details and are looking out for it. You think he's heading back home?'

Frankie had jotted down the registration number as it came through.

'Aye. He won't expect us to know he played any part in this, so I don't think he'll be trying anything clever. He's at most a few hours ahead of us, maybe less if he dumped the car back at the church.'

'Got it! I'll put out an alert to watch for him on the A82 through Glencoe. We're heading that way now. There's no way he can avoid us. We'll catch him.'

There was a pause until DI Brown's questioning tone came back over the airways.

'You're not thinking of going after him yourself, are you, Corstorphine?'

He could see Frankie's expression out of the side of his eye.

'I'm sorry, you're breaking up. Can you repeat? Over.'

Corstorphine turned off the police radio and glared at the road ahead.

'Are you still going after him, sir?'

Corstorphine's jaw clenched. 'I'm not going to risk him getting away.'

He turned to face Frankie. 'I can let you out here. You needn't be a part of this.'

She looked coolly into his eyes. 'Don't know what you're talking about, sir. The radio signal went just after DI Brown said we're all going to catch him.'

Corstorphine gave her a tight smile of acknowledgement.

'He'll want to avoid any routes with cameras. He's too clever to take the main road south.'

Corstorphine took the road north towards Spean Bridge.

'He's played us for idiots the whole time. My bet is he'll take the B862 and make for the A9. If we cut across on the A86, we should reach Kingussie before him.'

Frankie reached for her mobile.

'Before we lose the signal,' she explained in response to Corstorphine's questioning glance.

'Bill, DI Corstorphine thinks Gyles Lambert will be taking the road north, then cutting across to join the A9 south. Are you with Lamb?'

She nodded as a voice issued tinnily from her phone. 'We're taking the A86 across to cut him off at Kingussie. You and Lamb take the Dalwhinnie road in case we miss him.'

The sound of the PC's response was too quiet for Corstorphine to make out, but he understood the gist of the comment from Frankie's response.

'The police radio is unreliable north of the town, Phil. I don't think you heard DI Brown's instructions.'

She finished the call. 'They'll be waiting for him at Dalwhinnie in case we've missed him.'

Corstorphine gave a curt nod and turned on the siren, pushing the Land Rover as fast as he dared.

They'd been waiting in a layby for over an hour and Corstorphine was beginning to doubt the wisdom of his approach. PCs Lamb and McAdam hadn't seen the camper van either. It was only the lack of any announcement over the police radio that gave him the determination to stay put.

'Do you think he's given us the slip?' Frankie voiced his own concerns back at him.

Corstorphine reluctantly took his gaze off the stream of vehicles heading south.

'We'll give it a bit longer, Frankie. He could have taken another route entirely. We can't even say for sure what it is he's driving.'

A wave of despair washed over him. Shamila would never be safe until Gyles was behind bars. He shuddered at the prospect of him remaining at large and always being a threat to them both. The lack of sleep and unrelenting stress was catching up on him – he could feel himself slipping into a trance.

Frankie's touch on his arm shocked him back into alertness. She pointed to a light blue Volkswagen camper van driving towards them.

'Can you see the reg?' he asked urgently, fumbling for the binoculars in the dash.

'It's him!' Frankie asserted. 'I can read it from here.'

She was forced back into her seat as Corstorphine accelerated out of the layby, cutting into the traffic just behind the camper van. He hit the siren and motioned for the van to pull over. Frankie was working the radio beside him, putting out a call to all cars as the van accelerated away.

'First mistake you've made.'

He pulled out from behind the camper van, accelerating into the fast lane until they were neck by neck.

'Watch out, Frankie. I'm going to hit him with a PIT manoeuvre.'

Frankie leaned towards him, away from the impact as the Land Rover turned to swipe the camper. He could see Gyles frantically wrestling with the wheel as the van veered violently towards the soft verge, attempting to return to the road. Corstorphine saw he'd lost control and touched the brakes as the camper swung wildly across the tarmac. The rear wheels slewed in the grass embankment and the camper tipped onto its side, leaving a trail of sparks until it came to a halt across both lanes.

Corstorphine pulled to a stop and wrenched his door open, running towards the van. The air was thick with the smell of petrol leaking from the fuel tank. He spotted the passenger door lifting into the air, a hand reaching for purchase and straining as Gyles began lifting himself out.

Corstorphine grabbed the arm and heaved until the man's body lay draped over the side of the van.

'It's over, Gyles.'

He saw the calculation in the man's eyes as he worked the odds and something in Corstorphine wanted him to resist the arrest. Frankie advancing with a Taser held high stopped him.

'You win, Corstorphine.' Gyles Lambert spoke without any visible sign of emotion. He held his arms out in readiness for the cuffs. The sound of PC McAdam's siren drew closer from the other side of the dual carriageway, coming to a halt beside them. Any fight that might have been in him died with the appearance of the two PCs.

Corstorphine read Gyles his rights, then secured him in the back seat with PC McAdam keeping a close eye beside him.

'Can you deal until the traffic cops arrive?' Corstorphine felt an intense wave of weariness as he spoke to PC Lamb. 'Forensics will need a look at the van, and you'd better ask the fire brigade to stand by too with the petrol spill.

They edged around the camper van, the Land Rover making good use of its four-wheel drive as they mounted the embankment, then headed back towards home.

'Why did you do it, Gyles?' Corstorphine fixed the man in his mirror.

Their eyes locked together.

'You of all people should know why,' he responded calmly.

Corstorphine forced his attention back to the road. He'd caught the man who'd threatened Shamila. He should be feeling relief, but his overriding emotion was one of confusion. Gyles

Lambert appeared calm and completely sane – as far removed from a psychopathic killer as he could imagine.

'I loved her.' Gyles spoke quietly. 'I loved her and she felt nothing for me. Do you know what that feels like, Corstorphine? To be in love with someone who doesn't even acknowledge your existence?'

Corstorphine remained silent, concentrating on the road ahead.

'She thought she was too good for me. Took the promotion that should have been mine. I could have coped with rejection, but she chose to humiliate me as well.'

Frankie exchanged a sideways look. They knew each other well enough not to voice concerns over their prisoner's mental state.

'Love and hate share the same neural pathways,' Gyles continued. 'People think they're opposites, but they originate in the same parts of the brain, manifest with identical physiological symptoms. You've no idea how much I loved her. She'll never know.'

Gyles Lambert had nothing more to say, although his cool eyes remained fixed on Corstorphine every time he checked the mirror. The scent of cedarwood permeated the car until he opened his window. He needed to breathe fresh air.

EIGHTY-ONE

COMPLETELY SANE

DI Brown insisted that he and his DCs would interview Gyles Lambert when Corstorphine finally returned to the police station. The MIT weren't even trying to hide their anger at being sent on a wild goose chase whilst the local cops had made the arrest.

'We'll take it from here.' The DI had more to say but had to be satisfied with sending Corstorphine home.

Frankie had offered to drive him, but he'd told her he would be fine on his own. His first stop was the hospital where he'd been made to wait until the medical staff reluctantly let him see Shamila again. She'd reacted calmly to the news of Gyles's arrest, then held out her arms to draw him in close. Her body convulsed with sobs as they held each other tight.

'I'm so sorry love. I'm sorry I didn't protect you.' He buried his face into her hair until she quietened.

'You caught him. That's all that matters.' She let him go and wiped the tears from her face.

'He'll end up a patient at Carstairs.' She took a shuddering breath, regaining her composure. 'He knows how to work the system to avoid prison. I don't envy his replacement, having to treat the former head of clinical psychology.'

She'd managed a smile and reached for his hand. They'd stayed like that until the nurse apologetically asked him to leave.

'If there are no side effects, then your wife will be home later tomorrow. The doctor wants to keep an eye on his patient overnight.'

The next morning he called the hospital as early as seemed reasonable and had been asked to arrive after the doctor had been on the ward rounds at 11:00.

There was enough time to buy flowers. It was all he could think of to celebrate Shamila coming back home. When he returned to the house, a large bouquet in his hand, DI Brown stood waiting for him on the doorstep. Corstorphine's heart sank – today was about having Shamila back, not having an official reprimand delivered by the Chief Constable's messenger.

'Corstorphine.' The DI's tone gave the impression that he had bad news to deliver.

'You'd better come in.' Corstorphine glanced at the clock as he led the DI through the house. 'This can't take long. I'm picking Shamila up from the hospital at eleven.'

'No, shouldn't take up much of your time.' DI Brown searched for a stool to sit on as Corstorphine fussed with the flowers, placing them in a vase and adding water before turning his attention to his unwelcome visitor.

DI Brown laid a tape player down on the counter.

'Gyles Lambert's statement. I thought you should hear it – off the record.'

Corstorphine responded to DI Brown's raised eyebrows with a single nod, and the DI pressed the play button. The DI's Glaswegian tones issued tinnily out of the small speaker advising Gyles of his rights and introducing the duty solicitor before they started in earnest.

'Can you tell us where you were on the evening of Friday 24th October after leaving Carstairs Hospital at 17:00 hours?'

'No comment.' The bored tones of the duty solicitor automatically prompted his client.

'I went home and had a shower. The hospital has an antiseptic smell that tends to linger. Then I went to Richard Bryce's house with a glass I'd given Duncan Lewis to drink out of.' Gyles's voice was interrupted as the duty solicitor finally reacted.

'You say no comment to every question like I told you. Strike that from the record!'

The tape recorder was silent for a few seconds, then Gyles's measured tones issued a chilling threat.

'You can either stay quiet unless I ask you to speak, or I can silence you myself before these officers have a chance to react.'

The sound of chairs scraping across the interview room floor filled the air, followed by a short struggle and DI Brown advising that the duty solicitor had left the room.

'You don't have to continue the interview now your solicitor has left.'

'No, I want to tell you everything. I give my consent.'

DI Brown continued. 'You were with Duncan Lewis before meeting Richard Bryce?'

'Yes. I had my shower, then drove my camper van to his flat and gave him a large dose of ketamine in one of Richard's glasses. I'd told him I was adjusting his medication. I'd offered to take him to the supermarket in Lanark. He walked to the van before passing out in the back and I put him on a drip to keep him quiet.'

'Why target Richard Bryce?' the DI questioned.

'Richard knew I'd been taking ketamine from the hospital stores. He had to be dealt with.'

'So, you murdered him?' DI Brown's caustic voice interrupted.

'Strictly speaking, no. I'd expressed an interest in his allotment, and he managed to walk as far as the level crossing before the ketamine hit. I suggested he took a seat in his wheelbarrow until he felt better, then laid him out on the tracks so it was the train that killed him.'

'But you tied him to the rails,' DI Brown's tone expressed incredulity at his apparent defence.

'I couldn't risk him moving once I had him positioned just

right, could I? Besides I had no idea how long it was until the next train. I waited in the camper van until the goods train went past.'

'What time was that?'

'Around half nine. I wasn't really paying much attention. I was listening to Mart McKeown's greatest hits. Have you heard of him?'

The question was asked in eagerness.

'I have now,' came DI Brown's laconic response. 'How did Richard Bryce's body end up dressed as a scarecrow not very far from here?'

'Put his body in the back of the camper, along with his head and feet. Luckily, I'd prepared the van with plastic sheeting. Do you watch American forensics programs, officer?'

'Not if I can help it. You were explaining how Richard Bryce came to be dressed as a scarecrow.'

'Yes. The old church. I used it as my base. That wheelbarrow came in useful. I drove up on the Friday evening – just another camper van on the road. Tied Duncan up, made sure he was well dosed and then went looking for a scarecrow. She doesn't like scarecrows.'

Manic laughter filled the air.

Corstorphine felt his blood chill. Gyles Lambert had managed to sound completely rational up to then, now his insanity was clear. If he hadn't managed to catch him... He shut that thought down to listen to the final part of his statement.

'Then I was busy. I'd already booked an appointment with Shamila after she returned from her honeymoon, but I needed to see what her routine was like before taking her. That girl patient of hers – I'd read about the case. She was perfect. I waited until Shamila returned with that detective she married before putting Richard where he'd be found.'

'In farmer Haddow's field where you'd taken his scarecrow from?'

'If that's his name.'

'Duncan Lewis's DNA and prints were found at every crime scene. Why did you want to frame him?'

'He should never have been released!' Gyles sounded indignant. 'The man's a danger to society. I did what needed to be done.'

'You admit to deliberately abducting Duncan Lewis, drugging and holding him captive whilst leaving traces of his DNA and fingerprints at crime scenes?'

'Haven't you been listening?'

'And to the unlawful murder of Richard Bryce and leaving his body dressed as a scarecrow?'

'Is there any other murder than unlawful?'

'Why do it? Why murder Richard Bryce, Trudi McKeown and attempt to murder Shamila?' DI Brown's questioning became personal.

'Have you ever loved someone, DI Brown? Truly loved someone so much that life isn't worth living without them? That you'd do anything to have them back? And when they treat your love like it's nothing – no more than a joke to them – then have you felt the hate that fills that vacuum?'

One of the DCs coughed nervously to break the silence.

'No. I thought not,' Gyles eventually responded.

'Would you say you're completely sane, Gyles? Seeing as mental health is your speciality.' DI Brown attempted another line of questioning.

'Oh, I'm completely sane, detective. I was insane, for a while. Driven insane by love. You can tell Shamila I forgive her. Tell her that I'm over her now. And tell DI Corstorphine he was only able to solve the case thanks to his wife. He's not that good a detective.'

DI Brown pressed the stop key.

'That's essentially it. A full confession. I've met a few murderers in my time but not one as cold-blooded as him. I hope they never let him out, he's fucking insane – and clever with it! He gave us more details about Trudi's murder – said she was onto him but never let on what he'd done with the jewellery. Your man McCoach will have to claim that on his insurance.'

He stood to leave, pocketed the recorder before offering Corstorphine a hand to shake.

'We're done here. The office will be all yours on Monday. Gyles Lambert will be locked away for life, so you don't need to worry about him again. Goodbye, Corstorphine.'

'Goodbye – and thanks. For letting me hear that.' Corstorphine couldn't help but notice where DI Brown had chosen to end the recording.

'You're welcome.'

Corstorphine watched the detective drive away, lost in his own thoughts. Lambert had killed two people without any sign of remorse and had left Shamila for dead. He'd never have been able to forgive himself if he'd found her too late, and life without her wasn't worth living.

A skein of geese called overhead and he searched the sky until finding them, an unmistakable sign that another winter lay in wait. He returned to fetch his keys. It was time to bring Shamila home.

EIGHTY-TWO
GARDEN IMPLEMENTS

It was the start of a new week and Corstorphine was at his desk, putting the finishing touches to last week's report. He'd been given leeway in sending in the figures – it was the least the Chief Constable could do in the circumstances. Shamila's face smiled at him from the photograph beside his monitor and he gave silent thanks that she had physically recovered from her ordeal.

She'd left hospital after staying the night under observation. He'd tried to talk to her about everything that had happened, but she'd said it was too soon and she just needed time to work through it.

'You're the best therapy I can have, love.' Her words remained vivid in his mind. He'd give her as much time as she needed, but somewhere along the line she'd have to provide a statement and a clinical appraisal of what drove Gyles Lambert to commit such crimes.

'Why do *you* think he did it?' he'd asked when she'd nestled into his arms at night, the two of them wrapped closely together as if nothing could ever tear them apart again.

'I'm not sure,' she'd answered hesitantly. 'That's for someone else to find out. He became obsessed with me, then had an irrational hatred because I was seen as more successful than him and it manifested in attempting to kill me and framing it all on Duncan Lewis.'

'You say irrational. Do you think he'll evade justice if the clinical decision is that he's not of sound mind?'

She'd pressed her finger to his lips to stop him talking any more.

'Then he faces something worse than a prison cell.'

He'd had to be content with that.

Phoebe had missed the worst of it and the kidnapping apparently had a negligible effect on her. She was still being given psychological counselling, but Shamila had said that spending most of her life locked away in solitary was the best preparation for what had happened to her.

Outside his office he could see Frankie, Lamb and McAdam having an animated conversation as they waited for his team brief. The sound of laughter signalled that things had returned to normal in their small police station – although not everything would return to how it was.

He glanced at the envelopes propped up on his desk. One was a card wishing Hamish a happy retirement. Every retirement card he found had a similar message, or some quip about time for golf or travel. None of those things applied to Hamish, not when he faced being Molly's carer for years. The other held happier tidings. He put those thoughts to one side and opened his door, walking towards the blank crazy wall as the team gathered around.

'Morning, all.'

A series of muted responses came back. The laughter had gone.

'As you know, Hamish has now officially retired. I've a card for us all to sign and he specifically asked for no presents, so I've gifted our collection to Alzheimer Scotland with his blessing. I think you all know the outcome from the preliminary MIT investigation, but I'll summarise the main findings.'

Corstorphine referred to the single A4 sheet in his hand before looking up at his team again.

'Gyles Lambert has been imprisoned pending trial.'

'Do you know why he did it, sir?' PC Lamb's hand was held up high.

'It very much looks like some form of psychosis; we have to wait for a clinical assessment. He'd put a cover story in place – touring around in his camper van. Nobody would have suspected him if Shamila hadn't survived.'

'Wouldn't Duncan Lewis have accused him, sir?' Frankie asked.

Corstorphine nodded. 'He was relying on it.' The three of them looked at the DI in confusion.

'Duncan was Gyles Lambert's patient. Who's going to believe the allegations of someone suffering from psychosis against the word of the professional tasked with treating him? It was almost perfect. The more Duncan argued that Gyles was behind it all, the madder he would have sounded. Nobody would have believed him.'

'What's Shamila saying about it, sir?' Frankie's question went straight to the heart of it, as always.

'Seemingly Gyles Lambert had been in love with her to the point of obsession – she termed it limerence but don't ask me what that means. Added to that he was jealous of her being promoted above him. He'd recommended that Duncan Lewis never be released and Shamila had overruled him. She had no idea how obsessed he was with her until she tried to rationalise with him after being taken, then it had all spilled out.'

Phil Lamb raised a hand and Corstorphine nodded for him to speak.

'But why kill Trudi? If this is all about a crime of passion or professional jealousy or whatever, why murder a young woman who had nothing to do with it?'

'Simple answer is that she already had suspicions that the person calling himself Duncan Lewis wasn't who he said he was.

Added to which she was writing the biography on the basis that Duncan was cured of his mental illness, which wasn't the story Gyles wanted told. Trudi was pushing to meet with Duncan so he could sign his name to her project. I think Gyles took the opportunity to remove both problems at once. It's the same with Richard Bryce. From what I can gather, Gyles had been reducing Duncan Lewis's anti-psychotics dosage in the hope he'd become ill again. Richard had begun to suspect something was wrong with his treatment. He'd also noticed the ketamine supplies were being raided and raised it with Gyles. Lanark police have confirmed the tyre tracks belonging to a wheelbarrow found at the church match those at Farmer Haddow's field. They also match tracks found at the site of Richard Bryce's murder – they think that's how his body was transported.'

'Is there a garden implement you *can't* use as a murder weapon?' Lamb asked loudly.

Corstorphine silenced him with a look. 'You'll be pleased to hear that both Shamila and Phoebe have made a good recovery, thanks to the medical team at the hospital. Duncan Lewis is undergoing more detailed evaluation, but early reports suggest he'll be fit enough to return to the community soon now he's back on his medication.'

PC Lamb raised his hand.

'What is it, Lamb?' Corstorphine said wearily.

'What about Robb's ransom – the jewels? Did anyone find them?'

'They're still missing. They recovered the drone from the old church, but no sign of the earrings.'

'What are we doing about replacing Hamish, sir?' PC McAdam asked hesitantly.

Corstorphine locked eyes with the PC. It was no secret that he wanted the job – especially now that he was a dad.

'We'll be raising a vacancy request this week, Bill. I'll make sure you're kept in the loop.' He reached for one of the envelopes he'd carried through from his office.

'This is for you, Bill. From all of us with our congratulations.'

Bill took the card and opened it in front of his expectant audience, holding the picture of a stork carrying a bundle up for them all to see. A voucher fluttered down to the floor and he stooped to pick it up, his eyes opening wide as he read the amount.

'I wasn't expecting anything like that. Thanks. Thanks, everyone.'

'We'll be wanting to see your new daughter, as soon as Caitlin's feeling up to it.' Corstorphine covered the PC's awkwardness.

'She'd like that. I'll pass it on.' Bill returned to join the others.

Frankie's hand went up.

'Sir, what's happening with Mikey? Michael McKay. Alex asked me to try and find out if charges are being brought.'

'Suzie doesn't want to press charges. Bill paid for a new lock out of his own money, and I've agreed with Alex that if Mikey works to repay that – and spends time helping the community instead of being a bloody nuisance – then I'll put in a word for him.'

He waited for further questions, but none were forthcoming.

'Alright, back to work.'

He returned to his desk, saw the two constables head out on patrol and Frankie typing away on her keyboard. Bit by bit the station was returning to normal. He waited until Frankie was on her own and stood by her desk.

'Sir?' she asked expectantly.

'Frankie. I just wanted to thank you for your help finding Shamila.'

'I didn't do much, sir. It was mostly your work.'

'No,' Corstorphine asserted. 'You were the one who steered me towards those passages in the book. I'd have never worked out what he intended without that.'

'Glad it all worked out, sir, in the end.'

He saw the sadness in her eyes. It wasn't working out for her and her fireman boyfriend – he was a good enough detective to make that deduction.

'So am I, Frankie. So am I.'

He turned away, glancing at Lamb's desk as he returned to his office. Printouts displayed a selection of metal detectors. He recalled Lamb's question about the earrings and smiled to himself. Maybe the lad would make a detective, after all.

EIGHTY-THREE
DONE WITH CRYING

Please don't pretend to me
I know it's just a lie
And yet I take your loving
I can't resist you if I try.
These days are numbered
I can see the end draw near
You run away to him
You think it isn't clear?

Our kisses just bring sorrow
Our love will turn to hate
I'm done with crying
This will be our fate.

There are none so blind
As those who choose to be
I watch you both together
You stand in front of me.
I'll take my time as
Time is all I have
You took my heart

And that I can't forgive.

Our kisses just bring sorrow
Our love will turn to hate
I'm done with crying
This will be our fate.
I'm done with crying
All that's left is hate.

Mart McKeown

A LETTER FROM THE AUTHOR

Thanks so much for reading *Murder of Crows*. If you want to join other readers in hearing all about my new releases, you can sign up for my newsletter here.

www.stormpublishing.co/andrew-james-greig

Please consider leaving a review. This can help new readers discover a book you've enjoyed and gives us all a big boost!

I very much look forward to sharing my next book with you. You can peer under this author's bonnet at:

andrewjgreig.wordpress.com

instagram.com/andrew_james_greig

facebook.com/andrewjamesgreig

tiktok.com/@andrewjamesgreig

x.com/AndrewJamesGre3

www.ingramcontent.com/pod-product-compliance
Lightning Source LLC
Chambersburg PA
CBHW010427170726
48283CB00011B/3098